MONUMENT
IN THE STORM

by

John A. Truett

SUNSTONE PRESS

SANTA FE

Cover Illustration by Stu Pritchard.

Sunstone books may be purchased for educational, business, or sales promotional use. For information please write: Special Markets Department, Sunstone Press, P.O. Box 2321, Santa Fe, New Mexico 87504-2321.

FIRST EDITION

Library of Congress Cataloging in Publication Data:
Truett, John A., 1927–
    Monument in the storm / by John A. Truett. —1st ed.
        p. cm.
    ISBN: 0-86534-266-0
    I. Title.
PS3570. R813M66   1977
813' .54—dc21   97-24802
                                           CIP

Published by   SUNSTONE PRESS
                  Post Office Box 2321
                  Santa Fe, NM 87504-2321 / USA
                  (505) 988-4418 / *orders only* (800) 243-5644
                  FAX (505) 988-1025

To Jimmie Cooper

For so kindly opening his Monument Spring ranch to a stranger who wanted to write a novel.

Preface

Many of those residing in Monument, New Mexico, are unaware of an incident that took place over a hundred years ago, from which their little community ultimately got its name.

There is scant mention in history of Lieutenant Colonel William R. Shafter and a contingent of brave Negro Buffalo Soldiers who, on a hot summer day in 1875, found themselves dying of thirst on the desolate Staked Plains and stumbled onto a large spring that saved their lives.

It was at this spot, on a high rise of ground near present-day Monument, New Mexico, that Colonel Shafter had his men dig slabs of white rock out of the ground and erect a seven-and-one-half-foot tall monument as a guide to future settlers where water could be found. Glinting in the sunlight, the desert lighthouse could be seen for over twenty miles.

Along with Shafter and his Buffalo Soldiers, the accomplishments of many hardy souls have received little or no recognition. Hidden in the background, but no less important, are the many soldiers, wives and Indian scouts whose courage and strong will to survive in a forbidding land have lent a solid support to the shaping of our American west.

A heavy debt of gratitude is owed to all these magnificent men and women who sacrificed so much to lay the groundwork for today's many thriving cities—and for a little town called Monument.

Prologue

Darkness finally lifted from Elizabeth Doolan's mind. With a painful moan, she slowly opened a bruised eyelid and choked in horror. Her husband, still lashed to the wagon wheel, dangled head down over a glowing fire; his brains had boiled and the skull burst open.

Lying on the hard ground, unable to move her broken arm, Elizabeth turned away with a sickening cry, praying it was all a ghastly nightmare. But the scenes of carnage raced through memory like flashes from Hell:

Terrifying Indians appearing from nowhere, surrounding the little farmhouse . . .

Rough hands throwing her to the ground . . .

Tom grabbed by the arms and forced to watch . . .

The repulsive odor of a naked heathen writhing over her body . . .

Tom's yell of outrage; swinging a heavy boot to the red man's face . . .

The Indian's nose smashed to the side, hot red blood spurting down his chest . . .

Angry commands shouted in Comanche . . .

A sharp knife whipped around her husband's head; the awful suction of his scalp being ripped off . . .

Tom, dripping with blood, tied upside down on the wagon wheel . . .

A blazing fire kindled beneath his head . . .

Vicious flames licking over Tom's face . . .

Screams of agony and the nauseating smell of burning flesh . . .

A black cloud rushing to dull her senses . . .

Merciful sleep.

Elizabeth felt a hand on her shoulder. She cringed and turned to see a man down on one knee. "Go away!" she sobbed. Leave me alone . . . leave me alone!"

He was Indian, a face of carved granite. But not like the others; tenderness floated in the shiny black eyes. He spoke in English.

"Have no fear. We are Tonkawa, friends of the white man."

She caught her breath and saw two horses. Astride one sat a stocky Indian woman, gazing with a smooth bronze countenance void of expression; straight black hair plunged to the shoulders over a necklace of tiny colored stones glinting in the last rays of sunlight.

The man spoke again. "I am Quiet Bear. This is my wife Blue Dove. Our hearts are sad for you. I know of the Kwahadi Comanche who has done this bad thing. He has sworn death to all white men who are taking his land away . . . we know what the Comanches do to white women."

She shook her head in despair. "Why . . . why?"

"To defile a white woman gives everlasting shame, even to her spirit in death. But Tonkawas do not hold to Comanche beliefs. We have learned to live with the white man. We can speak and write his language. For this, we, too, are hated by the Kwahadis."

Quiet Bear stood up, observing the charred body hanging over the still-warm fire and the burned-out sod house. "Your husband is dead and you cannot stay here alone. Your

8

body needs healing. We have a small farm. You are welcome to stay with us."

Elizabeth tried to stand but the day's numbing events made her knees buckle. Quiet Bear caught her around the waist as she broke into mournful sobs.

Blue Dove, sitting quietly on the horse, stared with curious wonder. How remarkable that the white people's eyes carried so many different colors. This white woman's eyes were like the clear turquoise sky on days when Quiet Bear rode out to hunt buffalo.

PART ONE

- 1875 -

Chapter One

"I will *not* become a nun!" Cassandra Vosburg hissed through her teeth.

A group of Magdalene sisters had just appeared, bustling on their way to morning prayers. To Cassandra, the poor things, huddled together in their white habits, were nothing more than a flock of obedient doves; no doubt itching with sweat, wrapped in those voluminous folds of starched muslin with only blank faces exposed. Lifeless eyes staring in silence.

To punctuate her words, Cassandra kicked at a lump of dirt in the little convent garden and her long blonde hair sparkled with defiance under the bright San Antonio sun.

"But Cass, what choice do you have?" Sister Angelica replied. The small nun stood nearby, holding a large basket against her pristine habit. "You've lived at the Little Company of Magdalene from the time you were six."

"Yes—working in the kitchen, tending the garden, milking a cow every morning!"

"And if you don't take the vows when you become eighteen next month, where would you go?"

"I don't know, but I'll find some way to leave this place!"

Cassandra's mood changed to sympathy for the thin little nun; the girl's plain face held dark shadows around the eyes to compliment a faint line of hair on her upper lip. When Angela had reached the same age as Cassandra, there was no prospect for marriage and the unattractive girl joined the Little Company of Magdalene out of desperation, taking the name Angelica. But unlike Cassandra, Sister Angelica had made the best of it.

The nun gave a plaintive look. "I wish you wouldn't talk about leaving, Cass. You've been the only bright spot in the convent!"

"Thank you, Sister, but let's not waste our time beating a dead horse. Besides, we mustn't let Mother Sabrina know we've been dawdling!"

Cassandra moved a sleeve across her damp forehead and knelt down in the moist soil to dig up a bunch of carrots. The vegetables, all growing to fruition under her tender care, offered their fresh pungent smell of gratitude and Cassandra recalled a passage from one of the few books she had collected. It was Keats who wrote, "Where soil is, men grow, whether to weeds or flowers." She liked to think of it as a sign of hope, for there were no weeds in her garden. She handed the carrots to Sister Angelica.

The nun placed them gently in the basket, then lifted her snowy hemline, making sure it didn't brush the dirt as she followed Cassandra to the potato rows.

"I'd help you dig, Cass, but you know what Mother Sabrina would say if I came in with my habit dirty!"

"I know." Cassandra dropped three potatoes into the basket. "Since I'm not a member of the order, she'd find a reason to blame me!"

Sister Angelica put a hand to her mouth, but couldn't suppress a giggle. "Like the time *someone* let those two mice run loose during Vespers?"

The memory brought a smile to Cassandra's pretty face. "You'll have to admit, it broke the monotony!"

A flutter among the onions caught the nun's eye. "Look

over there, Cass—it's a little bird, trying to fly!"

Cassandra rose and walked over to a small starling struggling among the green onion tops. "Why, the poor thing must have injured its wing!" She gently picked up the bird, cupping it in her hands.

Sister Angelica came over for a worried look. "Is it going to die?"

"It will if we leave it out here." Cassandra tried to kiss the tiny creature's head but it pecked at her lips. "Maybe I can keep it till it gets better—I still have that old canary cage." She gave the basket a quick glance. "Go ahead to the kitchen, Sister. I'll see you there later." She stepped quickly over the low, white picket fence and went to her room.

The little nun shrugged in resignation and started to leave as Sister Terressa came rushing from Mother Sabrina's office.

A gust of hot dry wind lifted Terressa's habit like a billowing white sail and she clutched at the starched wimple about her porcelain-smooth face. "Have you seen my sister? I thought Cass was working in the garden."

Sister Angelica carried her basket over to the fence. "We just finished. Cass found an injured little bird and took it to her room."

Terressa sighed with agitation. "Thank you, Sister."

In her little room, Cassandra put the bird into its cage with some water and a crust of bread, then turned at the sound of a light rap on the door. Terressa's muffled voice called, "Cass, we have a visitor in Mother Sabrina's office. Come with me, quickly!"

Cassandra opened the door. "Visitor? We never have visitors."

"Nevertheless, we mustn't keep him waiting." Terressa eyed her sister's clothing. "My goodness, look at you!" She bent down to brush dirt from Cassandra's rough cotton dress and straightened the cloth belt around the waist.

Cassandra gave her a loving smile; with Terressa being thirteen years older, sometimes she was almost like a mother.

"Well, that'll have to do," Terressa judged. "Come, now, let's go!"

As they hurried to the convent office, Terressa frowned at the profane rustle of her habit in the quiet hallway, then forced a pleasant look as she tapped on the office door. After a short moment, the Mother Superior opened her door with a disapproving look at Cassandra's appearance.

It came as no surprise to Cassandra who often thought that the sixtyish woman, with a silken face and only tiny wrinkles at the corners of her mouth, might be beautiful if she could just smile.

"Sister Terressa and Cassandra," the Good Mother said, "a friend of your family is here to see you—Captain Ian Shaw, of the United States Cavalry." She stood aside for them to enter. "I'll leave you alone to talk."

The two women entered and Mother Sabrina drifted from the room as if on a small white cloud, the door closing softly behind her. Cassandra caught her breath at seeing their visitor standing in the drab office.

Captain Ian Shaw radiated like a Christmas tree in his uniform—a single-breasted frock coat of dark-blue broadcloth with matching trousers and a sash of silk net wrapped twice around the waist, tied at the left hip and dangling over a foot with a tip of bullion fringe. A belt hook carried his saber, guard to the rear, while he cradled a yellow-plumed helmet in his left arm.

"Captain Ian Shaw of the United States Cavalry," he said. His rusty-gold moustache tilted with a roguish smile as he smoothed back a lock of unruly auburn hair and extended a hand. "You must be Sister Terressa."

Terressa took his hand briefly. "Yes, Captain, and this is my sister Cassandra Vosburg. Would you like to take a seat?"

Ian settled onto the worn leather chair beside Mother Sabrina's desk and the two women sat on a nearby banquette.

"Let me explain my visit," Ian continued. "My father asked that I look you up, if I passed through San Antonio. He and your father were close friends back in Pennsylvania."

"Yes, I remember him—Brian Shaw," Terressa said. "Is your father in good health?"

"Just the usual aches and pains of old age. He wasn't even sure your parents would still be around after all these years. I was sorry to learn of their passing when I asked at the post office how I could find you."

"Thank you, Captain. They died when our home burned eleven years ago."

"I'm sorry to hear that. But, thankfully, you and your sister were spared!"

"With my living at the convent and Cass going to school, we weren't home at the time. Cass was only six and there were no living relatives. I persuaded Mother Sabrina to let Cass have a room with me here at the convent—until she's old enough to be on her own."

Cassandra had been staring in fascination. Captain Shaw was not a tall man; a bit thick in the waist, perhaps, but handsome in a comfortable way. Probably in his thirties and with a cheerful nature that was infectious. His green eyes swept over her slim body and she wondered if he found her attractive, even in a soiled work dress.

Terressa looked apologetic. "I'd offer you tea, Captain, but the convent rarely receives visitors and we're not prepared for such an occasion."

Ian chuckled. "Thank you, but I'm not much of a tea drinker and besides, I can't stay long. You see, I'm in San Antonio for only a few days, on my way to Fort Concho."

Cassandra's eyes widened—what an exciting life Ian Shaw must lead as an Army captain. A daring thought stirred in her mind. "Fort Concho," she remarked, "is that far from San Antonio?"

He graced her again with his sparkling shamrock eyes. "About two hundred and thirty miles. I've just been put in charge of some Negro troops there." With a hint of embarrassment he added, "Hardly any white officers would take such a command, so it was easy for me to get the assignment. I don't mind the color of a man's skin."

Cassandra had to ask a burning question. "I suppose you have a wife waiting for you back in Pennsylvania, Captain Shaw?"

Terressa gave her a sharp look.

Ian seemed unperturbed and winked impishly. "So far, I've managed to escape the grasping arms of matrimony!"

Terressa veered away from the subject. "I'm pleased to see you harbor no prejudice with your Negro troops, Captain Shaw. You're a kind man."

There was an awkward silence, so Ian got to his feet and adjusted the saber. "Well, I really should move on . . . just wanted to let you know my father thinks about you. He'll be happy to learn that his good friend produced two such lovely daughters."

Terressa blushed slightly as she and Casssandra rose from the banquette. "When you write to your father," Terressa said, giving Ian a quick handshake, "please tell him we send our regards."

"I'll do that, Sister." He took Cassandra's hand, holding it a fraction longer than necessary. "I still have a few idle days

18

in San Antonio, Cass. Since you're not a member of the Order, maybe you could get away for a little buggy ride if it's a nice day this Sunday?"

"Oh, I'd love to!" Cassandra answered before Terressa could shoot down the invitation.

Terressa gave her a look that said, *"I'll talk to you later,"* then smiled at Ian Shaw. "If Cass has finished her chores, Captain, I'm sure it will be all right."

He beamed. "Fine! I'll stop by Sunday, right after the noon hour."

Cassandra thought Sunday would never come. Just after the noon repast, she stood before her little wall mirror, clad in a pale yellow dress, and adjusted a wide-brimmed straw hat over creamy blonde hair. She saw the reflection of her sister who had stopped in the doorway; her wistful admiring smile gave Cassandra a tiny pang of sadness.

Terressa was no doubt recalling the time so long ago when she, too, had put on a pretty dress to meet her fiance. But then an accident had cruelly taken away the handsome, young man who was to be her husband. Unable to shake the grief from her soul, Terressa had given herself to God by joining the Little Company of Magdalene.

Terressa shook her head, as if chasing away forbidden memories, and walked over to Cassandra.

"I can't believe my little sister has grown into such a lovely woman! But seriously, Cass, I must offer a word of caution—you're going out alone with an Army man, so you must watch your step. Although Captain Shaw does seem to be a gentleman, you have to be careful!"

Cassandra smiled with assurance. "Oh, Terressa you're acting like a mother hen. It's just a buggy ride, what ever could happen?"

19

"You shouldn't be so trusting. The world is full of smiling faces hiding dark thoughts!"

Cassandra looked around her sad little room. She had struggled to make it cheerful with a brightly-colored bedspread and now the little bird in its cage; but even with the nuns' constant scrubbing and cleaning, the whole convent still carried a musty smell. "It's just so nice to get away from this dreary place for a change!"

Terressa gave a hopeless sigh. "Dear Cass, you're as headstrong as our father . . . I sometimes wonder what will become of you!"

"We'll just have to wait and see!"

Cassandra's dancing eyes only added to Terressa's worry and she automatically fingered the rosary hanging at her waist.

Early afternoon finally arrived with Ian Shaw appearing at the convent. He still looked gallant in a dark-blue jacket over a blouse buttoned to the neck, gray trousers and a jaunty forage cap.

He helped Cassandra into the black-lacquered buggy that was drawn by a handsome brown horse, then climbed in and started it forward. Cassandra waved to Terressa, who stood watching with concern, and also to Sister Angelica and the other nuns peeking with jealousy through the tiny convent windows.

Ian guided the buggy through San Antonio's dusty streets, all teeming with hardy settlers migrating west and Army personnel going to various forts that waited forlornly on the arid plains.

Finally they moved out of the noisy city and to the crest of a hill, stopping beside a lonely elm that stood like a sentinel guarding its domain.

Cassandra felt overwhelmed by the view. "Why,

Captain Shaw, you can see all of San Antonio from up here!"

"Now look," he chided, "we have to get something settled right away. If I can call you 'Cass,' you can call me 'Ian.'" He followed her gaze. "I take it you've never been out of the city before, Cass?"

"I've never been anywhere." She leaned back with dejection. "All I know about the world is what I read in books—and *they* don't tell me very much."

"You mean you've stayed in that convent all this time, no boyfriends or anything?"

"Oh, I wasn't restricted by the nuns' regulations, but I did have to earn my keep. I went to school in town and was allowed to go to a dance now and then—but everything had to be approved by Terressa."

"Then you've never been serious about a boy?"

"Not really." She was quick to add, "But that doesn't mean I *couldn't* be!"

The sun kindly lingered behind a small cloud and Cassandra took off the straw hat, fluffing her honey-blonde hair; after this morning's washing, it glistened like soft flax. She noticed Ian marveling at her profile and the ever-so-slight tilt of the nose; her father once said it gave her a delicate inquisitive expression.

Ian loosened his collar and leaned back, taking a small flask from his coat pocket.

"Care for a sip of brandy?" He unscrewed the lid.

"Goodness, no!" she replied with a gasp. "I've never had a drop of liquor in my life, and besides, Terressa would do a hundred Hail Marys if she knew I tried it!" Her eyes narrowed wickedly, "But I *am* curious—let me see what it's like."

She took the flask and raised it until the brandy just touched her lips. With a grimace she shoved it back to him.

"Oh, that's like fire, how can you drink it?!"

He laughed heartily. "The luck of the Irish. Seems to be one of our sinful delights!" He took a good swallow, wiped his moustache with the back of a hand and returned the flask to his coat pocket.

"It must be like living in a box," he said. "The convent, I mean. You plan to stay there the rest of your life, Cass?"

She frowned at being reminded of her dilemma, and on such a lovely day at that.

"I really don't know what I'm going to do, but I have to decide by the end of next month. I'll be eighteen then and Terressa expects me to take the Magdalene vows."

"Don't you want to be a nun?"

"Oh, *no*!"

"Then, what would you really like to do?"

"You'd laugh if I told you."

"I never laugh at a beautiful girl with a problem."

Her eyes turned dreamy. "My Uncle Emil has a little farm in the Territory of New Mexico and he writes us now and then. It must be exciting to know that you're the first person to gaze on a raw, new land . . . the first one to plow earth that has never felt a blade . . . to build a whole new world. Well, if I were a man, that's what I'd like to do!"

"I like that strong will of yours! You have the same spunk my mother had. Nothing ever stood in her way—till pneumonia took her while I was attending West Point. Her name was Rose."

"Rose. That's a nice name. I'm glad I remind you of your mother."

"Daddy called her his 'Rose of Tralee.'" He cleared his throat, getting back to the subject. "Now, about your situation. Lots of women are going west every day. You ever see all the settlers moving out of San Antonio, and all the women in those wagons?"

"Yes, but they have husbands with them."

"Then it looks like you'll just have to find a man who's on his way west."

Her eyes sparkled as she turned to him. "When do you have to leave San Antonio, Ian?"

"Another three days."

"Take me with you, Ian!"

He sat up as if kicked in the stomach by an angry mule. "Are you sure you didn't take a swig of that brandy?"

"Oh, Ian, you're my last chance . . . my *only* chance to get away from that convent! Isn't there some way I could go with you to Fort Concho?"

He quickly retrieved the flask and drained the little container. "If you went with me, you'd have to go as my wife," he croaked. "It's the only way, but that's impossible!"

"I don't see why!"

"Look, Cass, we've only just met . . . seen each other twice in our lives. You don't know anything about me, and the only thing I know about you is that you're a beautiful young thing with a head full of wild ideas!"

"My father and your father were good friends. You're a nice, likeable man, Ian. I know we could make each other happy!"

He shook his head. "Cass, a woman doesn't propose marriage—the man's supposed to do that!"

"Then, just treat it like a business arrangement."

"But you don't know anything about marriage! There happens to be a thing attached called Love."

"We could grow to love each other, Ian. I'd make you a good wife, I know I would!"

His eyes grew soft with understanding. "I can't blame you for being a little desperate with the drab life of a convent

23

lying ahead." He took her hand. "You're young, beautiful and full of spirit . . . and Saints preserve, it wouldn't take much for me to fall in love with you! But Cass, being an Army wife isn't the excitement you think it is. It's a hard life and lots of women can't take it."

"*Any* life would be better than the convent, Ian. Why, I've been working for years, cooking, milking a cow, growing vegetables. Isn't that what a wife does?"

"You've been protected all these years by a covey of nuns. How would you adapt to the grueling life on some desolate Army post?" He leaned back, arms folded across his chest. "Besides, I can't just take you away—that's the same as kidnapping! What would your sister say?" He shook his head. "She'd never allow it!"

"We'll talk to her . . . I know I could make her understand!"

He gave her a hard appraising look. "Are you cross-your-heart-hope-to-die serious about this, Cass?"

"Oh, *yes*, Ian!" She clutched his arm. "You'd be doing me the greatest favor of my life!"

His eyes rolled heavenward. "Please look down with forgiveness on a poor Irishman being lured into the valley of temptation!" With a deep sigh, he studied her lovely pleading face. "All right, m'love, we'll go back and see what your sister thinks about all this." He wagged a finger. "But I'm not going to fight her. If she says 'No,' then I'll leave you here and skedaddle on to Fort Concho without you!"

Her heart seemed to burst with joy. "Oh, thank you, Ian!" She threw her arms around him for a loving hug.

He grinned. "I believe this kind of business deal should be sealed with a kiss!"

She moved back in surprise.

"You mean you've never been kissed?"

She looked down with embarrassment.

He placed a finger beneath her chin and raised her blushing face. "Well, you'll have to start getting used to it. That's what marriage is all about!" He lowered his head and gently kissed her soft lips.

Cassandra stiffened at first, but he pulled her close and she melted, receiving him warmly. After all, it was her own decision and she had to go through with it. Realizing the door to a strange new life was opening, she tightened her arms around him and tingled with excitement.

Chapter Two

Traylor Doolan reined Pardo to a halt and gave his faithful horse a loving rub behind the ear. The Rockies were behind him, now, and with his keen senses Tray could taste the sweet clean desert breeze gently caressing his ruddy face. It felt good to be back in Texas again.

He took off the slouch hat and brushed aside a wisp of black hair, his sharp blue eyes moving over the stark Panhandle floor that swept below. Two hundred miles to the south a new assignment lay waiting—the longest and most dangerous one yet, in a part of the country he hadn't yet explored. He itched to get started.

Tray settled with ease in the Pueblo saddle that had been custom-made for him in Colorado. It cost a pretty penny, but he still had some pay left over after scouting the wagon train from Fort Sill. The new saddle held his slender body like a comforting hand and even Pardo seemed pleased with the lighter weight now carried on his back.

"Well, Old Friend," Tray said to the drab-brown horse, "we've got a good ways to go, so better keep movin'."

He used his spurs gently and the horse took him down into the Staked Plains, a wide nothingness of red baked clay. In the west, colorful battlements rose in shiny reds and dull yellows, mixed with somber dark brown and purple. With his knowledge of the plains, Tray carried ample water; if any were found here, it would be bitter as gall and eat through a man's guts with a single mouthful.

By late afternoon, Tray had reached the upper Brazos while a molten-red horizon signaled time to make camp. He stopped, freeing his horse of the saddle.

"Go ahead, Pardo, get that sweat off!"

The animal rolled happily in patches of finely-woven mesquite grass, rubbing away the dried itchy perspiration.

Tray fed and watered his devoted companion, then dug up some mesquite root to make a fire and prepared a small meal of coffee, beans and unleavened bread.

Soon the tired sun wrapped itself up for the night and Tray, likewise, rolled himself into a blanket. He lay content under a black velvet sky strewn with thousands of sparkling diamonds while the moan of a lonely coyote broke the prairie's silence.

Tray relaxed, but he always slept with one eye open; hostile Indians, hungry for white man's blood, still roamed the plains and a lone traveler was easy prey.

In the half-light of early morning, Tray continued south and arrived at a more hospitable area where a little farm used to be. Now, it was just a flat expanse of dirt and hardy grass, raked smooth by years of harsh desert winds. Only four mounds of earth showed that anyone had ever lived in the area. The wooden markers were long gone, probably trampled by buffalo and blown away.

Tray climbed down from the saddle and stood in reverence, his soft blue eyes resting on the graves. Two of them held Quiet Bear and blue Dove, the kindly Tonkawa Indians who had taken Tray as their own after his birth twenty-five years earlier. He could still picture their soft features and feel the love they had spread over him like a warm buffalo robe. It was from old Quiet Bear that Tray learned the ways of the prairie and languages of its people.

Tray's eyes moved to the other two graves and his loving ache turned quickly to vengeful anger. He clenched his fists against the painful memories and quickly climbed back into the Pueblo saddle, urging Pardo southward.

The endless flat plains had a calming effect on Tray's mind and he glanced at the clear sky. If the weather held, and no hot-headed Indians showed up, he'd soon be at Fort Concho to take part in the biggest campaign of his life.

Chapter Three

Cassandra felt like the little starling she had nursed back to health and set free, the happy bird stretching its wings to fly off, unrestrained, into an endless blue sky. Now, she, too, was about to fly away, but under the new name of Mrs. Ian Shaw. However, one thing shadowed her happiness—she had to convince Terressa.

Cassandra and Ian broke the news with the effect of a spring tornado sweeping over the little convent.

"Marriage?!" Terressa cried with a stricken face. "Cass, have you taken leave of your senses?"

Cassandra took a deep breath to deliver a well-rehearsed speech. "Terressa, I love and respect you for raising me like Mama would have wanted. But the convent isn't for me. I'd just die a lonely old woman if I had to spend the rest of my life behind these walls!"

Terressa dropped into a chair and clutched the rosary at her waist. "But you have love and security here, Cass . . . what kind of life will you have, married to an Army officer?"

Ian bridled at the remark. He had planned to say very little and maybe back out of the whole thing, but now felt compelled to speak up.

"Sister, as an Army officer, I am a man of honor. I promise to give Cass love and security—and I swear to you that I'll let nothing stand in the way of her happiness!"

Tears filled Cassandra's eyes and she took her sister's

hand. "Terressa, please try to understand that it's my life and I'm the one who should decide what to do with it."

Terressa finally leaned back in resignation. "Dearest Cassandra, I know it's useless to argue. You've always carried the strongest of our father's German blood!"

Cassandra turned ecstatic. "Then you'll give us your blessing?"

Terressa rose slowly from the chair, looking like the sole survivor of a terrible war. She walked over to Ian. "You gave me your word, Captain Shaw, and I'll just have to trust you. We are taught here to forgive our trespassers—but if you let anything happen to my little sister, I'll have to break that vow!"

Ian smiled and took her hand for a gentle kiss. "You needn't worry, Sister. You are a brave and understanding woman."

Terressa shook her head with a grim smile. "Being brave and understanding has nothing to do with it, Captain. I'm simply powerless. It's easier to move a mountain than to change Cass's mind!"

During the last furious days, much had to be done in so little time. Immediately following a quick wedding at the post chapel the newlyweds parted momentarily, Ian making arrangements for the wagon train taking them to Fort Concho and Cassandra gleefully cutting the ties that bound her to the convent.

But when the moment came to say goodbye, Cassandra felt pangs of remorse as she and Terressa tearfully hugged each other in the stark little convent room. Cassandra realized she was giving up everything she ever loved and prayed that she had chosen the proper road, with Ian guiding her toward a good new life.

The only consolation was the memory of her dear Papa's words. As a child, she would sit on the floor beside his big worn chair near the fireplace, blue smoke from his pipe filling the air with the woodsy smell of maple leaves in autumn. The words he spoke then, while stroking her soft blonde hair, had never left her mind: "If your back is ever against the wall, little *Liebchen*, I know, with my German blood running through your veins, you'll find the way out!"

Before they parted, Terressa brought out a well-worn Bible, its pages slightly charred around the edges.

"This was Mama's," she said, handing the Book to Cassandra. "It was the only thing not burned in the fire. Our family's names and dates of their births and deaths are all written on the first pages." Terressa's eyes misted sadly. "Since I'll never continue the family's heritage, it's your duty now, Cass, to record all forthcoming history of the Vosburgs in this Bible."

Cassandra opened the Book to see a page filled with records going back to a host of unknown relatives who had lived and died in Germany. She sat at the little table and took a pen in hand. Beneath the last entry—the date Mama and Papa died—she carefully entered her and Ian's wedding date.

Cassandra packed the Bible along with six other volumes of literature collected over the years. She possessed few belongings; a good thing, for the wagons had scant room for unessential goods.

On the morning of departure, fresh morning sun spread its warmth over the little caravan assembled outside the San Antonio Army post.

"You'll be riding in this wagon," Ian told Cassandra. "It's called an ambulance. During the war these wagons carried the wounded, but now we use them for transporting people and equipment."

31

Cassandra gave her conveyance a doubtful look. It was nothing more than a stout spring wagon equipped with a wood-and-leather seat in front and topped with canvas, supported on wooden bows.

The train included another ambulance with supplies and rations plus two pack mules and ten mounted Negro recruits who would join the Tenth Cavalry at Fort Concho.

Ian had assigned a Negro sergeant to drive the two mules pulling Cassandra's ambulance. Slightly older than the young recruits, he wore dark-blue trousers and gray flannel shirt with a little Confederate forage cap tilted devil-may-care to the back of his head.

As Ian helped Cassandra aboard he introduced them. "Cassandra, this is Sergeant Eben Carruthers. He'll be your driver and companion on the trip." Then he grinned at Carruthers. "You take care of my little wife, now, Sergeant."

"Don' you worry none, Cap'n," Carruthers replied.

Ian rode to the head of the train and gave the signal to start. Eben Carruther's big black hands gently urged the mules forward and the group began its arduous trek across a portion of the dry Llano Estacado, its stark expanse relieved only by clumps of yellowed buffalo grass.

Eben guided the wagon in silence and Cassandra thought perhaps he was reluctant to talk for fear of saying the wrong thing.

"Do you have a family, Sergeant?" she asked casually as the wagon struggled with harsh bumps over the thirsty ground.

"No, Ma'am." He kept his eyes squinting at the backs of the plodding mules.

"Are your folks living?"

"No, Ma'am."

"I was born and raised in San Antonio. Where are you

from, Sergeant?"

"Little place in Georgia . . . Antonville."

"What made you join the Army?"

"After slaves was freed, weren't no place fer me t'go. Army looked pretty good. They gimme food, clothes an' a place to sleep."

"And you get paid, too!"

A tiny smile cracked his solemn lips. "Fer what it is, I could almos' do without that."

Tiny beads of perspiration formed on his dark forehead; the wrong words might have slipped out. He wiped his face with the large yellow kerchief tied around his neck.

"You must have been stationed in San Antonio for some time, since you're a sergeant—what takes you to Fort Concho?"

"They needed somebody with rank t'oversee these recruits. 'Sides, I wanna see some action. I'm gonna be a Buffalo Soldier with the Tenth Cavalry at Fort Concho."

"Why are they called Buffalo Soldiers?"

"Indians give 'em that name. T'them, a black man's hair's like the buffalo's."

"It doesn't seem very nice of the Indians, comparing you to a buffalo!"

"Ain't no offense, Ma'am. The buffalo's brave, and he's sacred to the Indians. The Ninth and Tenth think it's a honor t'be called Buffalo Soldiers!"

"Well, I know that my husband thinks very highly of the Negro soldiers. He says they can always be depended upon."

"It's jes a job, but I guess us black folks wanna do it the bes' way we can."

He felt comfortable again and his dark eyes sparkled with pride while he jiggled the reins.

✻   ✻   ✻

33

Ian had positioned Cassandra's ambulance just behind him so that she caught very little of the dust stirred up by the company. She glanced with pity at the men in the rear, their faces covered with bandannas to block out the dirt and grime.

The plodding, little wagon train averaged twelve miles per day, traveling from daybreak until ten o'clock when they stopped for a "nooning," as the rest was called. After the blistering sun had moved from overhead, at two or three in the afternoon, the group started out again.

Firewood proved to be nonexistent on the flat treeless plains. Any piece of wood or buffalo chip that happened to lie in their path was picked up and thrown into a mule skin that hung beneath the supply wagon.

They made camp at sundown with only three cheerful campfires coaxed into life while the men began raising their little tents.

Cassandra felt downhearted, being able to prepare only fried bacon, beans and strong Arbuckles coffee for their supper.

"Terressa taught me how to prepare some of Mama's German dishes," she told Ian. "But out here, I don't even have an oven to make biscuits!"

"Well, when you're on the plains, you just have to improvise," he said. "If you'll mix up some flour, lard and water with a little salt, I'll give you a lesson in prairie cooking."

She did as he suggested and Ian rolled the mixture into strips, then wound them around two wooden sticks. They held these over the fire until baked and Cassandra enjoyed the "bread" that accompanied their meal.

Afterwards, Cassandra stood beside the tent, taking in the last remnants of daylight fading slowly beyond distant hills. A patch of soft aquamarine sky gave way to rolling gray clouds in the northwest, their dark forms broken intermittently by little

34

streaks of lightning.

Ian appeared at her side and put a large arm around her waist. "Reckon that little storm'll be gone by morning," he said.

"I see the lightning, but I don't hear any thunder."

"Sound of thunder curves upward. If it's more than fifteen miles away, you don't hear it."

She breathed in the clean air and pressed against his large body. "I've never felt so free in my life—it's like you can see to the ends of the earth! I wish we'd never get to Fort Concho, Ian. Maybe we'll become lost and have to stay out here on the plains forever!"

He laughed and pulled her closer. "I do believe I've married me a wild one! Don't ever think you want to be lost on the Llano Estacado. She's like a fickle woman who'll make love to you at night and leave you dying of thirst in the morning!" He turned her around for a tender kiss. "Now, little one, it's time you rested up for another long day. There're lots more sunsets waiting for you, even prettier than this one."

They snuggled together under a blanket in the big tent and Cassandra tried to convince herself that marrying Ian was the right decision after all. She kissed his cheek, recalling her words that they could grow to love each other.

She felt safe, now, in Ian's strong arms; but still, there was a savage new world lurking out there. Just the thought of it made her tremble.

Chapter Four

Cassandra wore one of Ian's big slouch hats to fend off the intense sun while she rode beside Eben in the ambulance. After enduring several days of bleak monotony, her backside ached from the bumping, hard wood seat.

At intervals, the men on horseback dismounted and walked for several miles to give their animals relief. On these occasions Cassandra climbed down from the torturous wagon and also trudged along, staying beside the ambulance as it moved slowly onward.

Eben sat undisturbed with reins in hand and she wondered how a person with dark skin could tolerate such a harsh climate.

"Sergeant Carruthers, why do they call this place the Llano Estacado?" she asked while plodding in the dust.

"Spaniards give it that name when they discovered it." He wiped sweat from his brow. "Means 'Staked Plains' in English."

"Why Staked Plains?"

"Nobody knows f'sure. Some folk say the Spaniards drove metal stakes t'mark where they went. Then some folk say it's 'cause o' the cactus that looks like spikes. Other folk think it's 'cause them mountains in the west look like a stockade."

Cassandra ran a handkerchief around her perspiring neck. "Well, if I hadn't been raised in a convent, I could think of something else to call it!"

During midmorning they came upon the remains of a wagon abandoned by some hapless traveler who had struggled before them. Since it offered a good supply of firewood, the train stopped while Eben Carruthers had two recruits tear the boards apart.

Cassandra welcomed the break in routine and sat in the ambulance, idly watching.

One tall lanky Negro by the name of Joshua Barnes lifted a board. Suddenly he jumped back with a startled yell; a large diamondback rattlesnake, disturbed in its cool retreat, had lashed out, sinking its fangs into the man's flesh.

Cassandra stared in horror as Joshua danced around in panic, the ugly reptile dangling from his arm.

"Git 'im offa me!" he yelled. "Somebody git 'im offa me!"

The snake finally dropped to the ground and Eben quickly pulled his revolver, blasting off its head with a single shot. He then led the shaking Joshua to Cassandra's ambulance.

"Miz Shaw," Eben said, "if you'd kindly let me have some salt, and somethin' fer a bandage, I'll fix this man up."

Cassandra retrieved the items, then cringed as Eben took his sharp knife and cut two deep gashes on the bitten area of Joshua's arm.

The poor man gritted his teeth in silence, but when Eben packed the wound with salt Joshua yowled in pain.

Eben tied a bandage around the arm and turned to Cassandra. "Would you happen to have any kerosene, Ma'am?"

"Why, yes, we brought some to use in the lamps." Cassandra handed him a tin of kerosene.

Eben carefully poured a little over the bandaged arm until it was thoroughly soaked. "There, that oughta do it," he exclaimed with a satisfied grin. "Now, you git back t'work,

Josh!"

"Sergeant Carruthers!" Cassandra said. "You mean you're sending a man back to work right after getting bitten by a horrible snake?!" She looked with pity at Joshua Barnes. "Couldn't Private Barnes ride with us till we know that snake venom isn't going to kill him?"

Eben tried to hide his amusement. He motioned for Joshua to get into the wagon while the other men snickered behind their hands. Joshua climbed in and gave his fellow recruits a large, defiant smile.

At the end of the day Joshua Barnes seemed in good health and strutted back to his unit with a privileged glow on his face.

One of the Negro soldiers spit tobacco juice at Joshua's feet. "Some men'll do anythin' to get a ride with a pretty white gal!"

Ian eventually halted the party as it approached a slight rise in the flat stretch of prairie. He trotted his horse back to Cassandra, which he often did to see how she was faring.

"That's Saint Angela, way ahead," he said, pointing to the horizon. "Can you see it?"

Cassandra shaded her eyes and looked very hard. At first she saw nothing but a faint, shimmering mirage, then the tiny shapes of buildings took form.

"Just across the river is Fort Concho," Ian said. "We oughta be there by late afternoon."

Cassandra had quickly lost appreciation for the long stretch of nothingness and looked forward to the pleasures of civilization. But as they pulled into Saint Angela her heart sank.

A far cry from San Antonio's wide, bustling streets and tall buildings, here sprawled a dirty collection of stick-and-mud hovels, gambling dens, bawdy houses and a number of saloons.

They passed through the dust-filled community in short order and were soon across the river, entering Fort Concho where another depressing scene confronted them. The garrison was nothing but a sad accumulation of dilapidated buildings, sagging porches and broken windows stuffed with rags and old blankets. Trash-strewn ditches were everywhere.

"Do people really live here?" Cassandra uttered with disdain.

Eben shrugged. "Concho's had a string o' commandin' officers, one right after the other. Reckon none of 'em has been here long enough t'keep it lookin' right."

A row of stark two-story limestone houses on one side served as officers' quarters, while opposite the quadrangle squatted six long, wood-and-adobe barracks for the enlisted men. The only other buildings were a two-story hospital, storehouses for the commissary and quartermaster, a powder magazine and a small, eight-cell guardhouse.

The entire post, including the parade ground, sat almost hidden by weeds, some three-feet high, their only saving grace being that they masked the odious droppings of a multitude of dogs. Some could be seen romping in the distance. Rising out of the weeds and trash on the parade ground, a flagpole stood with the American banner hanging forlornly in the hot, dead air, as if ashamed to be seen amid such disgrace.

Cassandra slumped with dejection on the wagon seat. "I wonder how long I'll have to call this dreadful place my home?!"

"Don't you fret, Miz Shaw," Eben told her. "The way officers get moved around, you might be outta here in no time!"

She recalled Ian saying that Army officers were continually shunted from one fort to another; maybe they would soon be transferred to a more welcome establishment.

They waited in the hot dusty ambulance while Ian reported his arrival. After a few minutes he returned to let Cassandra know which house would be theirs.

"It's that second one up there," he said. "We'll be sharing it with another captain and his wife." Then to Eben, "Sergeant, you help my wife unload the wagon and I'll get the recruits assigned. I'll be back before dark."

Eben pulled the ambulance to a stop in front of the forlorn building and Cassandra climbed down. As she approached the tilting front stoop, a thin, dark-haired figure stepped out of the doorway.

"Welcome to Fort Depression," the woman said. "I'm Millicent Adams, but please call me Millie. My husband is Captain Henry Adams. We heard you were coming—they told us you'd be our roommates!"

Cassandra guessed that she and Millicent Adams might be about the same age, however Millie's face carried a worn-out look that added a year or more to the listless, dark eyes. Straight, black hair, dull even in the sunlight, touched her shoulders while a nondescript skirt and blouse begged for the touch of a kindly iron.

Cassandra walked up and shook the woman's rough-skinned hand. "I'm Cassandra Shaw, but I'd like you to call me Cass. My husband is Captain Ian Shaw . . . he's busy with the recruits right now." She peered through the open door. "All right if I start moving in?"

"Make yourself at home." Millie showed Cassandra into the house.

The building had smooth pecan wood floors, a fireplace at each end, a small kitchen and sitting room downstairs with a pecan wood staircase leading to the two bedrooms above.

"I hope you have a strong stomach," Millie went on. "I wanted to vomit, my first day here. Henry keeps telling me

40

there are worse forts than Concho, but I find that hard to believe!"

As Cassandra stood appraising her new home, a large brown scorpion ambled across the floor. It stopped near her feet, and curled a tail forward. She stepped back in alarm.

Millie uttered something under her breath and grabbed a broom. "You'll get used to these little house guests!" She gave the ugly creature a heavy swat. "It's the centipedes you have to watch out for, they can really sneak up on you!"

She swept the dead scorpion out through the open doorway as Eben appeared with a box under each arm. He stepped around the squashed insect and came inside.

"Sergeant Carruthers," Cassandra said to Eben, "this is Millie Adams. Ian and I will be sharing the house with Millie and her husband, Captain Henry Adams."

Eben and Millie nodded politely at each other and she led them up the staircase.

"The bedroom on the left is yours," Millie advised. "Henry and I have this one across the hall. I'll stay out of your way while you unpack. If you need anything, just give a holler." She disappeared into her own room.

Eben deposited the boxes in the empty bedroom, then went back downstairs for more. Cassandra stepped cautiously inside and looked with misgivings at her new quarters.

The sun's fading rays struggled through dirt-encrusted panes of a small window to reveal the only pieces of furniture—a double bed and crude chest of drawers.

Cassandra walked across the creaking wooden floor and sat on the edge of the bed. She was welcomed by the sound of rusty springs and a cloud of powdery dust that rose from the coverlet. She sneezed and realized that dust was everywhere.

Her heart turned over in despair; the neat little room back at the convent, now, didn't seem so drab after all. And this was to be the first bedroom she and Ian would spend the night in!

Tears welled in her eyes. If the bed hadn't been so dirty, she would have thrown herself face-down for a good cry. But there was no turning back. She'd just have to make the best of it.

Cassandra wiped her eyes, then went across the hallway to the Adams' bedroom and knocked lightly on the open door.

"Millie, could I bother you for a moment?"

"Come on in, Cass. I'm only making up the bed."

Cassandra entered and found the Adams' bedroom a little more cheerful than her own. At least the windows had curtains and a hooked rug lay on the hard wooden floor.

"I really ought to clean up our room before Ian returns," Cassandra said. "Is it possible to get hold of a broom, a pail of water and some rags?"

Millie laughed. "I guess it is a mess, nobody's lived in there since the last officer and his wife got transferred four months ago. I think we can find what you need downstairs."

Cassandra noticed a framed picture resting on the bureau and walked over to study it. The photograph showed an attractive young girl with glistening black hair, clad in a white gown and on the arm of a Cavalry officer. He was slender, handsome and wore round, wire-frame spectacles.

"That's our wedding picture," Millie said. "Taken two years ago in Ohio."

Cassandra almost gasped. Only two years ago! She could hardly believe the comparison of the lovely girl in the photo with the same worn-out-looking woman standing here beside her.

Millie saw the surprise in Cassandra's eyes and smiled ironically. "Yes, that's me, but those were better days. Before I married, I lived in a big house—even had a maid to do my hair. With Daddy's money, I had anything I wanted."

"It must have been hard to give it all up when you married Henry," Cassandra said.

"Oh, I thought I'd still have everything, being an officer's wife living in Washington. But I learned fast that you can't outguess the Army!"

"You never got to Washington?"

Millie shrugged. "Henry's orders were changed right after the wedding and our first assignment was here at Fort Concho—the ends of the earth. I wanted to kill myself when I saw this place, but I'd bitten off my piece of cake and had to swallow it."

Cassandra nodded with sympathy. "I think I know how you felt!"

"You'll see, Cass. Existing in this dried-out purgatory, life has no meaning. You won't have a reason to put on a nice dress . . . fix your hair . . . make your face pretty. Nobody here gives a darn!"

"There's always your husband Henry."

Millie shrugged. "Even *he* doesn't care anymore! The only thing that'll keep you from going crazy, Cass, is remembering all the nice things you left behind!"

Ian Shaw and Henry Adams had become instant bosom friends. At the end of the day they burst into the house, laughing uproariously over some racy joke, while Cassandra and Millie busied themselves in the kitchen over a simple evening meal.

"Cass, m'love," Ian called to his wife, "think you can find that bottle of brandy we packed? Henry and I need to wash this Concho dirt out of our throats!"

Cassandra took the brandy bottle from a top shelf and carried it to the sitting room. Millie followed with two chipped glasses.

Ian grabbed Cassandra for a loving hug. "Henry Adams, meet Cassandra, the beautiful bride I've been telling you about!"

Henry's eyes lit up through the large, round wire spectacles, as if he were seeing an attractive woman for the first time in years. "Welcome to your new home, Cassandra—such as it is!" He turned to Ian. "When the rest of the men see what you've brought to the fort, you'll have to fight 'em off like flies!" He took Millie's hand. "Ian, this is my wife, Millie. Hardly a bride, but she's had two years' experience!"

Cassandra gave Henry his drink and said, "I feel like we've already met. Millie showed me your wedding picture this afternoon."

He raised an eyebrow. "Now, you see what two years of Army life can do to a happily married couple!" His remark, intended as a joke, seemed more like a warning.

The two men collapsed into chairs, pulled off their boots and began swapping hilarious Army adventures.

Henry, in his late thirties, seemed nearly lost in the big, wingback chair, his prominent spectacles making him look like a happy, young school boy, just home from class.

In appearance, the two were as different as night and day, Ian large and burly in his uniform and Henry's clothes hanging loose on his short thin frame; but they shared the same appreciation for a mocking laugh at the vagaries of life.

Late in the evening, a bugler's jolting signal for lights out punctured the quietness surrounding Fort Concho and Ian yawned. "Don't know about you two," he said to Henry and Millie, "but Cass and I've had a long day!"

"Well, reveille comes early and we've talked enough," Henry replied. "Let's call it a night."

44

Henry and Ian took kerosene lamps and led their wives upstairs where the two couples said good night.

After closing their door, Millie Adams changed into her nightgown and turned to see Henry already in bed, his spectacles resting on the night table. She extinguished the lamp, then lifted the blanket and crawled in beside her husband. They lay silent for a moment.

"Nice having someone else in the house," Henry finally said. "What d'you think of the Shaws?"

"They're a nice couple. She's quite lovely."

"I wonder how long it'll be before she . . . " He stopped, realizing he was about to say the wrong thing. He turned his face to her in the dark. "I know it's rough for a woman living out here, Honey. I'm just sorry I couldn't have gotten a better assignment."

"You could have, if you weren't so stubborn."

He sighed in exasperation, hoping the subject wouldn't be dredged up again.

But she kept on. "You know Daddy could've arranged it. Being an arms supplier during the war, he knew all the right people in Washington."

"I told you I didn't want to be helped that way. Anything I get out of the Army, I want to do it on my own."

"Poor Daddy is so disappointed. You could be holding a high position, now, and we could be living in a decent officer's home, instead of this . . . " She shuddered, unable to find the right despicable word.

He turned on his side, their bodies touching, and placed a hand on her shoulder. "Millie, it won't be long. Look at all the others who've been transferred. There'll be a big field expedition here in a few months, then I'll try to get a transfer to Fort Davis. I hear that's officers' heaven, you'll love it!"

"That's wishful thinking and you know it. I know I'm

going to shrivel up and die at Fort Concho!" She turned her back to him with a little sob.

Henry rolled away and stared at the dark ceiling. She was right. He *could* have sucked up to all that brass, but damned if he was going to be a toady. Even with all the glamour that came with it, he could never live with himself. But look at what he was doing to Millie. Well, if she could just hold out a little longer, things would get better. He closed his eyes and tried to sleep, but knew it would be a losing battle.

Even though Cassandra had been able to chase the dust away, their bedroom stubbornly refused to look friendly. Ian extinguished the lamp and climbed in between cold sheets, the bed springs protesting with shrill squeaks. He pulled Cassandra close to his large body for both warmth and affection.

"Do you realize this is our first real bedroom?" she said. "It doesn't look like much now, but I promise I'll have it looking nice in a few days."

"Doesn't matter where we are," he mumbled. "As long as I've got you in my arms, I'm happy!"

She smiled in the darkness. The anguish and despair she had felt upon arrival at Fort Concho were now all in the background; with Ian's warm body breathing next to her, she felt content and secure.

After the last twenty-four hours she was completely exhausted, but her thoughts kept roaming over the day's events and Millie Adams came to mind. The poor girl's face carried a haunting, resigned look. It was a gloomy portent of what life at Fort Concho had to offer.

While pondering the subject, Ian's light rhythmic snoring lulled Cassandra into a restful sleep.

Chapter Five

Cassandra's eyes flew open at the earsplitting sound of "Reveille" delivered by a bugler hidden somewhere among the weeds and trash on the parade ground. She covered her ears and waited until the end, sighing with relief; then it started again and she endured an agonizing repetition.

Her little clock, sitting next to the glowing lamp, showed five o'clock and she turned sleepy eyes to see Ian nearby, buttoning his coat.

"You awake, Honey?" he asked with a bright smile.

She wanted to throw a pillow at him, but yawned instead. "Isn't everybody from here to San Antonio awake now? That poor man must be getting revenge for having to blow his horn at this ungodly hour!"

"Sorry I don't have time to eat breakfast with you, I'll just grab some of Millie's coffee. And don't forget to shake the scorpions out of your shoes!" He gave her a quick kiss and left.

With reluctance, Cassandra vacated the warm bed and dutifully shook her shoes—no scorpions, thank goodness. She put on a robe and made her way downstairs to find Millie in a sad-looking house coat, pouring a cup of coffee.

"Did you enjoy our little musical greeting?" Millie asked. "That's why I get up so early—to beat that bugler at his own game!"

Cassandra laughed. "Guess it's one of the things I'll

have to get used to."

"We can whip up a breakfast, if you have an appetite. I lost mine the day I came to this place!"

Cassandra still felt a little confused and shook her head. "Thank you, Millie, but coffee will do me fine."

Millie poured another cup and they seated themselves at the rough table.

"Are we the only women here at Fort Concho?" Cassandra asked with a tiny yawn.

"Only one other, so far. Major Thomas Manning and his wife Anne have the house next door. I understand more personnel are arriving in the next few days, with probably a wife or two." She snorted with derision. "Of course, we always have the laundresses, but they live in those awful shacks behind the enlisted men's barracks."

With Millie's strong coffee, Cassandra now felt able to face her new environment. "I think I'll dress and have a look around the fort, Millie. Care to go with me?"

Millie winced. "Please let me beg off, Cass. I don't want to see any more of this place than I have to!"

Cassandra dressed and put on a light shawl to protect her shoulders from the cold morning air. She had no longer stepped off the creaky porch into the morning sun when two men approached, a mature-looking colonel and a young lieutenant.

"Pardon me," the colonel said cheerfully, "I take it you're the wife of Captain Shaw who just arrived yesterday?" He had a longer beard than most men and his eyes were sharp but kind.

"Why, yes, I'm Cassandra Shaw."

"May I present myself—Colonel Benjamin Grierson, the post commander of Fort Concho."

Cassandra felt honored. "I'm so happy to meet you,

48

Colonel. I was just about to get acquainted with your establishment."

"Precisely why we're here. I've brought along Lieutenant William Burger to show you around."

The young man clicked his heels together and made a little bow. He seemed just a boy with short platinum hair topping a shiny face that looked freshly scrubbed. "Pleased to be at your service, Mrs. Shaw!"

Colonel Grierson looked chagrined. "I must apologize for the deplorable look of this place, Mrs. Shaw, but with the men your husband brought along, I can get a good start, now, on cleaning it up. I promise by tomorrow, at least the weeds will be gone from the front of your house!"

Cassandra glanced at the eyesore. "It looks like you'll have your hands full, Colonel!"

"More officers and their families are arriving tomorrow, so we have to work quickly." He added with a chuckle, "And I don't dare ask my wife and children to come out until I have this place sparkling!"

Cassandra brightened. "Really? I'll be anxious to meet them!"

"No as much as I!" He gave an agitated look. "If you'll excuse me, Mrs. Shaw, I do have to run." He took her hand for a quick shake. "I'll leave you in Lieutenant Burger's care. If you need anything, please feel free to call on me."

After Colonel Grierson departed, Cassandra and Lieutenant Burger began their tour, stepping carefully around the weeds and fly-encrusted dog droppings. She wondered how long it would be before she could walk the grounds of Fort Concho with confidence.

"I'm afraid it's going to be a while before the colonel can ask his family to join him," she said.

He caught her inference with a grin. "He'll have to get

the place in order before June. Not only for his family's sake, but that's when Colonel Shafter comes in to prepare for a large campaign."

They stopped in front of the two-story hospital. "This is where I stay," Lieutenant Burger said. "I have a room on the second floor, since only higher-ranking officers occupy the limestone buildings."

Cassandra looked sheepish. "You make me feel guilty, Lieutenant!"

"Think nothing of it. If an officer arrives with a higher rank than your husband, you'll have to move out and give your quarters to the newcomer."

Cassandra's eyes widened. "Why, that sounds like a caste system!"

"Call it what you will, it's Army regulations!"

They stopped at the far end of the parade ground and Lieutenant Burger waved his arm across the field. "The enlisted men's barracks are over there." He turned to the modest building behind them. "And this is the quartermaster's office. There's little to do here for amusement, so if you ever want to read a book, just call on him."

"Oh, he keeps a library?"

"Something like that. One thing Fort Concho can take pride in is a collection of several hundred volumes."

Cassandra, feeling more at home, now, said, "I have a hunch, Lieutenant, that you're from German background. Am I correct?"

He looked pleased. "You have a good eye, Mrs. Shaw. Yes, my parents came from Germany and settled in Pennsylvania where I was born."

Cassandra smiled with delight. "Then we're kindred souls! My maiden name is Vosburg and my folks are from the old country, too. We're going to have lots to talk about."

During the personnel's noon meal break from eleven-thirty to one o'clock, Major Thomas Manning and his wife Anne, the next-door neighbors, stopped by.

"We've been here only a couple of weeks, ourselves," the tall, fortyish major said. "Hope you're coping with Fort Concho better than we are—we're still trying to get used to it!" He appeared quite distinguished with long, graying hair, moustache and short-cropped beard.

Anne Manning, also in her forties, small and frail-looking, had delicate skin and straw-colored hair. She seemed to have just stepped from a cool bath. Anne waved a hand in the air. "It shouldn't take much longer. Thank goodness we have Colonel Grierson here, now, to clean up this ghastly place!"

"Can you come in for coffee?" Cassandra asked.

"Thank you," Manning said, "but I must return to my duties. I'll leave Anne in your good hands."

The two women went into the sitting room and Millie poured them all cups of coffee.

"I know Tom is as happy as I am to see more ladies here at the fort," Anne Manning said. "I do love to visit and I've been talking my dear husband's ear off!"

"Colonel Grierson says more personnel will be here tomorrow," Cassandra said. "And his family will be arriving soon."

"The Colonel is such a nice man," Anne rattled on, then frowned slightly. "It's a shame he has to keep such a long beard to cover that dreadful scar on his face!"

Cassandra smiled over her coffee cup. The dear woman wasn't joking—she did love to talk.

"When he was just a boy," Anne continued, "a horse kicked him in the head. He was in a coma for over a day, I understand." She gave a small laugh. "He's been leery of

51

horses ever since!"

Millie sighed with boredom at the idle chatter. "Cass, would you believe that Anne actually brought her piano out to this God-forsaken place?!"

"Well, I do love to play and couldn't bear to part with it," Anne explained. "Since it's only a spinet, I thought I'd try to bring it along in the ambulance, and it made the trip quite well. Colonel Grierson has promised to tune it for me this evening."

"Oh, does the Commander play, too?" Cassandra asked.

"Indeed so! He has quite a musical background and plans to have a band here at the post. I hope by day after tomorrow the colonel and I can give a little musical on my piano for all the new arrivals."

It was Millie's turn to laugh, but in derision. "Don't hold your breath Anne. The colonel's so busy cleaning up Fort Concho, it'll be another year before we hear any music from that piano of yours!"

Colonel Grierson proved Millie wrong. Within two days, the dog population quickly disappeared, along with the ugly weeds, and the Mannings announced a welcome tea at their house for the new arrivals.

The guests sipped lukewarm tea during the hot dry evening, recalling better times when there was ice to swirl in their tall glasses, while Colonel Grierson and Anne Manning entertained with duets on the spinet.

Just when Cassandra thought she had met everyone, another new face appeared at Fort Concho. The ruggedly handsome young man stood at the sitting room door, waiting for the music to end, and looked conspicuous in buckskin clothing with a dusty slouch hat in his hands.

After the guests had applauded, Tom Manning and his

wife greeted the new arrival, Anne giving the man a loving kiss on the cheek and Tom grabbing his hand for a warm shake. They brought him over to Ian and Cassandra.

"Traylor Doolan, I'd like you to meet Captain Ian Shaw and his wife, Cassandra," Manning said. He added with pride, "We're going to be honored in having Tray as a scout on the Shafter expedition."

Traylor Doolan took Cassandra's hand and a shiver ran through her body while his incredible blue eyes impaled her like some captive prey. Groping for the right words, she said lamely, "Then you must be a member of the United States Army, Mr. Doolan."

He looked down at his rough clothing and chuckled. "Well, these ain't exactly Army issue, Mrs. Shaw. No, the Army's just hired me as a scout."

To Cassandra's relief, he turned to shake Ian's hand.

Tom Manning laid an arm across Tray's shoulders and said, "I want you to know, I owe my life to this man! I was with Colonel Mackenzie up at Palo Duro, chasing that old Comanche Gray Panther—now, there's the meanest Indian that ever lived! Tray saved me from a horrible death!"

Ian perked with interest. "The devil, you say! You mean you were captured?"

"Very much so! Stripped naked and tied down. Gray Panther and his boys were ready to cut me up, piece by piece!" Manning gritted his teeth. "To this day, I can still feel those leather straps cutting into my wrists!"

Anne Manning frowned at her husband. "Tom! Do you have to tell that gruesome story when we're having such a nice time?!"

"Please don't stop now," Cassandra said, "I've got to know what happened!"

Manning patted Anne's arm. "I'll make it short, Dear."

He turned to Cassandra. "I was about to be torn apart when Traylor Doolan, here, stampeded the Indians' horses. Gray Panther and his braves scattered after their mounts and Tray cut me free, then swung me up behind him on his horse. I can tell you, we rode like the devil was after us till we reached Mackenzie's camp!"

Anne ended his story on a happy note. "I've always been grateful to Tray." She put a loving hand on his arm. "He's been like one of the family ever since!"

The party had been a bright moment for everyone in the drab life at Fort Concho and the guests reluctantly departed in time to be home before Lights Out.

That night, Cassandra snuggled next to Ian in the noisy bed, their bodies warming each other beneath a puffy comforter, while her mind went over the evening's events. Soon, Traylor Doolan's haunting eyes floated into her mind like two relentless blue phantoms. Though she had come to love her husband dearly, Traylor Doolan stirred something in her she had never felt with Ian.

Struggling to push it out of her mind, she said, "Ian, I've heard people mention Colonel Shafter so often. What is this 'expedition' they're all talking about?"

Ian's large frame stirred as if troubled by the question. "Oh, that. I didn't want to worry you about it till later. Lieutenant Colonel Shafter's coming here from Fort Duncan in a couple of weeks. He has orders to lead a big expedition up the Llano Estacado. I expect most of the men at Concho'll be involved."

Cassandra frowned. "What kind of expedition?"

Ian cleared his throat slightly and Cassandra knew he was reluctant to say any more, but he continued.

"Shafter's supposed to sweep the plains of any remaining Indians. Also gather information for future settlers going that way, especially where water can be found."

"Indians," Cassandra repeated with concern, recalling Tom Manning's horrifying story about one called Gray Panther. "That sounds like it could be dangerous."

He pulled her closer with a kiss on the forehead. "Not really. Colonel Mackenzie's got most of those devils cleared out. Old Chief Quanah even made peace this year. All Shafter has to do is chase any Indians up Mackenzie's way so he can push them over to Oklahoma and into the reservation. You don't have to worry about anything."

"How long will you be gone?"

"Probably six months."

"Six months?!" Cassandra raised on an elbow. "Why, by that time, you're apt be a father!"

Ian lay for a moment, absorbing her remark, then sat up to peer at her in the moonlit room. "What do you mean, 'father?' Are you tellin' me you're . . . ?

She giggled and put a hand on his cheek. "I admit I've been holding out on you, but I wanted to be sure before I said anything. Right now, I do believe you'll be a father by December at the latest."

Ian fell back in amazement. After a moment of realization, he erupted into a loud whoop and grabbed Cassandra with a tremendous hug that brought forth a scream of protest.

In seconds, Henry Adams was knocking on their door. "Ian," he called, "is everything all right with you two?"

Ian bounded out of bed in his underwear and flung open the door.

"This calls for a drink!" he boomed. "Come on downstairs, Henry—and get Millie up, too. I'm gonna be a daddy and we've got to celebrate!"

Chapter Six

Ian Shaw and Henry Adams sat with forced patience in their saddles, the hot sun adding to their discomfort.

"I've got a feelin' Colonel Shafter's gonna drive us till our butts are draggin'!" Henry breathed in the hot air. "Sure will be glad when this thing's over." He wiped the steam off his glasses, but when he put them back on they only clouded up again.

On this blistering July fourteenth, Lieutenant Colonel William Shafter's huge company had gathered, preparing to leave Fort Concho. It filled not only the parade ground but a large area outside the fort's perimeter.

Inside the fort, ready to move forward, six mounted companies of the Tenth Cavalry Buffalo Soldiers, the backbone of Shafter's force, mingled with two companies of the Twenty-Fourth Infantry and one company of the Twenty-Fifth. Waiting outside the fort stood sixty-five wagons drawn by six-mule teams and a pack train of seven hundred mules. They all carried supplies for at least a four-month campaign, along with a large beef herd to provide fresh meat.

"It'll be a piece of cake," Ian laughed. "If the going gets tough, I'll just think about that son of mine. Why, you know, he might even be waiting for me when we get back."

"Ian, what makes you so danged sure that baby's going to be a boy? Ever think a little girl might show up, instead?"

"No matter," Ian said, cheerfully. "Just the thought of

bein' a daddy is enough to get me through this thing!"

Henry shifted irritably in his saddle. This campaign was nothing new to Ian; he'd already tasted battle as a young man during the War Between the States.

Henry, though, had been stuck behind a desk and spared the horrors of conflict. With the Cavalry after the war, he'd supervised Indians being sent to reservations, but never forced to kill one. Colonel Shafter, however, would ferret an Indian out of a prairie dog hole. If he did, Henry didn't relish the thought of having to shoot the man down.

Directly behind Ian and Henry, the enlisted men fidgeted in their casual but scratchy field gear, sweat already staining the gray flannel shirts. Wide-brimmed Jeff Davis hats failed to keep beads of perspiration from dotting their brows.

Each had a Colt revolver strapped to his waist and Winchester rifles hung from the saddles. Their sabers, too clumsy for field duty, had been neatly stashed back in the barracks.

Although thoroughly trained, most of the Negro Buffalo Soldiers had yet to experience Indian warfare. Now, they sat on their horses, joking nervously among themselves.

Joshua Barnes looked almost comical in the saddle, his long legs reaching nearly to the ground. "I heerd tell them Injuns like to cut you up, if they catch you," he mumbled. "They take off yer ears—even yer pekker!"

A soldier next to him chuckled. "They'd have a heap o' cuttin' to take off that dingus o' yers, Josh!"

The other men laughed, masking the dread that nagged them like an itch.

Major Thomas Manning, with a reserve acquired through years of service, sat quietly in the saddle, although uncomfortable in a snug-fitting officer's jacket with high-standing, yellow-braided collar. His Custer's hat was "looped up," as the Army called it, the left side of the brim folded up and pinned to the crown with a U. S. eagle coat of arms.

He saw Anne among those lined up in front of the officers' stone houses. Now turning forty, the dark areas around her large almond eyes seemed to add years to the sweet face.

A brave little lady, Tom thought. Not the type for the kind of life he had to offer. A worry tugged at his heart and he wondered what would become of her if anything happened to him.

Tom's reverie was interrupted by Traylor Doolan who rode up, stopping his faithful dull-brown horse Pardo beside Tom. Tray gave the animal a loving rub behind the ear and Pardo nodded with pleasure.

"Nice day for a picnic, ain't it?" Tray said, pushing back his hat to get a little air.

"That it is," Manning chuckled. "We could fry eggs on a rock."

"Sure wish ol' Shafter would get this bunch t'movin'!" Tray removed the hat to wipe sweat from his forehead. "*Hurry up and wait* oughta be the Army's motto!"

Nothing could keep Traylor Doolan in one place for very long and Manning laughed. "Patience is the first thing you have to learn in the Army, my boy. The colonel's just as anxious as the rest of us, but he and Colonel Grierson have to say their goodbyes, first."

Inside the post commander's house, Lieutenant Colonel Benjamin Grierson peered through the window and saw Colonel Shafter about to get onto his horse.

"Damn this military protocol!" Ben fumed to himself. "I don't know why I have to dress up, just to say goodbye!" He slipped on the coat in front of a long mirror. "Downright embarrassing, having to be cheerful when an Infantry officer is leading half my regiment into the field!"

He quickly pushed the buttons through their holes and recalled his hard work in organizing and preparing the Negro Tenth Cavalry for service, all the time fighting against racism for their rights.

Now, Infantry Colonel William Shafter seemed to be taking over. Since arriving at Fort Concho, Shafter's heavy-set body had been everywhere at once, putting together the expedition force with military precision while giving commands through a thick walrus moustache.

"Just another slap in the face," Ben muttered, straightening the collar. "I'm still being punished by those higher-ups in Washington!"

Because of his reluctance to wage an all-out war against the Indians, Ben had been too often passed over for promotion, while those beneath his rank received theirs. Even his assignment to this deplorable Fort Concho seemed to be an insult.

Satisfied with his appearance, Ben heaved a determined sigh and rushed out to bid farewell to Lieutenant Colonel William R. Shafter.

The ponderous colonel had just settled his ample frame with enviable coolness in the saddle when Benjamin Grierson walked up and took the man's gloved hand in a parting shake.

"Looks like you're taking the whole damned fort with you!" Ben said amiably.

"Not so," Shafter replied with a straight face. "I was kind enough to leave you the laundresses!"

The man's wit could be disarming, uttered with no hint of a smile, but Grierson had to admit that William Shafter was a logical choice to head the undertaking. Two years earlier he had explored the southern Staked Plains and was familiar with its hostile environment.

"We needn't worry, since you know this territory better than any man west of the Mississippi," Grierson said. "Just don't take any chances with that stubborn determination of yours!"

"And don't you forget that Christmas dinner you owe us when we get back!"

Colonel Grierson stepped away while Shafter gave the go-ahead signal to Sergeant Eben Carruthers.

Eben turned to the long line of men and equipment behind him. "Stretch 'em out!" he hollered.

It was quite a show. Even a few people from wicked Saint Angela had come across the river and stood in awe at the spectacle.

The remaining members of Fort Concho began to wave as the huge column of men, wagons and animals started off slowly toward the northwest in a mixture of popping whips, oaths and shouts.

"Gee up, thar . . . gee up!"

Cassandra and Millie watched from their porch. Cassandra felt a stab of emptiness, knowing it would be months before she would ever see Ian again. Her heart twinged with anxiety as clouds of gray dust rose slowly behind Shafter's moving force, blotting it out like a huge dirty curtain.

Chapter Seven

The large company made one of its early stops at Rendelbrock Springs, sixty miles from the Upper Concho River and found the spring dry. It was to be expected in mid-July, however their water supply was ample and they made camp for the night.

"Before it gets too dark," Traylor Doolan said to Colonel Shafter, "I'd better see if we got any signs of Indians for company."

Tray rode in a wide arc ahead of the company and returned as night fell to give his report.

"Looks like a party of maybe a dozen Indians goin' north, camped this mornin' just five miles west. Then they split, half of 'em goin' west."

"Wonder why they'd want to change direction?" Colonel Shafter muttered.

"Water," Tray said. "They probably hoped there'd still be some here. When they found it dry, my guess is that half of 'em headed for Mustang Springs about a hundred miles west and the other half went lookin' north."

"I want you and Major Manning to take his company first thing in the morning and follow those tracks north," the colonel said. "Be sure to take at least a week's rations. I'll have Captain Henry Adams follow those other Indians west. He can catch up with us on our way to the base camp at Brazos Fresh Fork."

At three o'clock the following morning, Henry Adams' eye muscles ached from a fitful sleep, not anticipating the job that lay ahead. He went to join Ian Shaw at the campfire.

"Didn't think we'd be chasing Indians so soon," Henry said, filling a tin cup with coffee. "Colonel Shafter said we're to kill them or run them up north and destroy their camps."

Ian saw the worry in his friend's eyes. "Well, Traylor Doolan says they've split up, so there shouldn't be too many."

Henry rubbed his chin. "Even so, I'll be glad when it's over and done with!"

After they had eaten their bacon, beans and hardtack, the two men said goodbye and Henry Adams gathered his two companies with one Tonkawa scout.

Ian Shaw joined Major Thomas Manning's group, consisting of the scout Traylor Doolan, Sergeant Eben Carruthers and sixty members of C Company. They headed north, Tray's keen eyes following the Indians' trail, until the group came to a rise.

"Think maybe you oughta call a halt," Tray said to Tom Manning. "They could be on the other side of that hill. We don't wanna risk ridin' up there and takin' a chestful of arrows."

"I agree," the major said and waved the unit to stop. He rode over to Eben Carruthers.

"Sergeant, keep the men here on their horses while Traylor Doolan and I check the other side of that hill. Have all guns ready in case of an attack."

Eben guided his horse among the troops and gave instructions to stay mounted with their guns loaded. He knew the men were nervous and he felt just as edgy.

"Now, I don't want none o' you tenderfoots get bug-eyed scared when you see a Injun," he warned them. "We gonna show the major we're real soldiers. If you see any o' them redskins comin' over that hill, you start shootin', hear?!"

After Manning and Tray had edged their way to the hill's crest, Tray parted a tuft of grass and gazed downward. "There they be!" he whispered.

Manning followed his gaze. True enough, there was a small Indian village of five lodges nestled around a smoking fire. The major could make out about ten ponies tethered nearby. Two women sat cross-legged on the ground, scraping buffalo hides stretched on wooden frames. A warrior with an ugly crooked nose and clad in only a loin cloth emerged from one of the tepees. He walked over to the women for a brief conversation.

Tray's eyes narrowed with the stir of an old loathing. "Well, I'll be damned, if it ain't ol' Gray Panther, himself! I'd recognize that broken nose twenty miles away."

"By Jove, you're right!" Manning said. "But I thought he and his people were on the reservation at Fort Sill."

"Not for long. He has a born hate for the white man. It wasn't three days before he sneaked off. Took some of his men and squaws with him. Mackenzie's been lookin' for 'em ever since."

"How about us doing Colonel Mackenzie a favor and ambush them?"

"That's your job, Tom. I just find 'em for you!"

They moved quietly back to the group of soldiers who were mounted and waiting with guns loaded. Manning explained the situation.

"There's an Indian village on the other side of this hill. We're to split up, half entering the village from the east, the other half from the west. Ride fast and shoot every Indian on sight, except women or children who'll be taken captive. Now remember, we've got to surprise them!"

Tray knew it would be easy, for strangely enough, Comanches never bothered to post guards.

As soon as the two groups rounded the hill they charged at full speed, racing into the village from both sides with excited whoops and roaring gunfire.

Bedlam erupted as the two women screamed and ran in terror while warriors poured out of the lodges, heading for their ponies. The confused Indians tried to escape, too surprised to fight back. Only a few grabbed their bows and let loose an arrow.

Joshua Barnes, with wild eyes, raised his gun toward a fleeing brave. It didn't seem right to shoot a running man in the back, but those were his orders. He fired and the Indian dropped to the ground. A strange thrill ran through his body and he reloaded the rifle.

Before he could fire again, something hit him in the shoulder with a force that nearly bent him over and pain burned through his right arm. He looked down at the bloody point of an arrow sticking out through his shirt. A shot roared from behind and he turned to see that Eben Carruthers had gunned down the brave who still had a bow in his grasp.

An angry snarl curled Joshua's lip and he took the rifle in his left hand. "Ain't none o' you buzzards gonna take my pekker!" He fired and brought down another Indian.

At least six Indians had been killed during the wild ambush while the others leaped to their horses, Gray Panther one of them. Several yards away, the menacing chief reined his pony to a halt and looked back to survey the havoc sweeping through his camp.

Major Manning had quickly dismounted and grabbed the arms of a wild, struggling squaw. As he bound a rope around her hands, he caught sight of Gray Panther glaring at him through the billowing clouds of dust.

The old chief's grotesque face with its misshapen nose and beady eyes full of steaming hate cut like a knife into

Manning's gut.

Gray Panther shook a red-feathered war lance above his head and shouted angry words at Manning, then turned, galloping off with his braves through a clump of mesquite.

After the dust had settled and the captive women's hands were bound behind their backs, Major Manning gave orders for his men to destroy the entire village. "Burn everything—food, clothing, cooking utensils and tepees!"

Eben Carruthers rode up to Joshua Barnes who was panting with excitement, unmindful of the arrow sticking out of his shoulder.

"You damn fool," Eben shouted, "get down offa that horse so's I can yank that thing outta you!"

Joshua climbed down and sat on a rock. Eben grasped the feathered arrow shaft and broke off a good portion, bringing a howl from Joshua. "Go easy, there!"

"Cain't help if it hurts," Eben told him. "You jes grit yer teeth and let me pull this damned thing on through."

He gripped the flint head of the arrow and withdrew it with a hard yank as Joshua yelped again.

"Now git yerself back t'the supply mule and we'll put somethin' on that," Eben said, then laughed. "You gonna git some respect 'round here, now, bein' the first one t'get a arrow stuck in 'im!"

Tom Manning and Traylor Doolan stood watching black smoke curl into the sky from the smoldering debris.

"Well, I'd say this was one successful raid," Manning exclaimed. "Not a man lost, only one wounded." He looked at the fading dust left by Gray Panther's retreat. "Too bad, though, Gray Panther got away."

"I don't think you've seen the last of 'im," Tray replied. "Did you see the way he looked at you?"

Manning scowled. "Yes, and that ugly face sent a

shiver up my spine! Wonder what that was he shouted at me?"

"He's got you marked, now, is what he said. Swore he's gonna get even with you for stealin' from him."

"Stealing?"

Tray glanced with a wry smile at the Indian woman whose hands Manning had bound together. "Yep—you just captured his squaw!"

Chapter Eight

A scattering of pony tracks in the dusty earth, easily led Captain Henry Adams, his scout and two companies for six days. They finally arrived at Mustang Springs where the men refreshed themselves, filling their canteens and water barrels.

"Those six redskins have been here, all right," the company sergeant told Henry. "Joined by a passel more, I'd say, from all these tracks!"

Henry uttered a soft curse. He had expected to deal with only a handful of Indians, not a mob.

The Tonkawa scout shaded his eyes, looking west. "Grass gets heavier in that direction where the tracks lead. They might have a village over that hill where it's greener."

"Then let's get a move on." Henry turned to the Negro sergeant. "Tell your men we're going west. We're apt to meet resistance over that hill, so be at the ready!"

Henry called his group to a halt just below the crest of the hill. He and the scout dismounted and crouched up to the top to see what lay below.

In the distance a village of thirty or more tepees nestled around several fire dugouts, but no signs of life.

"What do you think?" Henry asked, squinting through his spectacles.

"They probably saw Colonel Shafter's large party and moved on, thinking he'd follow," the scout replied.

"Must've been in a hurry, didn't even take down their

tepees. Come on, let's get down there and see what we've got."

The men rode cautiously into the village and indeed found no living creature, not even a skinny dog. They poked into each lodge and saw piles of buffalo robes, clothing, food and cooking utensils.

"All right, sergeant," Henry said, relieved that there had been no conflict. "We've got our work cut out for us. Set fire to all these tepees and equipment. I don't want anything left, understand? Destroy is the word!"

The lodges were gutted and skins, clothing, equipment and lodge poles thrown into piles, then burned. Columns of black and white smoke rose, spiraling into the hot dry air.

"If any more of them redskins are around," a sergeant muttered, "that smoke's a sure sign we're on their behinds!"

Henry and his men later followed tracks to another village five miles away. It, too, lay empty, clearly vacated in haste.

"Looks like we've got about forty tepees to get rid of here," Henry said. "Let's get to work!"

Again, the soldiers laid waste to the settlement, together with robes, saddles and a large supply of food.

Now, Captain Henry Adams began to feel proud of himself. At the end of the afternoon he called for camp to be made nearby on the grassy plain.

"Get a good night's sleep," Henry told his men. "We'll pick up the trail in the morning."

But the group had little rest. A hard rain poured down soon after midnight, sweeping across the camp in wind-driven sheets. Streams of cold water rushed through each man's dog tent. Morning arrived, making it impossible to build a fire, so they had to make do with only hardtack, cold water and a strong desire for body-warming coffee.

At about noon the rain dwindled to a sprinkle and the

68

men packed and mounted for another try at finding their quarry.

"I can't see any tracks," Henry said with discouragement as they plodded through the muddy terrain.

The scout riding beside him seemed determined. "If we keep going, we might see a fresh sign."

The sun came out, turning the atmosphere to a clammy swelter and Henry wiped sweat from his face.

"This is useless," he said. "That rain didn't leave us anything to trace. We've gone four miles and there's not a sign!"

"True," the scout replied, "but the trail yesterday was in this direction. They probably camped overnight till the rain ended."

"What are you getting at?"

"A large group like that wouldn't scatter to confuse the enemy like they usually do. If we continue this way, it shouldn't be any trouble to pick up their trail in the wet ground."

After four more miles, with still no signs, Henry grew impatient. "We're getting nowhere," he said in disgust. "I'm going to call this to a halt and join Colonel Shafter on his way to the base camp."

The scout shrugged in disappointment. "You're in command!"

"Well, we have just enough rations to get us back. I'll send a courier to Colonel Shafter telling him it's hopeless to catch these sneaky devils, then we'll leave tomorrow morning and catch up with the main group."

Captain Henry Adams and his men looked forward with aching bodies to the comforts of Shafter's main camp. The group had ridden for two hard days and all felt relief as they trudged in, glad to be back in any hint of civilization. Henry went immediately to Lieutenant Colonel Shafter's tent to make his report.

The colonel's heavy moustache twitched in agitation as he briefly shook Henry's hand.

"I was pleased to read the report your courier sent me on the destruction of the two Indian camps," Shafter said. "However, I fail to understand why you didn't locate the Indians."

"We probably could've run them down," Henry replied, "but with the rain washing away the trail, I found it hopeless to continue the search."

"Then you admit there was a possibility of finding them, anyway, if you had pursued a few miles more?"

Henry's spectacles began to fog. "Well, yes, sir, there's always that possibility, but . . . "

"A good soldier never let's a possibility get away from him!"

"But our rations were getting low . . . we had just enough to get back here."

The colonel's answer was sharp. "You have been trained to cut rations, Captain, when it becomes necessary to stretch a campaign a few days longer!" He paused for a cold, hard look. "Do I have to remind you that the main purpose of this field trip is to eradicate any remaining hostiles? Those Indians were obviously in your vicinity, yet you failed to give vigorous pursuit . . . I find that a clear dereliction of duty!"

Henry clenched his fists, barely able see through the clouded spectacles.

Shafter seemed reluctant to deal with the unpleasant subject, but added, "It is therefore my decision, Captain Adams, to relieve you of your command. You will return to Fort Concho tomorrow, taking Major Manning's captured women with you. You will also await there for court-martial!"

Chapter Nine

Long before daylight, Henry Adams, still wide awake, sat beside his campfire like a water-soaked bird unable to fly. With no desire for breakfast, he pulled a blanket over his drooping shoulders and nursed a tin cup of strong hot coffee.

"Got an extra drop of that Arbuckles?" a voice asked and Henry looked up to see Ian Shaw standing with a cup in hand.

Henry grumbled, "Are you sure you wanna be seen drinkin' coffee with me?" He took a glove and removed his blackened pot from the glowing coals.

Ian squatted down to accept a half cup of the dark brew, then pulled the small flask from his coat and poured a spot of brandy into the coffee.

Henry looked around quickly. "Ian, you crazy? You'll get a court-martial, too, if the colonel sees you drinkin' that stuff!"

Ian laughed softly. "Everybody's still asleep. Here, looks like you need a shot of this."

Henry pushed the flask away. "No, thanks, I've got enough against me already."

Ian returned the flask to his coat pocket. "Look, old friend, nobody here blames you. They probably would've done the same thing you did."

"If that's the case, then the whole damned bunch of us would be goin' back for court-martial!"

"No, Colonel Shafter's just a stickler for carrying out orders, that's all. Don't let him make you think you've failed in your duty."

Henry's metal-framed spectacles glinted in the firelight. "Thanks for sayin' that, but it still makes me mad as a bull stuck in a mud hole!" He banged a fist on his knee. "That officer goin' back with me has a written order to give to Colonel Grierson at Fort Concho. They won't throw me in the guardhouse, but it's like I'm under arrest—I won't be allowed to leave the fort under any circumstances!"

With nothing more he could do, Ian got up to leave. Trying to sound cheerful, he said, "You have a good trip back, now, you hear? I'll see you at the fort in December."

An hour later Major Thomas Manning got his small fire going and set a coffee pot in the flames. After a few minutes the coffee began to simmer and Traylor Doolan joined him.

Tray yawned and stretched his arms wide, taking in the crisp, morning air. "Anybody shot a bear? I could sure eat one right now!"

Manning smiled. "Haven't heard any shots lately. Would a cup of coffee and some fried mush do?" He put a small frying pan on the fire and scraped some mush into it with a bent spoon.

Tray squatted beside him and used a glove to pick up the coffeepot. He looked at its black contents.

"I'd say this has boiled enough! With all that high-class education of yours, Tom, how come you never learned to make a good pot of coffee?" He poured some into a cup and tasted it with a grimace.

Manning laughed. "When you lose that dew behind your ears and get to be my age, you'll need strong coffee, too."

Some distance away Captain Henry Adams climbed into his saddle and fastened a rope leading a pack mule with provisions. An officer and three mounted Buffalo Soldiers joined him with two mules carrying the Indian women, their hands bound behind their backs.

Manning and Tray watched as Adams and his party trudged off into the early morning light, Henry's small shoulders hunched in defeat.

"I'd like to be going back to Concho right now, too," Manning thought aloud with Anne's gentle face in his mind. "But not under his circumstances."

"Just hope the Indians don't get 'im," Tray said. "Findin' a small party like that out here on the plains would make any redskin mighty happy."

"Well, he made his own bed, as they say. The colonel won't stand for any backsliding, no matter how redeeming the circumstances. Adams should've gone after those Indians, even if it meant going hungry and doing without water for a day or two. Wouldn't surprise me if Shafter tries to run down those hostiles himself!"

In fact, Colonel Shafter did just that. While the men were finishing breakfast, he began organizing a search party and the colonel's stocky body soon appeared at Manning's campfire.

"Major Manning, I want you and Doolan here to join me in going after those Indians that Captain Adams let get away. The rest of our command will continue north. We'll join them there."

"Yes sir," Manning replied.

Colonel Shafter turned to Tray. "Doolan, I wonder if you share my opinion. When Adams left the Indians, they were headed north, no doubt to Casas Amarillas. It's over a hundred miles, but that's the only water I know of in that direction. What do you say?"

Tray grinned. "You'd make a right good scout, Colonel.

I'd say that's a fair conclusion."

The Colonel turned back to Manning. "Major, round up three companies of the Tenth for this party. We'll need a wagon and some pack mules with rations for about two weeks. I want to leave tomorrow before the sun comes up over those mountains."

The morning sky began turning a golden pink as Colonel Shafter and his group moved out, going due west. Captain Ian Shaw, in charge of one of the companies, rode with Eben Carruthers as his sergeant in command.

When they arrived at the lake called Casas Amarillas, Ian shook the brandy flask next to his ear. For six days he'd been trying to make it last, but the little container didn't sound encouraging. He returned it to his coat pocket and rode up to join Colonel Shafter and Traylor Doolan who sat with disappointment in their saddles. Cakes of dried mud spread before them in the river bed.

"Those Indians obviously found the same thing we did," Tray said, "and went toward the Pecos."

Colonel Shafter muttered through his large moustache, "Then we'll continue on and try to overtake them."

Ian and the others had hoped to at least refill their canteens here. "And if we don't find them, Colonel," he ventured, "how far do you plan to go before turning back? Our rations are half gone now."

Colonel Shafter turned a stony face. "Rations will be cut as soldiers have been taught, Captain. We'll camp here for the night and then go on to the Pecos. Indians or no Indians, we can make it to Fort Stockton and restock our supplies before returning to Fresh Fork."

Morning arrived with a dark and chilly gloom as the

party left Casas Amarillas and began the trek southwest. Their water ran out in two days. Only a few spots were found where water stood, but it was muddy and strong with gypsum.

"Don't touch that water," Shafter ordered, "and keep your horses away from it—one mouthful can kill you!"

By late afternoon the sky blackened and the men turned their parched faces upward, letting a few skimpy raindrops cool their sunbaked skin. As the rain became harder, each man scrambled to catch the precious water in hats, cups, buckets—anything that could possibly hold water. But the shower was brief and the sun quickly took back its domain.

"Go easy with that rain water," Eben Carruthers told his men as they refreshed themselves. "We still got a ways t'go! Reckon when we hit the Pecos, we can get us a good drink."

"I wouldn't try it!" Traylor Doolan warned, pouring a thin stream of water from his hat into a canteen. "Pecos water is full of alkali. It'll just make you sick!"

The group finally arrived at the Pecos River, but its steep banks prevented them from reaching the other side.

"Keep moving south to Horsehead Crossing," Colonel Shafter urged. "Then it's only twenty miles to Fort Stockton."

Rations had already been cut to the bone, but Shafter kept pushing them onward. The following day stretched like an agonizing week, but at sundown the beautiful sight of Fort Stockton loomed on the horizon and the men quickened their pace. At last they staggered into the garrison, gasping for water and a good meal.

Captain Ian Shaw was hungry and thirsty, too. But he also hoped the sutler store could replenish his brandy flask.

Chapter Ten

Fort Concho buzzed with surprise as Henry Adams rode in, accompanied by another officer and two captive squaws on pack mules behind them. After Colonel Shafter's strict written order had been delivered to Colonel Grierson, Henry made his way to the limestone house to greet an astonished Millie and Cass. He broke into a tired grin behind the wire-frame glasses and took Millie in his arms for a long embrace, then Cassandra gave him a welcome hug.

Millie knew something was wrong by the worried slump in Henry's body; he was much thinner and his uniform made him look like a scarecrow.

"Why didn't the others come back with you?" she asked.

He answered in a tight voice, "I had to deliver two Indian squaws we captured."

Cassandra couldn't hold back her anxiety. "Please tell me about Ian," she broke in eagerly. "Is he all right?"

"Last time I saw him was weeks ago," Henry told her, "but don't worry, he's just fine."

Millie kept studying Henry's anguished face. "Couldn't they have waited and brought those captives back with everyone else?"

Henry plopped wearily into the big chair as if he'd walked all the way back to Fort Concho.

"No," he said and averted Millie's eyes. "Colonel Shafter ordered me back . . . to wait for my court-martial."

76

"Court-martial!" Millie cried in disbelief.

"It's all a mistake! The colonel thinks I was lax in my duties, but he just doesn't know all the facts . . . I swear, I did my duty the best a man could under the circumstances!"

Millie bit a finger to hold back her tears and rushed upstairs to the bedroom.

Cassandra walked over to the chair, putting a soothing hand on Henry's shoulder as he stared after his wife.

"We know you did your best," Cassandra said. "Everything will work out, Henry. When Ian gets back, he'll stand up for you!"

Later in the evening Cassandra prepared a small welcome-home dinner for Henry. Millie, however, refused to come down and join them, leaving Cassandra and Henry to only pick at their meals without any appetite. He finally said a painful goodnight and trudged upstairs.

Millie lay on the bed, face turned on a tear-stained pillow, as Henry walked into the gloomy bedroom. The bedside lamp had been turned down low, but he didn't raise the wick; it would be mockery to brighten the room. He sat on the bed and stroked her arm.

"Millie, I'm sorry this happened, but you've got to try and see my side of it."

"Can't you understand?" she wept. "Daddy's going to be crushed when he hears about it . . . how can I ever face him after this?!"

Henry felt drained of words. "I guess we can talk about it later," he said and lay down beside her, without taking off his clothes. He reached over to the lamp and turned the wick down until the room was lit by only the sad light of a new moon shining through the cold window panes.

Chapter Eleven

A warming August sun greeted Colonel Shafter as he led his men out of Fort Stockton. It would be a long trek to Fresh Fork and the main supply base, but all were well-fed and with rations for ten days.

They followed the Pecos River north and made camp at Pecos Falls, forty miles north of Horsehead Crossing. It was territory that Colonel Shafter had ridden through two years before.

"There's a big stretch of white sand 'bout three miles ahead," Traylor Doolan reported to the colonel. He had done his usual look-see of the area as soon as they arrived. "Looks like it'd blind a man if we try to cross it in this sun!"

"Yes, I know the area," Shafter replied. He recalled the previous mission and his men slogging painfully through the treacherous sand.

Tray learned quickly to use tact in dealing with Shafter and said, "We could cross this thing at night."

The colonel shook his head. "That white sand is too dangerous. We'll avoid it by proceeding northeast in the morning."

But tact was hard for Tray and he began to lose it. "That area's too big. Goin' around it will double our travel time from ten to twenty days at the least. We don't know for sure if we'll run into any water holes on the way."

"Then we'll cut our rations when necessary!"

Tray could see disaster hovering like a buzzard over a dying rabbit. He shoved aside protocol. "I may be outta line sayin' this, Colonel, but in my mind, you're takin' a gamble—we'll just be damned lucky if we make it to Fresh Fork!"

The group struck out, moving away from the ominous sand dunes; however, the barren plains seemed just as forbidding. On the eighth day, each canteen held only a few drops of water, with not enough in the barrels to even hear them slosh as the mules plodded over the sun-baked terrain.

Colonel Shafter had to admit that without finding water they'd never make it to Fresh Fork. He went to Traylor Doolan for advice.

"I've heard there's a place called Dug Spring, over in New Mexico Territory," Tray said through cracked lips, "about seventy miles to the west. Now, I know it's out of our way, but I'd say it's our only choice. And then, we'll just have to pray it ain't dried up!"

The colonel tried to lick his lips with a dry tongue. "Then we'll just have to chance it. Tell Major Manning we're pushing west."

Temperatures on the Staked Plains during late summer soared high enough to burst any thermometer. For three days the small group of men forced themselves through the heat, dust and sand with throats too dry to swallow the few pieces of hard tack left in their saddle bags.

By some miracle they reached Dug Spring, however their hope plunged to despair on finding it dry. The men used spades, digging into the dried mud, but produced only dark moist earth. A few smeared the wet mud over their dried-out faces while others put it into their mouths in a vain effort to ease the thirst.

Tray searched for the sight of a bird. The dove watered daily and flew straight to the source; and the mud dauber, with mud in its beak, would be coming from water. But no birds existed in the bright expanse of hot, blue sky.

While scouring the desert for signs of water, Tray discovered a large Indian trail leading north.

"With so many of 'em goin' that way, there's gotta be water there somewhere," he told Colonel Shafter. "But we might have to fight 'em for it!"

The colonel got his men mounted once more and they proceeded north. As the sun began its descent, a few soldiers slid from their saddles in delirium; others with more strength pushed their comrades back onto the mounts. Two of the hardier ones helped the mule pulling its small wagon of supplies while the rest walked in order to spare the poor horses.

A few animals, however, went blind without water and collapsed in a heap of dying flesh on the parched earth. Their throats were cut immediately and the soldiers tried to drink the blood, but it proved to be so thick with dehydration the men had to squish it between their teeth to get it down. The horse blood quickly resulted in bad cases of diarrhea, going through the bowels almost as soon as it was ingested.

Even with pangs of hunger, the men couldn't masticate or swallow hard tack with dry mouths and throats. It stuck in the teeth and had to be removed with their fingers.

The mad desire for water became overpowering; some men drank their own urine and one slashed his arm for the red liquid he could suck out.

Ian Shaw was appalled at the sight of two soldiers rushing with tin cups to catch the small amount of urine trickling from a horse.

"My God, Sergeant," he said to Eben Carruthers, "are your men drinking that?!"

"Ain't too bad," Eben told the captain solemnly, "when you stir a little sugar in it."

Finally Colonel Shafter called a halt for camp. No one could move a wretched limb to pitch his tent. Instead, the soldiers merely dropped where they were and tried to sleep; but hallucinations of cool waterfalls splashing over their heads made them fill the darkness with moans of agony.

Only the few able to think coherently were assigned guard duty, Captain Ian Shaw and Eben Carruthers being the first. Too weak to stand, they sat on the ground, leaning against a wagon wheel.

"Hell of a situation," Ian breathed, tipping his little flask upside down. "Not even a drop of brandy left!"

"Good thing," Eben replied with a thick tongue. "Only make you thirstier."

Ian turned to study his friend's dark face. "How do you do it, Eben?"

"Wha's that?"

"Keep your men from dropping around you like flies on a hot griddle."

"That's jes it. They's my men, an' yers, too. They look up t'us. 'Magine what they'd be like if they seen us drop like flies . . . wouldn't be a man of 'em left alive, now."

Ian chuckled with admiration. "Eben, remind me to submit you for promotion when we get back!"

Eben had to smile. "I'll hold you t'that, Cap'n." Then he added, "An' look at yerself. You ain't any worse off than the ol' colonel. Both o' you still runnin' around like a couple o' strong bulls!"

"Reckon if it wasn't for Cassandra, I'd just say, 'what the hell,' and kick it all over," Ian sighed. "She's going to have a baby, did I tell you? Yessir, when I get back, I'm going to be a daddy—and that's the only thing that's making me damned sure I do get back!"

Their shift ended at two o'clock in the morning with Major Thomas Manning and Traylor Doolan taking over for the rest of the night. Tray and the major sat against the wagon with blankets over their shoulders, listening to the dry coughs of men trying to sleep in thirst-crazed misery.

"Tell me the truth, Tray," Manning said. "You know this country. How does it really look to you—are we going to make it?"

"I've scouted all over the upper Llano," Tray replied quietly. "Ain't been down this way much and don't know all the water holes. Only thing I can do is look for signs." He shrugged in despair. "But it's like lookin' for snow in Hell."

"If either of us gets back to Concho, it'll most likely be you," Manning said. "You're young and you know better than me how to survive on the plains. Anne thinks the world of you and I'd be grateful if you'd see that she gets along all right. She'd be all alone."

"Ain't nothing I wouldn't do for the both of you," Tray said with a warm heart. "But ain't no reason to be talkin' this way, either. We always got ourselves out of tight spots before, and we're gonna get outta this one."

Suddenly a burst of gunfire shattered the night and a bullet tore through the wagon above their heads. Tray jumped up, drawing his Colt, while Manning struggled to his feet with rifle in hand. A second blast came out of the darkness and Tray fired toward the flash of light. They heard a scream of pain, then another shot rang out.

Colonel Shafter, along with two soldiers, rushed over and the men began firing into the darkness. After the din stopped, they heard hoof beats fading into the night.

"Must've been only two or three," Tray said. "We probably made 'em think we're all able to fight back." He put his gun back into its holster. "Sounds like they've taken off to the north, now."

"Those devils know where the water is!" Colonel Shafter rasped. His voice sounded unreal through lips barely discernible in the large, now-shaggy moustache and growth of beard. "Major," he decided, "as soon as we get some daylight, pick out forty-five men—those able to ride—and we'll follow their trail."

At sunrise, Manning, Doolan and the colonel, with forty-five half-crazed men crawled into their saddles and began pushing their shriveled horses north.

Minutes later Tray spotted a mesquite bush, then another. It was a good sign, for he knew the mesquite bean did not germinate unless passed through the bowels of an animal. And wild animals did not venture more than four miles from water.

Soon the group saw in the distance a sight worthy of the Garden of Eden: Shimmering in a grove of cottonwood trees, surrounded by mesquite, lay a large body of water. But a group of Indian lodges sat in a small clearing near the lake.

"I don't see any horses," Tray said, squinting ahead. "My guess is that those Indians we ran off last night must've warned this group, and now they're all on the run. But that water's all ours now. What say we go down there and get us a drink, Colonel!"

The rest of the dazed men had been staring with bleary eyes at the spring, believing it was only a mirage; but their horses knew better and strained forward with the smell of water in their nostrils.

Shafter waved his arm forward and the soldiers galloped down to the spring. They fell out of the saddles, throwing themselves face down into the water while the horses plunged their noses in alongside.

"Go easy, men!" Colonel Shafter ordered. "Take only a little at a time or you'll drown yourselves!"

He dismounted and walked unsteadily to join the men who choked down water as fast as they could; their unaccustomed stomachs, however, kept vomiting it up.

Some time later, the men lay on their backs, panting and slowly regaining strength. Colonel Shafter ordered a group to fill their canteens and go back to guide the remainder of the party to the spring.

In the afternoon, the company set to work destroying all signs of the Indian village, burning the lodges and buffalo skins, breaking the cooking utensils and saving only the amount of food that was useful to themselves.

Colonel Shafter and Major Manning rode a quarter of a mile up from the spring to a high plateau overlooking the entire area.

"Why, a man can see for at least twenty-five miles in every direction from up here," the colonel said. "Tell you what I'd like." He looked down at the hard ground, which was embedded with large, white stone. "Major, have a few men bring their spades up here. I want these rocks dug up and placed in a pile, a good seven or eight feet high so that anybody can see it as far as the horizon. It'll be a sign that there's an abundance of water just down there."

Manning rode back down to the spring and rooted out Eben Carruthers who was supervising the village's destruction.

"Sergeant, I've got a rather unusual assignment for you," Manning said. "Colonel Shafter wants a pile of rocks put on top of that rise over there." He waved his arm toward the plateau. "Make it about eight feet tall. High enough for settlers to spot it when they travel this way."

Eben selected ten Buffalo Soldiers with picks and shovels and took them to the plateau. He walked around the area for several minutes before deciding on the highest point, then started the men digging until they had enough rocks to begin.

First, Eben had them dig an eight-foot-square hole about a foot deep for the larger rocks to be embedded as the base, then the soldiers unearthed more stones and began fitting them together into a stack.

"I want them rocks to fit tight!" Eben ordered. "And make 'em smooth enough so's you can run yer hand over 'em. This thing's gotta last a hundred years!"

Joshua Barnes glared in amazement through sweaty eyes. "What you 'spect t'be here in a hundred years?!"

"They's gonna be big towns . . . roads . . . farms . . . lots o' people, that's what!"

"You dreamin', Sarge!" Joshua heaved another stone onto the pile. "This here dried-out land ain't never gonna 'mount to nothin'."

Eben bristled. "You wrong, Josh. When settlers see this, they'll come like ducks t'water and turn this land into another Atlanta . . . or Kansas City. And you, jug haid, oughta be proud to know you a part of it!"

"If they's gonna be a town here, what you 'spect they'd be callin' it?"

Eben smiled at the growing pile of white rock. "*Monument* wouldn't be bad fer starters!"

By the end of the following day the soldiers had constructed, under Eben Carruther's approving eyes, a four-sided stone monument. It tapered from the eight-foot-square base to a height of seven and one-half feet with a four-foot-square summit. Its carefully-fitted surface picked up the dying light of day and Eben Carruthers gave the edifice a satisfied pat before trudging back down the hill.

During early morning, the party began preparing for the

long trek back to the main supply camp and Colonel Shafter turned for a final look at the neat assemblage of white rocks standing atop the hill.

"Sergeant, you and your men have done an excellent job," he told Eben. "I have to congratulate you!"

"Thank you, Sir," Eben answered, swelling with pride at his accomplishment.

As the rising sun spread its golden rays over the glistening stone, the monument stood out like a shining beacon against a dark blue sky.

"I'll call this spot Monument Spring," Colonel Shafter proclaimed. "Word will be spread to all the settlers. When they see that beautiful pile of rocks, they'll know this is where they can finally wash the infernal sand out of their throats with a good drink of water!"

Chapter Twelve

The dry heat of early afternoon lay heavily over Fort Concho as a carriage, ambulance and two wagons with an escort of Buffalo Soldiers pulled into the establishment.

All the ladies had appeared for the occasion, dressed in their finest and fluttering among themselves as they stood in small groups along the walks, which were now laid with neat gravel.

This was no ordinary wagon train with a delivery of water and supplies; the vehicles carried Alice Grierson, the post commander's wife, three of their children and a young cousin.

The Grierson family had been on everyone's tongue for weeks, since they had nothing else to talk about at the dreary fort. Now, the women watched with subdued excitement.

Lieutenant Colonel Benjamin Grierson, who had met his family in Denison, Texas, climbed out of the carriage, then helped his wife and the others emerge.

"That's their little daughter Edith—isn't she a dear!" Anne Manning remarked to Cassandra as they viewed the homecoming. "And the two boys are Harry and George. I don't which one is which, but we'll find that out later. I'm told there are two older sons attending school back east."

The young attractive girl was last to be helped down from the ambulance.

"That must be the cousin we heard about," Cassandra said, embarrassed at being caught up in the gossip.

"You're right," Anne replied. "Her name is Amanda. Alice Grierson brought her along as governess and maid, but some of us think she really came out here to catch a young officer for a husband!"

"Well, she certainly came at a bad time, with most of the men away on the Shafter expedition!"

Alice Grierson wasted no time in getting her new home in order. She quickly announced an informal get-acquainted tea for the officers' wives and the women found their post commander's wife a delightful but strong-willed woman.

During the party, the commander's wife introduced her family. "This is my cousin Amanda," Alice Grierson said to Cassandra and Anne, taking the hand of the lovely, young dark-haired girl. "She's a God-send to help me get settled!"

"I'm sure you'll find it pleasant here," Cassandra said to Amanda. "Please let us know if we can help with anything. We all work together here at the fort."

"That's very nice of you," Amanda replied. An eager sparkle shone in her eyes. "This is all new to me . . . and so exciting!"

The Grierson's twelve-year-old daughter Edith appeared, holding a tray of small tea cakes.

"And here's our little Edie," Alice Grierson said, putting a loving arm around her daughter. "She's Ben's pride and joy. I'm afraid he's spoiled her, though—besides me, she's the only girl in the family!"

Edith gave the women a shy smile and moved on to her duties.

"I'm delighted to find such comfortable quarters in this stark area of Texas," Alice continued.

"We all have your husband to thank," Anne Manning said. "He's done wonders for the place." Then her smile faded. "But I'm afraid you're going to find life at Fort Concho to be terribly desolate!"

Alice pressed her lips in determination and said, "Well, you just let me take care of that! I'm going to start right away thinking up ways to keep our minds busy."

Without Ian's presence, Cassandra found it difficult to enjoy the rash of pleasant activities that Alice Grierson had dreamed up. To make things worse, the brick wall Millie had built between herself and Henry cast gloom over the entire house. When they were alone, Cassandra tried to talk to Millie and learned of Henry's refusal to let Millie's father help with the Washington assignment.

"I'm sure it was a big disappointment," Cassandra said, "but you really ought to feel proud of Henry for wanting to stand on his own."

Millie shook her head helplessly. "And now this court-martial thing . . . Daddy will look at Henry as if he's a traitor or something!" She held her face, almost crying. "I just wish I were dead!"

Cassandra took Millie's hands. "Now, you stop talking like that! You've got to let things work themselves out." She switched to a more cheery subject. "Why don't you come with me to the Grierson's house? Alice has started a sewing circle and you can learn how to make a new dress."

Millie looked shocked. "Why, I've never sewed anything in my life!"

Cassandra laughed. "About time you started! You could use a new dress, and just think of all the baby clothes I'm going to need. Let's work together, Millie!"

With so few personnel, the fort seemed wrapped in a strange silence as the group of women sat in Alice Grierson's living room, working with patterns and material.

"My, that's a beautiful cloth!" Cassandra said to Anne Manning. "The sutler's store has practically nothing—where did you get it?"

"At the store in Saint Angela," Anne replied.

Another woman raised disdainful eyes. "That sinful place?! None of us would go there without a soldier escort!"

"That's true," Anne said, "but Tom took me across the river before he left on the Shafter expedition. There's only one dry goods store in Saint Angela, but supply wagons bring in shipments from San Antonio twice a year."

Millie looked up with sudden interest from her sewing. A new spark came to life in her usually drab eyes and she asked, "Do they go back to San Antonio right away?"

"Yes, almost like clockwork, every May and November."

Cassandra wondered at the strange expression on Millie's face, then changed the subject. "Well, it's certainly been quiet around here with nearly all the men away, hasn't it?"

"We still have a few officers," one of the wives said. "That Lieutenant Burger, for one. I'm sure there's a certain laundress who's happy he didn't go on the expedition!"

Cassandra glanced up in surprise. "Lieutenant William Burger? Now, don't tell me that fine, young man is mixed up in the fort gossip."

"Well, they've got to talk about something in this dismal place." The woman turned to Alice Grierson. "Alice, surely your husband knows about this?"

Alice Grierson had said little, for she was smart in the ways of a commander's wife. She kept eyes on her working needle and said, "Maybe Ben knows and maybe he doesn't. But I'll never say anything. It's my policy to see to household matters and let Ben see to military matters."

Cassandra couldn't stand it and said, "I'm not one to gossip, but you've got me curious! Is the lieutenant involved with one of the laundresses?"

"There's an attractive little Mexican laundress," the woman continued eagerly, "living in one of those shacks behind the enlisted men's quarters, down by the river. Dorotea, I believe her name is. The way I hear it, Lieutenant Burger takes his soiled clothes to her place in the evening instead of during the daytime. It's been known that he isn't seen leaving until quite a late hour of the night!"

Cassandra grinned. "Well, being stuck out here in the wilderness, you can't blame a young man for succumbing to temptation."

Alice Grierson added with authority, "But you must remember, that's strictly against Army regulations. Only the enlisted men with laundress wives are allowed to fraternize."

As late evening fell, the soft cloak of night enveloped Fort Concho, swallowing the parade ground in near darkness. The only illumination came from a pale moon and the soft glow of kerosene lamps fluttering like fireflies trapped behind the buildings' windows.

Lieutenant William Burger brushed back his short straw-colored hair but the breeze caught it again in a tangle. *Never mind*, he thought, *it's dark and she'll not see it.*

He made his way beyond the enlisted men's barracks and to the shack where Dorotea washed the officers' clothes in two large kettles that sat before the hovel. He tapped on the door and it was quickly opened by a beautiful Mexican girl with glistening ebony eyes.

"Well, has my *Chico* come for his laundry?" she asked and leaned seductively against the doorway. A thin blouse and short skirt blatantly advertised every curve of her slender body.

The lieutenant swallowed at the sudden desire she ignited in his groin. "Yes, Dorotea . . . can we go inside?"

She took his hand and led him into the dark room, closing the door behind them. He put his hands on her narrow waist and she slipped into his arms like a soft bundle of feathers for a smothering kiss. When their mouths finally parted, she spoke again.

"I have your uniform all nice and clean. You have brought the money, yes?"

"Of course!" He took a breath and drew some bills from his trousers pocket. "And here's some extra so you can buy that dress you told me about."

"Oh, you are so sweet to your little Dorotea!"

She moved him to the bed, unbuttoning his shirt. Perspiration dotted his forehead and he took off the shirt, wiping his face with it.

Dorotea removed her blouse, sat on the bed and pulled him down to her warm body. "Now, I give you something for the extra money you let me have."

Somewhere on the parade ground, the bugler began his sad rendition, signaling day's end, and windows in the various buildings began to wink into darkness. Only the scratching sound of crickets, chirping their nocturnal song along the river banks, filled the night air as Fort Concho settled down for another sultry night.

Chapter Thirteen

Benjamin Grierson came home in the late afternoon and took off his coat. He breathed a weary sigh. It had been a long haul, cleaning up a cesspool, but well worth it; Fort Concho was finally looking more hospitable. He found his wife at the sitting room table with pen in hand.

"Dinner will be ready in a moment, Dear," she said and continued writing.

Alice had always faced a new challenge without hesitation and Ben knew she was not about to submit to the depressing environment of west Texas. She had already brought fresh air to the fort with all her activities. He studied her with curiosity. "I see you've been keeping yourself busy."

"Yes. In fact, I've just come from the stables."

He chuckled in surprise. "What on earth were you doing at the stables?"

"There are several fine horses the fort personnel can use for group horseback rides. I expect we can have picnics and fishing parties down by the Concho River!"

Ben stroked his ample beard with amusement. "I'd guess most of the ladies here at the fort have never been on a horse."

"Then we'll teach them! It's no problem, and besides, they'll find it more delightful than sitting in their dark rooms, brooding!"

Ben nodded approvingly. "There are Indians still

roaming the plains, but I suppose we can use soldier escorts."

Alice smiled with confidence. "If it becomes a problem, I'm drawing up a series of parties for each month of the year . . . we can all dress in costume for a particular holiday and enjoy ourselves in the large mess hall."

Little Edith Grierson heard her father's voice and rushed into the room for a welcome hug. She looked up with studious dark eyes as he ran a loving hand over her head.

Now that his favorite child's birthday was coming up, Ben pondered on what to give Edie as a present. He had already given her a pinto pony; this time, it would have to be something special.

"Edie, you'll be thirteen on the twenty-seventh," he told her. "That deserves a big party. You can have all your friends come by for birthday cake, and I'll even have the post band play a few tunes for you!"

Edith's somber eyes widened with expectation. "Oh, thank you, Daddy . . . I've never had a party before!"

For the next few days, Edith, usually a quiet child, talked about nothing but her coming birthday party. However, as the date approached the girl turned listless and seemed to have lost her excitement.

"Edie, dear," Alice worried, "let me see your tongue."

Edith stuck out her tongue while Alice put a hand on the girl's forehead.

"I think you'd better lie down for the rest of the day," Alice said. "You've probably been riding that pony too often in this cold morning air."

Ben Grierson returned from his duties that afternoon and missed his daughter's usual loving hug.

"Edith isn't feeling well," Alice told him. "I've put her to bed for the day."

"Do you think she'll be all right for the birthday party tomorrow? I have everything arranged."

"You needn't change anything," Alice assured him. "I don't think it's serious. But even so, let's keep the party simple."

A group of the fort's children stopped by the next afternoon for cake and sweet drinks while Colonel Grierson's band lined up in front of the house.

"The band has been practicing and they're anxious to play for Edith," Ben told his wife. "We can let her sit on the porch and listen."

Everyone knew the post commander's little girl was ailing and Cassandra, especially, was concerned. It could very well happen to her own child one of these days. She baked a cake and took it to the Grierson house. The pretty cousin Amanda opened the door.

"I'm so sorry to hear of Edith's illness," Cassandra said. "I thought this might be of some help."

"That's so thoughtful of you," Amanda said, "but I'm afraid Edie won't be able to enjoy it."

Cassandra's heart sank. "You mean she hasn't improved?"

"The poor dear was stricken with nausea and diarrhea this morning and hasn't been able to keep anything on her stomach. Ben called for the post surgeon. He's in the bedroom, now, looking at Edie with Ben and Alice."

In a moment, the doctor came out of the bedroom, followed by Ben Grierson. Both had long faces.

Through the doorway, Cassandra saw Alice sitting at her daughter's bedside.

"I stopped in to see about your daughter," Cassandra told the colonel. "I do hope she's better."

"That was kind of you," Ben Grierson said, "but I'm

95

afraid the news isn't good."

The doctor explained. "All indications show that the girl has typhoid fever, Mrs. Shaw." He turned to Ben. "I'll do everything I can for your daughter, Colonel."

Cassandra was stunned; typhoid could be deadly and she felt helpless. She put a gentle hand on Ben's arm. "I'll be glad to stay with you, if I can help in any way."

He gave her a brave smile. "Thank you, Cassandra, but I don't think there's anything we can do, now, but pray."

For the next eight days Amanda took turns with Alice and Benjamin Grierson, sitting by their daughter's bedside. They tried without success to keep fluids on Edith's stomach while the girl became more dehydrated and her fever still raged.

The doctor seemed at a dead end. "If only we had some ice in this blasted place!" he fumed. "That might bring her temperature down."

Alice dabbed at a tear. "Ben, is there any way we could get some ice? It's the only thing left we can do!"

Benjamin Grierson worked a miracle, although it took three days. A small amount of melting ice finally arrived at Fort Concho and the doctor placed it around Edith's face and body. But the temperature refused to abate while her stomach continued to reject all liquids.

Alice and Ben prayed diligently at Edith's bedside; however, at eight o'clock on the evening of September the ninth, Edith Clare Grierson closed her little eyes in final rest.

Benjamin Grierson covered his face and went to break the news to Amanda and his sons Harry and George.

Alice sat for a moment, her soul wracked in grief. She knew how devastated Ben must be and that he needed her now, more than ever.

She rose wearily to comfort her husband and found him standing before the big sitting room window, his eyes seeing nothing through the dark panes while his long beard sparkled from the warm tears pouring down his cheeks.

Alice placed her damp face on his shoulder. "Even though our daughter has been taken from us," she sobbed, "Edie will always be in our hearts . . . that will have to be our only consolation."

Fort Concho's bleak atmosphere turned even more somber as Cassandra and other close friends of the Griersons attended beloved Edie's funeral in the civilian cemetery.

The following day, Benjamin Grierson had some of his men construct a small rock wall around the grave; as if, Cassandra thought, to protect his daughter from any more harsh realities a cruel world might have in store.

Cassandra's heart ached to see Alice Grierson spend the early mornings at Fort Concho sitting within the enclosure, reading her mail and planning the day's activities.

No one was immune to the dangers of this inhospitable country, Cassandra realized with gnawing dread. Even her own child, due in just a few months.

When Cassandra lay down that night, she felt terribly alone and vulnerable. The usual prayer went through her mind, asking for Ian's swift and safe return. Only then could she face the perils that lay ahead.

Chapter Fourteen

The only thing that kept Cassandra from falling into Millie and Henry's doldrums was watching her belly grow larger each day. She felt almost giddy with the thought of bearing her first child.

November came in on the heels of cold gusting winds, and the good Colonel Grierson with his wife Alice began arranging a Thanksgiving dinner for the few personnel at the fort. Everyone was invited, including the laundresses. Cass hoped the gala might be the trick to change Millie and Henry's attitude.

"I don't know how the Griersons did it," Cassandra told them, "but they've managed to get apples, pears and pickles—both sweet and sour! And I'm helping Anne Manning with cake and cookies."

"I don't feel like going to the dinner," Millie said with a dark face, "but I don't want you to miss it because of me. Why don't you go with Henry. I'll be all right."

Henry knew how much Cassandra had been looking forward to the celebration. Not wanting her to go unescorted, he condescended. "I'll take Cassandra but we won't stay long. We'll be back right away to see how you're doing, Millie."

The tempting buffet-style dinner covered several long tables in the larger mess hall behind the number one enlisted men's barracks. Members of Grierson's post band played in the middle of the room, the small group of remaining officers dancing with the wives at one end and enlisted men dancing with laundresses at the other.

Soon after Henry and Cassandra arrived, Lieutenant William Burger, handsome in his dress uniform, appeared at her elbow.

"I've been saving a dance with you, Mrs. Shaw . . . that is, if you feel like it."

She smiled with delight. "I may be heavy with child, but it won't keep me from enjoying a dance or two!"

While leading her into a gentle waltz, the lieutenant's eyes kept glancing across the room at a pretty raven-haired laundress with cinnamon complexion. The girl was obviously enjoying herself in the arms of many of the enlisted men.

Cassandra noted the deep hurt on Lieutenant Burger's face. "Is it really that serious?" she asked.

He blushed in surprise. "You're such a wise lady, Mrs. Shaw. I've been rather foolish. I thought I was in love with a certain young girl. But, as you can see, her affections are available to any of the men here . . . for a price!"

"Well, don't let someone like that mess up your life, Lieutenant. There are many fine young women out here, just waiting for someone as good as you!"

She noticed Colonel Grierson's pretty cousin Amanda in an attractive dress, watching the dancers. "I think I've danced enough for a woman in my condition, Lieutenant. If you don't mind, let's find someone to take my place."

Cassandra led him by the hand over to the young girl. "Amanda, would you do me a large favor and finish this dance with Lieutenant Burger? I just can't keep going as long as I'd like!"

The girl's eyes widened with delight. "Why, of course, Cassandra, if Lieutenant Burger wishes!"

99

The concern on Burger's face turned to pleasure. He made a courteous bow and took Amanda's hand. "I would be honored."

Cassandra felt a warm glow as she watched them move onto the dance floor in a graceful waltz. She took a seat and after two more numbers, Henry Adams appeared at her side.

"I hate to be a party wrecker," he said with concern, "but I'd like to get back and check on Millie. If you want, I can find someone to see you home."

"Thank you, Henry, but it's getting late. I'll come along with you."

They returned to the house and Henry rushed upstairs to the Adams' bedroom while Cassandra stopped in the sitting room to undo the scarf from her head. She turned at the sound of Henry's grief-stricken voice.

"Millie's gone! I can't understand it . . . she's gone!"

With sudden dread, Cassandra pulled her awkward body up the staircase. "What do you mean, Henry?"

Henry held out a paper. "She's taken all her things and left . . . here's a note!"

Cassandra took the paper and quickly read Millie's hasty scrawl:

"I tried, Henry, but the disgrace was too much. I don't want to become a shriveled-up old woman at Fort Concho. Please forgive me. I'm going back to the world of the living! Millie"

Henry's face had turned to panic. "I've got to stop her, Cass . . . but where could she've gone?!"

Cassandra put a hand to her forehead. She recalled Millie's keen interest on learning that supply wagons left Saint Angela for San Antonio every March and November. Like clockwork, Anne Manning had said. And this was November.

"The only place would be Saint Angela," Cassandra told

100

him with reluctance. "She knows that supply wagons leave this time of the year, going east."

"Then I'm going to Saint Angela and find her!"

Cassandra took his arm. "But you're under orders not to leave the post, Henry—if you do, they'll arrest you!"

He gritted his teeth. "Then let them try. I'm not gonna lose my wife!"

Cassandra watched, helpless, as Henry stumbled down the stairs and out of the house.

Chapter Fifteen

"I'd like to see Colonel Grierson," Cassandra said to the orderly. "It's most important."

Ben Grierson heard her voice and came from the other room. "Cassandra Shaw, what brings you here at this early hour?"

She glanced at the enlisted man behind his desk. "It's rather personal, Colonel. Could we talk in your office?"

"Why certainly, do come in."

They entered the room and he closed the door. "Please have a seat, Mrs. Shaw." He leaned on the edge of his desk. "I rather think I know why you're here."

"Yes. It's about Captain Henry Adams," she replied and took a chair. "I just want you to know that when the guards arrested Henry last night, he was not trying to escape from his court-martial. He was trying to find his wife who had run away to Saint Angela."

Ben raised a surprised eyebrow. "Millie Adams has run away? Captain Adams said nothing about that when he was arrested."

"He wouldn't. It was a very personal matter."

Ben gave it a moment's thought. "Then, what you're saying is, we should release him since he has no desire to run away from court martial?"

"Yes, Colonel. If you could do that, it would make everything a lot easier for all of us."

"And what makes you think once Captain Adams is free, he won't try to go after his wife?"

Cassandra took a deep breath. "If you'll let me talk with him, I can assure you that Henry Adams will wait here at Fort Concho until Colonel Shafter returns for the court-martial hearing."

A sergeant escorted Cassandra to the deplorable jail and she peered at Henry Adams through a barred window. Her heart went out to anyone forced to spend even a minute in the horrible little cells.

"Henry," she began in a soft voice, "I hope you've had time to think this thing over. Maybe I'm putting my nose in where it doesn't belong—but you must realize that if you desert the Army in trying to find Millie, your life will be ruined forever. Even if you find her, what good will it do?"

He ran a hand through his tousled hair. It was obvious that he had worn himself out thinking about the situation. "Maybe I could change her mind. We could both run away somewhere . . . "

Cassandra shook her head. "And what kind of life would that be, hiding from military law? She would only leave you again. Besides, no one can ever change Millie's mind."

He looked up with baleful eyes. "Are you saying our marriage is over? I'll never see her again?"

"Did you ever really have a marriage? Ask yourself, Henry, if you both wouldn't be better off going your separate ways. If the answer is yes, then the only difference between you and Millie is that you're the one who took the right path!"

Chapter Sixteen

December arrived with gusts of icy wind moaning across the flat barren plains. It swept over Concho River, shaking a few dried pecans from the scraggly trees, and finally reached the fort to slip beneath Cassandra's door.

The resulting chill only added to the gloom of Henry Adams blaming himself for his wife's desertion. Adjusting to their separation was difficult but, in time, Cassandra knew both Henry and Millie would finally be at peace with themselves.

On the eighth of December, Cassandra's cold world turned suddenly to warm joy as Fort Concho erupted with excitement. At the first sounds of shouting and cries of laughter she rushed outside to see Lieutenant Colonel Shafter's party straggling in, surrounded by the happy wives, children and fort personnel.

She thought her heart would leap out of her breast as she scanned the crowd, desperately looking for Ian's face. At last he emerged from the throng and ran up the porch steps, taking her in his arms. With Cassandra's baby due any day now, they both laughed at their two stout bodies pressing together.

"Oh, Ian," she cried, happy tears rolling down her cheeks. "I've prayed you'd get back before the baby came!"

"I've been doin' the same!" He kissed her longingly. His eyes, too, were not exactly dry. "You look just beautiful, Cass. I still can't believe I'm gonna be a daddy!"

She uttered a delirious giggle. "If you hug me any tighter, it could happen right now!"

The joy of Ian's return was tempered by Henry Adam's impending court-martial and two days later the officers convened for the procedure. Only a few personnel were allowed to attend, but Ian lingered outside with others, waiting for the verdict.

Cassandra, working in the kitchen during late morning, turned to see Ian burst into the house.

"Is it over?" she asked with apprehension. "Is Henry all right?"

Henry Adams appeared a step behind, both men radiating smiles of relief.

Ian put an arm around Cassandra's large waist. "Captain Henry Adams was let off with only a reprimand," he announced, "due to extreme circumstances while on duty in the field!"

It was a time for celebration and what better occasion than at the Christmas dinner Ben Grierson had promised for Colonel Shafter and his dedicated Buffalo Soldiers.

Cassandra threw herself into the holiday spirit. She whipped up a batch of cookies and had just taken a tray from the oven when Anne Manning stuck her head in the front door.

"Cass, may I come in? I have wonderful news!"

"Of course, Anne, what is it?"

Anne came inside and closed the door behind her.

"First, here's a little something for you and Ian's Christmas." She handed Cassandra a little wrapped package.

"Oh, Anne, I wish you wouldn't. I haven't gotten a thing for anybody, not even for Ian!"

Anne shook her head. "Doesn't matter. I don't expect anything!"

Cassandra looked chagrined. "Now, what's the good news?"

"Tom's promotion to Lieutenant Colonel finally came through! And not only that, they're looking for a new post commander at Fort Union in New Mexico—Tom's put in his application!"

Cassandra was struck with a mixture of delight and sadness. "I'm so happy for you . . . but that means you'll be leaving!"

"Not unless Tom is selected. You know those military bigwigs, it takes them forever to make up their minds!"

After Anne left, Cassandra's head swam with confusion. So many things were happening all at once; and her life would be changed even more with a child to raise. The baby gave a strong kick and she eased herself into a chair to let it stop protesting.

Christmas would be so different out here in the middle of nowhere. She recalled the piney smell of a Christmas tree in the convent's anteroom; an aroma of spice cookies permeating the hallways; soft voices of nuns singing carols on Christmas eve; she and her sister Terressa exchanging some trivial little gift.

But here at Fort Concho, what could she give Ian—and poor little Henry? Maybe it'd be just a simple bottle of Irish whiskey from the sutler's store. Whatever, they would know it was the thought that counts.

Thomas Manning left the sutler's store and carefully placed a little wrapped package into his coat pocket. He hoped Anne would like the small bottle of perfume. She deserved better, but out here there wasn't much to choose from, and besides, his Army salary prevented any extravagance.

He warmed his hands in the deep pockets of the great

coat while walking back to the limestone officers' quarters. A light snow had fallen and the crunch of his footsteps made him think of their wedding day. There was snow then, too. In fact Anne was always disappointed if there wasn't a bit of white on the ground at each of their anniversaries.

He turned up the collar against an icy breeze whispering around his neck and wondered how many more Christmases he and Anne had left. The number was dwindling and he vowed to make each one more important than the last.

Chapter Seventeen

The wintry coldness only added to December's holiday spell that had crept over Fort Concho with everyone looking forward to the coming festivities. Alice Grierson found the means to scrounge some apples and raisins for Cassandra to use in a good German strudel for the Christmas dinner while Anne Manning would provide fresh-baked cookies. They had even fashioned a Christmas tree out of mesquite bushes trimmed with ornaments cut from tin cans and popcorn on strings.

Cassandra arose early on Christmas morning, knowing she had much to do. She went downstairs to start a warming fire and was delighted to see falling snow, although it was just a light dusting and would probably melt off by late afternoon. Even so, it gave a sparkling aura of Christmas.

Later, Ian came downstairs to find his wife humming a carol while preparing his breakfast. Walking up quietly, he slipped his big arms around her ample waist, kissing her on the ear.

Cassandra did not turn around, but closed her eyes dreamily. "Ian, do you remember that day when we sat in a buggy on a hill overlooking San Antonio . . . and I proposed to you?"

"Luckiest day of my life."

"And you said, 'But there's such a thing as love in marriage.' And I told you we could grow to love each other."

"In case we didn't, I'd planned to ship you right back to

that convent!"

She turned to him with mock horror. "Ian!"

He laughed and gave her a tender kiss. "But it worked out the way you said. I love you more than all the shamrocks in Ireland!"

Henry Adams appeared in the kitchen doorway. "Oh, sorry," he apologized. "Just wondered if there was any coffee yet."

"That's all right, Henry," Cassandra said as Ian released her. "It's on the stove. You two pour yourselves a cup and I'll have breakfast ready in a couple of shakes."

"Better make that one shake," Ian remarked, "or they're gonna hear our stomachs rumblin' all the way to Saint Angela!"

After the men had eaten, Cassandra shooed them out, saying she needed the entire table to make her strudel. By late morning the house swirled with the aroma of baked apples and cinnamon; the tantalizing strudel lay wrapped in a large basket to be taken to the dining hall.

Cassandra cleaned the kitchen and started upstairs to prepare herself for the festivities. At the top landing a sharp pain tore her insides and she gripped the stair post.

"Ian!" she called.

Ian and Henry, engrossed in a game of checkers, paid little attention.

"Ian, please come quickly . . . I need your help!"

Ian put down his checkers and rushed to the foot of the stairway.

Cassandra stood holding her stomach and looked down with a funny little smile of delighted awe. "Ian . . . I think you're about to be a father!"

He caught his breath and turned to Henry. "Get the post surgeon, Henry—and fast!"

As Henry rushed out the door, Ian ran upstairs and

helped Cassandra into the bedroom where he carefully eased her down onto the bed.

The doctor, about to leave for the Christmas dinner, listened to Henry's urgent request, then buttoned his coat collar and the two moved quickly down the gravel path to the house.

"This is it, Doctor," Ian said nervously. "For the first time in my life, I don't know what to do!"

The doctor chuckled. "Don't worry, just leave everything to me. What you *can* do is get me some towels and start heating a pot of water."

Cassandra's labor pains lasted mercifully for only two hours and by early afternoon the post surgeon came down the stairway, buttoning his shirt cuffs.

"Captain Shaw," he proclaimed with a satisfied smile, "You are the father of a beautiful daughter, weighing approximately six pounds, I would say. Mother and child doing nicely."

Henry clapped a congratulatory arm over Ian's shoulders.

Ian stared in a daze. "Is it all right to go up, now?" he asked the doctor.

The surgeon laughed. "Of course, your family is waiting for their daddy!" He threw on his coat. "Now, if you'll excuse me, I'm going to see if any of that Christmas dinner is left."

"I'll join you," Henry said. He grabbed his coat and the basket of strudel, then turned to Ian. "You ought to be alone with your new family, now, anyway!"

Ian started up the stairway and the surgeon called after him. "I'll stop by later this evening to be sure everything's all right."

Ian rushed to the bedroom and found Cassandra looking radiant, holding a tiny little red-faced thing wrapped in a soft blanket.

"Ian Shaw," she said happily, "meet your daughter . . . Rose Terressa Shaw."

"You gave her my mother's name!" He kissed Cassandra on the forehead, then moved the blanket carefully with a large forefinger to get a better look at his daughter.

"Oh, Ian," Cassandra fretted, "I had a little present I was going to give you after the dinner. Now I've gone and messed up your Christmas!"

He wiped his eyes with a sleeve.

"Cass, dammit, don't you ever tell anybody you've seen Ian Shaw with tears on his face! You've given me the best Christmas present any man could hope for . . . Cass, I love you so much!" He crouched beside the bed and put a large arm around his wife and child.

Cassandra's happy tears rolled down her cheeks to moisten the pillow. It was the most wonderful moment of her life and she gave a silent prayer.

Thank you, God, thank you!

PART TWO

- 1876 -

Chapter Eighteen

Although letters announcing little Rose's arrival had been sent to her sister Terressa and Ian's father, Cassandra chided herself. Here it was March already and she was just now entering her daughter's birth in the family Bible.

The year had started out brightly, first with an open house on New Year's day at Benjamin Grierson's house, then Alice Grierson's little parties, sometimes twice a week. But a small dread marred Cassandra's happiness; with the coming of warm weather, Ian and Henry were being sent into the field again.

"Nothing to worry about," Ian told her before leaving. "Won't take more than a week to string those telegraph wires."

"And we'll have twenty Buffalo Soldiers with us," Henry added.

The two men had just come downstairs and were buttoning up their uniform coats. Cassandra felt relief at the change in Henry Adams. With a lovable new baby in the house, he had regained his fun-loving self, joking with Ian as before.

Ian took Rose from the small cradle he had made and raised the baby above his head. She gurgled and made bubbles for him. At first, Cassandra had been concerned in not giving Ian a son; however, no father could lavish more love on his little daughter.

Cassandra hated the thought of being separated from Ian

once more and tried to mask her fear. "It's going to be terribly lonesome in this house with you two away!"

Ian ran his hand softly over her cheek. "With two beautiful girls waiting for us, we'll be back before you know it. Then you'll wish we'd stayed longer!"

He gave her a goodbye kiss and Cassandra put a hand to her heart, watching them walk out of the house.

The telegraph wire project, uniting Fort Concho with Fort Griffin to the north, had been started before Lieutenant Colonel Shafter's arrival. Now, with the passing of winter, they hoped to finish it without delay.

Ian, Henry and the group of soldiers arrived at the working point, ten miles outside of Fort Concho, to find that Indians had played havoc with the progress already made. Many of the tall poles stood bare, the hostiles having cut down the copper wire to use as ornaments.

"Well, they at least left us the poles!" Ian remarked in his good-natured way. "We'll just have to start over."

After they made camp, Ian supervised half of the men who began attaching rolls of copper wire. Henry led the other ten soldiers a few miles down the line to install additional poles.

Henry and his group were to return to the base camp by late afternoon. However, at the end of the day there was no sign of the men. Long, ominous shadows creeping over the desert floor gave Ian an edgy feeling.

"I think we ought to send out a search party," he said to one of the men.

Suddenly a burst of distant gunfire turned his insides cold—he had not placed a guard for his men and probably neither had Henry. It was a mandatory thing to do during the night, but here, in broad daylight, one could see for miles and

116

it seemed unnecessary. Now, it was too late to correct his mistake.

Forty Indians, like a crowd of angry bees, had rushed from behind a distant pile of boulders, swarming with bloodcurdling screams and a barrage of gunfire over the surprised soldiers.

Ian watched in agony as three of his men took arrows or bullets in their chests. The others grabbed rifles and returned the fire; three Indians dropped from their mounts.

Ian had only a Colt-45 strapped to his side. He pulled it quickly and rushed into the storm of milling horses and falling bodies, blasting one Indian off his horse and beating at another with his free arm.

Using rifles, bows and arrows, lances and clubs, the hostiles began slaughtering Ian's men and his ears rang from the terrifying mayhem. Blinded by the thick clouds of dust, he felt his body being thrown violently from side to side by the thrashing horses.

Through slitted eyes he saw one fearful red face with a crooked nose glowering down at him, then a blow to the head sent him reeling face down into the dirt. Ian Shaw's last thoughts were of his wife and newborn daughter before he sank into a painful sea of darkness.

Chapter Nineteen

Cassandra held little Rose close to her breast and shivered from the chilly evening winds coiling around Fort Concho like a cold invisible serpent. Thank goodness, it would be only a short walk to the Mannings' house where she was to have dinner with them and Traylor Doolan.

Anne Manning opened the door to Cassandra's surprise, for Anne had just put a shawl over her shoulders.

"Oh, Cassandra, I was about to come over to your place—Tom and Tray had to leave!"

The dark look on Anne's face gave Cassandra a twinge. "What's happened, Anne . . . is something wrong?"

"There's been trouble in the field. Tom and Tray have gone to see what the situation is."

Fear stabbed Cassandra's insides. "What kind of trouble?"

Anne wrung her hands, dreading to go on. "Lieutenant Burger just got back with a wagon full of wounded. It seems Indians attacked Ian's party this afternoon."

Cassandra's face turned white. "What about Ian?! Is he wounded?"

"He wasn't one of those brought back, but Henry Adams was. Tom and Tray have gone to check."

Cassandra gave a little moan. "Oh, dear God! I'll have to talk to Henry—maybe he can tell me if Ian is all right!"

Anne stopped her. "Please don't, Cass. They say the

hospital is bedlam right now. Besides, Henry Adams is in no shape to talk."

Cassandra pulled Rose close with a shudder.

Anne took her arm. "Please, Cassandra, don't think the worst. Ian may be all right." She pulled Cassandra into the house. "Now come in out of this cold."

Cassandra's face turned to stone as she sat on the sofa and checked to see that Rose was asleep, thumb in mouth.

Anne had removed the shawl and sat down beside her. "This is your first encounter with the bad side of Army life, Cass. You're just going to have to expect these things to happen and trust the Good Lord to work them out the only way He knows." With a weak smile, she took Cassandra's hand. "I want you and little Rose to stay here with me until Tom returns—who knows, it might've been just a minor skirmish."

Night had settled in when Tom Manning, Traylor Doolan and the group of soldiers arrived with two wagons at the site of battle. A half moon bathed the area in a foreboding ivory glow and the men's insides shrank at the sight of twisted bodies sprawled on the cold ground.

Tom Manning clenched his teeth. "All right, men, let's see if there's anyone still alive."

Torches were lit and lowered to each body with the hope of finding signs of life. A morbid dread swept through Tom Manning, something he hadn't felt since the war. He had seen men's heads blown off during the fight at Shiloh, even arms and legs dismembered, but nothing like the revolting spectacle here; the dead had their clothes ripped away and the bodies cut open or hacked into unrecognizable, bloody corpses.

One mutilated soldier had his head bashed in, but the face was untouched—Manning saw with anguish that it was Captain Ian Shaw.

"How am I going to tell Cassandra?" he said with a leaden heart.

At his side, Traylor Doolan surveyed the massacre. It was nothing new to him; he knew the ugly nature of a Comanche. "I think you're the only one she'd want to hear it from," he replied with quiet resignation.

As morning arrived, a morbid darkness persisted in keeping with the somber party that returned to Fort Concho, their wagons full of dead soldiers.

Colonel Tom Manning took a deep breath of reluctance. "I'd better go to the house right away," he said to Tray.

"I'd go with you," Tray replied, "but this kind of news don't need two men to tell it."

Cassandra and Anne Manning, unable to do any justice to the wonderful meal Anne had prepared, had waited through the long night for a word of hope.

Anne rose quickly from Cassandra's side and went to Tom as he came in. She gave him a hug of relief, then took his hat and coat.

Cassandra nestled Rose in her blanket and got up from the couch. "Tom, is Ian all right?"

He didn't answer right away, only firming his jaw. The pain in his eyes foreshadowed the terrible words that finally came out. "I'm so sorry, Cassandra . . . Ian's dead."

Anne was first to react with a gasp of horror and she clutched Tom's coat to her breast.

Cassandra stood frozen, as if unable to move in a bad dream. Then she uttered a plaintive cry and life suddenly drained from her body. The cozy sitting room turned quickly into a chilled cave, sending her plunging into a black abyss with those two ugly words echoing in her brain: *Ian's dead . . . Ian's dead . . . Ian's dead!*

Chapter Twenty

Cassandra opened her eyes to see Tom Manning kneeling beside the couch where she lay. Anne had placed a damp cloth on Cassandra's forehead and looked down with tear-stained cheeks. Reality struck back at Cassandra like the thrust of a saber and her face twisted with a cry of anguish.

"Ian! Please, God, not Ian . . . why . . . why?!"

Tom Manning held her shoulders, powerless to say anything, and waited until the sobbing grew weak. It was some time before she could sit up, rocking with grief in Anne Manning's arms.

"Can I see him?" Cassandra managed to choke through a flood of tears.

Tom replied quietly, "Cass, you don't want to see him, now. You must remember him as he was."

She turned red eyes to him. "What do you mean . . . as he was?"

"All the bodies were badly mutilated. It's the custom of the Indians, I hate to say."

A terrible shudder ran through Cassandra. "Savages! They're all savages!" Her voice rose to a pitiful cry. "I hate them . . . I hate every one of them!"

Cassandra had turned into a lost soul, wrapped in a haze of despair, as she spent the day and following night with the Mannings while Anne looked after Rose. The more Cassandra thought about what the Indians had done to Ian the more her grief was compounded by hate.

Then her dear father's words, spoken so many years ago, drifted into her mind and she found the strength to carry on, not only for herself but for her child, as well.

On the second morning, much against the wishes of Tom and Anne, Cassandra took Rose back to the empty house that used to ring with Ian's infectious laughter.

Soon after reveille Cassandra heard a light knock on the door and she opened it to see Lieutenant William Burger standing on the front porch.

"Just want to offer my condolences," he said.

"Oh, Lieutenant, I'm so glad you're all right! Won't you come in? I spent the night with the Mannings and just got home—haven't built a fire yet, so it may be a bit chilly."

"Please let me do it for you."

Cassandra shook her head. "No, no, it's not a problem and I know you have your duties."

He stepped inside and Cassandra paused beside the doorway. She moved a hand across her brow. "Lieutenant Burger . . . could you tell me how it happened?"

"But you've already been through so much . . . "

"I might as well hear it now. If I spend the rest of my life wondering about it, I'll go crazy!"

He gave a helpless sigh. "I wish I could have saved your husband, Mrs. Shaw, but I was down the line with Captain Adams' group. When the Indians attacked us, we lost some men, but were able to fight them off. I loaded Captain Adams and the other wounded into the only wagon we had. I drove back to Captain Shaw's camp, but couldn't see any signs of life. There was nothing I could do, since my men were badly hurt and I had to get them back to the fort as fast as I could."

Cassandra could only stare, her face like a silent white statue.

The lieutenant looked at the ground. "I don't know why it had to be your husband instead of me, Mrs. Shaw. With such a wonderful family, the captain had much more to live for than I do."

At last, Cassandra began to melt. "That's a wonderful thing for you to say, but you shouldn't feel that way. God has a plan for everything and you have a whole life ahead of you."

She recalled something Anne Manning had said about the budding affair between Lieutenant Burger and Grierson's cousin Amanda.

"If it's true from what I hear, you and a certain young girl have your own future waiting."

He looked chagrined. "I plan to ask for Amanda's hand in marriage. But maybe we should wait."

Cassandra put a gentle hand on his arm. "Don't wait, Lieutenant, or life will slip away before you know it. Enjoy it now, while it's in your grasp!"

His eyes softened with gratitude. "I think I've said before—you're a very wise lady, Mrs. Shaw." He took her hand and kissed it lightly, then did his polite little bow. He started to leave, but turned and said, "By the way, I saw the sergeant friend of yours, Eben Carruthers, at the hospital. There were several wounded, you know."

"Dear Eben!" Cassandra exclaimed. "I'd planned to go see Henry Adams . . . it's selfish of me not to think of the others! Is Sergeant Carruthers badly wounded?"

"I don't believe so. Just a bullet in the shoulder."

After the lieutenant departed, Cassandra dropped Rose off with Anne Manning and rushed to the hospital.

Repugnant smells of blood and medicine greeted Cassandra as she stopped inside the door. The single ward overflowed with beds of wounded soldiers, but Henry Adams face stood out among the many dark ones. She quickly made her way over to him.

"Henry! I'm sorry I didn't come sooner—how are you?"

Although his head was partially bandaged, he greeted her with a grim smile. "I'm fine. I really shouldn't be taking up room here, it's just a blow to the head." He frowned and bit his lip. "God, Cass, I'm sorry about Ian!"

The tears in his eyes made her choke back a sob. "Let's not talk about it, Henry. You just think about getting well, now!"

He wiped his eyes. "Don't worry. I'll be outta here soon as I can!"

She looked around the room of pitiful wounded men and spotted Eben Carruthers sitting up on a cot. "Oh, there's Sergeant Carruthers! I've got to see him, too." She patted Henry's shoulder. "You take care, now. I'll have a nice dinner waiting when you come home!"

Cassandra picked her way through the sea of beds with their moaning soldiers and stopped at Eben's side.

"Sergeant Carruthers, I didn't know until just this morning that you were hurt! How bad is it?"

He broke into a large smile. "Jes a bullet in the arm, Miz Shaw. It ain't nothin'. I'll be outta here tomorrow mornin'." Then he frowned. "I want you t'know how bad I feel 'bout the cap'n. He was a brave man . . . wish I could've saved 'im from gittin' kilt!"

A thought came to her. "Sergeant, there'll be a need for pallbearers at the funeral tomorrow. If you think you'll be able, could I ask you to be one of those carrying my husband's coffin? I know he'd want it."

His ebony eyes glowed. "I'd be right proud to, Miz Shaw. Ain't nothin' wrong with my right arm."

"Good. I'll arrange it with Colonel Grierson."

As she made her way back to the doorway, Cassandra

heard one of the Negro soldiers ask in a weak voice for water. She turned to see the poor man lying with his head wrapped in a bandage; even though it covered his eyes, the face was familiar. She walked over to him.

"Joshua Barnes, is that you?"

"Tha's right, Ma'am, I'm Josh Barnes."

"I'm Cassandra Shaw . . . Captain Ian Shaw's wife."

"Thought I knew yer voice. You was kind enough t'let me ride in yer ambulance back there on the plains."

A glass and pitcher sat on the little bedside table. Cassandra poured some water, then raised his head and helped him with a sip of water.

"Are you hurt bad, Joshua?"

"Some ol' Injun hit me in the face with his tommyhawk. Doc says I oughta be okay in a week or two."

She lowered his head back to the pillow. "There's only the doctor to see to all you men. Let me show you how to find the water if no one's around." She took his hand. "Now, feel the table here . . . then slowly move your hand up to the top. The pitcher of water and the glass are right here."

"Tha's real kind o' you, Ma'am. I 'preciate that."

Cassandra's eyes misted and she patted his hand.

"You're a brave soldier, Joshua. We're all proud of you. I've got to go, now, but I want you to take care of yourself. I expect to see you on the parade ground soon, doing that saber drill you do so well!"

She had just stepped out onto the graveled path, when Traylor Doolan joined her.

"I was leaving my room above the hospital when I saw you," he said. "That was a mighty nice thing you did in there."

"Why, hello, Mr. Doolan," Cassandra replied. "I do feel so sorry for those poor men."

"Ain't many women as thoughtful as you. I'd planned

125

to stop at your house and pay my respects. Reckon, now, you'll be goin' back to what they call civilization."

They began to walk slowly toward the officers' quarters.

"I'm not sure what I'll do," she sighed. "I feel like the whole world has been pulled out from under me. I wish I could be like you, Traylor Doolan, being a part of building this land. I suppose you'll be leading another group into the wilds?"

"As a matter of fact, yes. I'm goin' with Tom Manning's party to Fort Union in a couple of weeks. He just got his orders this mornin'."

She turned with surprise. "Oh, they finally came through? Anne's probably waiting to tell me when I get back to the house."

They stopped in front of the Manning's house where Cassandra would pick up Rose.

"Well," Tray said as he took her hand and held it gently between both of his, "I wanna say it's been real nice knowin' you. You're one brave little lady."

"Thank you, Mr. Doolan."

She studied his handsome face. It was strange how those eyes could be so riveting one time and soft and inviting the next.

Cassandra removed her hand from his. "I imagine we'll be seeing each other again before you leave." She gave him a parting smile and walked to the front door, fighting the desire to look back. She knew Traylor Doolan's gentle blue eyes were following her until she closed the door.

It seemed incongruous for the bright midmorning sun to be smiling down cheerfully on Fort Concho's grief-stricken souls gathered at the post cemetery.

Cassandra stood holding Rose and gazed, misty-eyed, at

the sewed-up canvas bags of enlisted men lying next to their open graves. Scarcity of wood at Fort Concho was a problem when it came to making coffins, therefore only the officer Captain Ian Shaw was placed in a box made out of crates scrounged from the commissary.

The pallbearers included Lieutenant Colonels Grierson and Manning, with two Buffalo Soldiers. Sergeant Eben Carruthers looked proud in his dress uniform and left arm in a sling.

Cassandra watched in tender grief as Ian's coffin was carried by, then she noticed something that made her gasp. Stenciled on the side of the wooden box, in large, black letters, were the words: "20 LBS. LARD."

She smiled and could almost hear Ian roaring with laughter at the incident. A warm comfort swelled in her heart and she knew Ian would want her and Rose to perpetuate his joyful love of life.

That night, Cassandra opened her Bible to the last entry she had made—one filled with happy words announcing the birth of her and Ian's baby Rose. Now, Cassandra added one more, written with a heart that had been torn to shreds.

March 10, 1876: Ian Shaw killed by Indians. Buried at Fort Concho, Texas.

Chapter Twenty-One

Alice and Lieutenant Colonel Grierson, still suffering from the loss of their beloved little Edith, knew too well of Cassandra's grief and stopped by in the afternoon to pay their respects. As they seated themselves, Grierson's tall body filled the wingback chair that always swallowed up little Henry Adams.

"Mrs. Shaw," Ben said hesitantly, "there's another matter that has to be brought up at times like these . . . "

Alice put a hand on her husband's arm. "Ben, does it have to be now?"

Cassandra gave him a kindly look. "I understand, Colonel. It's about my leaving Fort Concho, isn't it?"

He shifted uncomfortably. "Well, it's duty time and I'm compelled to follow regulations. Of course you realize that with the captain gone, now, you're no longer an Army wife. Do you plan to return to your home in San Antonio? I can make arrangements for your passage whenever you're ready."

"I don't really have a home there," Cassandra stated lamely. "The only way I could go back is to become a nun at the convent where I was raised . . . and I'm afraid that would be a little out of the question with my baby Rose."

"Then, do you have an alternative?"

"I've been giving it some thought." A small wrinkle creased her brow. "I understand that Lieutenant Colonel Manning is being transferred to Fort Union in New Mexico to be the new post commander there. He and his wife are leaving next week, I believe."

"That's correct."

"Well, you see, I have an uncle living on a small piece of land in New Mexico—Seven Rivers, the place is called. I know that Colonel Manning's itinerary will take him through that area. Is it possible that I could be allowed to travel with his party and be dropped off at Seven Rivers to live with my uncle?"

Colonel Grierson stroked his long beard thoughtfully and glanced at the baby as she kicked her legs playfully in the cradle beside Cassandra's chair. "With a three-month-old child, do you think that's a wise decision?"

Cassandra lifted Rose out of the cradle. "Rose is a strong healthy baby. I realize it would be somewhat of a hardship for both of us, but I know we could make it, and without any trouble to the others."

Little Rose smiled, wiggling her pudgy arms at Grierson. The colonel's reserve melted swiftly, remembering his own daughter at that age.

"You do have a beautiful child, Mrs. Shaw. Are you certain in your heart this is the direction you wish to take?"

"I really don't see any other choice, Colonel. It's been a dream of mine for years to go to New Mexico and this seems to be the perfect opportunity . . . it's as if God is showing me the way."

Grierson chuckled. "Well, far be it for me to interfere with God's plans. I can arrange for you and the baby to have your own ambulance, and I don't suppose the two of you will increase the rations noticeably." He stood up to leave. "I'll notify Lieutenant Colonel Manning of the addition to his party."

Cassandra got up with Rose in her arm. "Thank you,

Colonel, you've been very kind."

Alice Grierson rose and gave Cassandra's arm a little squeeze of sympathy. "You've been a brave Army wife, Cassandra. I know things will turn out for you."

"I wish you the very best, Mrs. Shaw," Colonel Grierson added. "You were a charming addition to Fort Concho and we're all sorry to see you go." He lovingly touched little Rose's cheek and the Griersons departed.

Tom and Anne Manning rejoiced to learn that Cassandra would be joining their party.

"How wonderful!" Anne cried. "I was dreading the trip, but it'll be like a picnic, now, having my good friend Cass along!"

Cassandra had accumulated very little during her short time at Fort Concho, so there was no problem in packing.

"Ian's clothes are too big for you," she told Henry Adams, "so I'll let you give them to some officer his size. But I'll keep Ian's Jeff Davis hat for the hot days and his overcoat for the cold nights."

He took the clothes with a sad face. "That's mighty kind of you, Cass."

With the difficulty in saying goodbye, Cassandra had tears in her eyes. "I really don't know what I'd have done without your companionship, Henry."

His cheeks had also become moist. "I'm the one who's beholding, Cass. You saved me from steppin' off the edge of a cliff. I'll never forget you!"

A soldier arrived to take her things to the wagon train that stood waiting and Cassandra gave Henry a parting hug.

"We must keep in touch," she said. "I'll write as soon as I get settled in Seven Rivers."

"I might be in Fort Davis by then," he told her. "I'll

just wait till your letter catches up with me!"

Morning greeted them, bright and crisp, as the party assembled for departure. They would have along several head of cattle to provide extra food and two companies of Buffalo Soldiers from the Tenth Cavalry serving as escorts and herders.

As Cassandra walked up to her ambulance with little Rose in one arm, Traylor Doolan appeared on horseback. He tipped his hat with a smile.

"Mighty happy t'see you goin' with us, Mrs. Shaw."

She laughed. "Well, you know what they say about a bad penny!"

Another man pulled his horse alongside Tray and raised an Army hat in greeting. It was Lieutenant William Burger. "Guess you haven't seen the last of me yet, Mrs. Shaw!"

Cassandra looked astonished. "Lieutenant! They're sending you on this long trip? What about Amanda?"

He grinned sheepishly. "Afraid I didn't take your advice, Ma'am. We decided to wait until I come back to Fort Concho to get married."

"Well, perhaps you're right. It certainly wouldn't have been much of a honeymoon, otherwise!"

The two men tipped their hats again before riding ahead, taking their places with Tom Manning.

Cassandra started to put Rose into the ambulance before climbing in and a dark hand reached down. She looked up in startled delight to see Eben Carruther's smiling face.

"Let me take the baby fer you, Miz Shaw," he said.

"Sergeant Carruthers! You're going to see me on another trip? I'm so glad! How ever did this happen?"

Eben took Rose in one hand and pushed back the forage cap with a little, embarrassed smile.

"I told 'em I wanted to be the one t'drive yer wagon."

He placed the baby and blanket in the cradle behind him, then helped Cassandra up onto the wagon seat.

She noticed a new insignia rank on his shirt sleeve. "Why, Sergeant, is that another stripe?"

He lowered his face, hiding a shy look. "It was a long time comin', Miz Shaw. Got it jes last week. I owe it to yer husband, though. The cap'n, he put me in for promotion after that field duty with Colonel Shafter."

"Well, congratulations, I know you've earned it!"

"Thank you, Ma'am."

At the signal to start, Eben urged the mules forward, his eyes shining under the bouncy cap.

Cassandra made sure little Rose was happily snuggled in her cradle, then turned to see Fort Concho fading away behind them. From this distance, the garrison looked like forlorn little match boxes scattered on the endless plains.

She felt a pang in her heart and thought what a desolate place it really was. But it had been a major part of her life, filled with many happy and tragic memories. Now, she was leaving them all there, among the stark buildings dotting the wide thirsty horizon.

Chapter Twenty-Two

Cassandra felt reassured to see how well Rose endured the continual jostling of the ambulance while the mules pulled them steadily onward. Ian's wide-brimmed hat fended off a glaring sun while Cassandra sat beside Eben as the miles of thirsty unchanging land passed by.

Finally, the eastern sky began to fade and they stopped to make camp. It was a desolate flat area with nothing but clumps of tall dead grass, casting long shadows across the sand.

Lieutenant Burger trotted his horse up to the wagon. "I'd be glad to put your tent up for you, Mrs. Shaw."

Eben Carruthers didn't give her a chance to reply. "Might as well let me do that, Sir. After all, Miz Shaw's my passenger!"

Cassandra suppressed a laugh. "That's right, Lieutenant. But I thank you for being so thoughtful."

While all the tents were being raised, Cassandra helped Anne Manning prepare a simple meal for everyone. Later, after the plates were cleaned, they sat around a crackling fire, chatting in low voices and sipping hot coffee.

Cassandra looked up at the huge full moon. It shone down with such brilliance, anyone could have read a book under its glow. Ian's face seemed to appear in the shadowy markings, like a guardian angel watching over her and little Rose.

"Well, ladies," Tom Manning said, wiping out his coffee

cup, "we'd better hit the tents. I'd like to start out before sunrise."

Anne got to her feet and rubbed an aching back. "Cass, do you need anything before bedtime?"

"Not at all, thanks." Cassandra pulled a coverlet around the baby. "Sergeant Carruthers has my tent all ready for us!"

After she had crawled into the tent and held Rose next to her breast beneath a warm blanket, Eben's voice came through the canvas.

"You all right in there, Miz Shaw?"

She smiled at his thoughtfulness. "You needn't worry, Sergeant Carruthers, we're just fine. Goodnight."

In the dark early morning, Cassandra awoke with a start at the crack of gunfire and excited shouting. A quick look through the tent flap revealed a line of flames licking the camp's perimeter. Then the ground shook with thundering hoof beats as the men continued their urgent yelling.

She quickly took Rose in her arms and crawled outside to find the camp half surrounded by fire, a few of the enlisted men's tents already engulfed in orange-red flames.

Cassandra made her way to the wagons where Anne Manning stood, trembling in fear and clutching a blanket around her shoulders.

"How did this happen?" Cassandra asked.

"Indians," Anne replied through chattering teeth. "They set fire to all that dry grass and stampeded the cattle!"

They heard more gunfire and Cassandra noted a few shadowy figures attacking the supply wagon. Flames glistened off their nearly-naked bronze bodies and Cassandra realized she was seeing her first Indians.

The hostiles turned the spigots on two water barrels

strapped to the side of the wagon, sending water streaming down onto the dry ground. Then they used hatchets on the other remaining barrels, ripping off the iron bands as the precious water cascaded into the dust below. Another shot rang out and one Indian fell backward while the others scurried off into the dark, the metal barrel hoops dangling from their arms.

Chaos reigned as men ran here and there, some beating out the flames with coats and blankets while others mounted their horses to go after the fear-crazed cattle.

Much later, the fire had been subdued and Tom Manning appeared, his face and clothing streaked with soot. "Thank God, you two are all right!"

Anne took her husband's arm, drawing him close with relief. "Are there any injuries . . . anyone killed?"

"Not as far as we can tell. They're trying to round up the cattle, but we won't know the real extent of damage till daylight."

A survey next morning proved, to some degree, that the camp was fortunate. There were no casualties and only five tents were burned to ashes—but the most crucial discovery was the loss of their water supply.

"Those devils left us in a bad spot," Tom Manning said. "They know we'll have a rough time of it without water!"

He and Lieutenant Burger had made the rounds to see how much water was available and found only the men's canteens—none entirely full—and a small keg in each of the two ambulances.

"Put the entire camp on water ration," Tom said to the lieutenant. "No one is to waste a drop!"

After Cassandra had breast-fed Rose, she joined the Mannings and Traylor Doolan at their small campfire where they enjoyed a breakfast of bacon, beans and hardtack. They had taken a small portion of water from the keg in Manning's ambulance and rationed only a half-cup per person.

"You'll have to pretend that's coffee, ladies," Tom said. "It'll be a while before we're able to brew any more."

"Just what is our prospect of finding water?" Cassandra asked.

"Not too bad, if we're lucky. We're changing course today for Monument Spring in New Mexico. Shouldn't take more than four days at the most. Colonel Shafter had a stone marker put up there last September, so we can't miss it."

Cassandra set down her now-empty cup. "I can understand the Indians wanting to deprive us of water, but why do you suppose they'd want the metal hoops from the barrels? I saw them run off with the hoops hanging on their arms."

"They use 'em to make arrowheads," Traylor Doolan spoke up. "Hoop iron's stronger than flint. But I'd rather take a flint head in the shoulder any day than one made of hoop iron."

"Dear me," Anne shuddered, "either one sounds bad enough! Why would you prefer flint?"

"If hoop-iron stays in the flesh very long, it starts to corrode. Can kill a man in a day or two."

"Those despicable savages," Cassandra muttered, "I'd like to see them all dead!"

Traylor Doolan gave her a grim smile, then stood up and wiped out his cup.

"If y'all will excuse me," he said, "I gotta go check on the horses."

By early morning the stampeded cattle had been rounded up with some unaccounted for, possibly taken by the Indians. With equipment secured, the party made its way on a new course to Monument Spring. Everyone used water

136

sparingly and felt a sense of duty not to take a sip unless absolutely necessary.

Disheartened, Cassandra watched three of the cattle fall to the ground, weak from dehydration. Rifle shots spared them an agonizing death.

While the other men slumped miserably on their horses, Traylor Doolan looked as if nothing was wrong. He appeared at Cassandra's ambulance, riding alongside, and extended a hand to Eben.

"You and Mrs. Shaw put these pebbles in your mouths," he suggested. "Might help a little."

Cassandra stuck her head out and took two pebbles.

"Too bad we don't have prickly pears around here," Tray added. "A peeled slice of that would keep your mouth watered for days."

"I'll try anything!" Cassandra told him and put the small pebbles into her mouth.

"'Course, if you roll a bullet on your tongue, it's better!"

Cassandra frowned. "Now, that's going a little too far . . . I don't think I could bring myself to put a bullet in my mouth!"

The next day Eben Carruthers' usually strong shoulders drooped while he guided the ambulance. Even with the wagon's stifling interior, it still offered Cassandra and Rose shade from the blistering sun. Unable to breast feed, little Rose cried from thirst and Eben turned to Cassandra, offering his canteen.

"Here, Miz Shaw," he said, "ain't much in it, but the baby needs it more 'n me."

"No, Sergeant," Cassandra choked. "That's your ration—you're out in the sun and you've got to have water."

"I'm doin' fine," he replied while his bleary eyes belied the fact. "I mean it. You give that baby o' yers somethin' t'drink!"

"You're a wonderful man, Sergeant, I'll never forget you!" She took the canteen and moistened a rag for Rose to chew on.

The following day proved even more unbearable and they lost five more head of cattle. Cassandra felt like a dried-out corn husk. She had given Rose all of the water and now slumped on the floor of the ambulance, her throat so dry she couldn't swallow. Through her delirium she heard Eben's raspy voice.

"There it is!"

Cassandra's eyes fluttered open.

"My monument!" Eben croaked. "Can you see it, Miz Shaw?"

Cassandra gathered enough strength to lift herself on an elbow and look through the ambulance opening. A plateau rose in the hazy distance. Under the striking rays of a blazing sun, Cassandra saw a pearl-like monument sitting proudly atop the summit; an angel in white, beckoning with a sun-bleached arm.

Rose began to whimper and Cassandra lay back down, pulling the baby close. "Thank God!" she whispered.

Fortunately there were no Indians at the spring, so Manning's party made camp and spent two days refreshing themselves. On the third morning they filled the two empty barrels with lifesaving water and began their journey west to the Pecos River.

Cassandra watched the gleaming stone marker grow smaller as their caravan trudged away from Monument Spring. They were only the first of many settlers who would follow Colonel William Shafter and his thoughtful pile of rocks to a brave, new world.

Cassandra hoped the beautiful monument would remain

there forever as a tribute—not only to Colonel Shafter, but to Eben Carruthers and his courageous Buffalo Soldiers who had slaved in the hot sun to make it all possible.

Chapter Twenty-Three

The angry Pecos River carved its way down the eastern side of New Mexico, in some places with more twists than a busy rattlesnake. High steep banks and treacherous water posed a challenge to the bravest of any traveler. Only two spots along the jagged course offered the safest crossing—and both had claimed many a life.

Southern Horsehead Crossing was favored by Indians and settlers alike, but Colonel Tom Manning wanted to cut days off the journey. He chose Pope's Crossing, farther north at a point separating Texas and the Territory of New Mexico.

Even with only half the water they started out with from Fort Concho, things seemed to be going well as the group rolled in at the crossing on a late afternoon. Colonel Tom Manning and Traylor Doolan reconnoitered the area.

"Think we should wait till morning?" the colonel asked.

Tray looked up at the sky. "See those clouds? I'd say we're in for one heck of a storm, comin' down from the north. River could be flooded by mornin'."

Manning followed his gaze. "Then we'd waste several days sitting here till the water subsides. I say we cross now before it gets any darker."

Tray rubbed his chin. "You might be takin' a chance. Ever see a flash flood? Can hit before you know it."

Manning scanned the north horizon again. "Doesn't look so bad to me. Let's get them moving. The shallowest place is over there." He spurred his horse to give orders for crossing.

Tray shrugged. Six of one, half dozen of another.

Soldiers moved the few remaining head of cattle first, but some became mired in quicksand. With wild shouts, the men threw a rope around each one's horns to drag them free.

The job took longer than Manning had expected and sunlight began to fade as storm clouds moved in from the north. Finally, with the cattle safe on the other side, all but a few of the troops plunged into the dark waters and swam across, their horses paddling behind. With darkness closing in, the river seemed even more determined to resist its trespassers.

The supply wagon had to be eased down the embankment and into water, the mules struggling to pull it across. Using extreme effort and goading yells, the wagon finally heaved up onto the opposite bank. Next came the Manning's ambulance, which laboriously made the hazardous crossing.

Cassandra had put the boxes containing books and clothing in the Manning's wagon, therefore her ambulance was lighter. It was the final one to cross and she crouched with Rose behind Eben Carruthers while he coaxed the mules down the steep slope. The ugly, mud-yellow water had risen considerably and it surged around them as they sank into its midst.

Just past the half-way mark, Cassandra heard a distant roar, the ominous sound growing even beyond the noise of the river surging around them. One of the mules lost footing and its head disappeared beneath the water, the other one working in vain to drag the wagon along. Men shouted futilely at the poor animal until Traylor Doolan and his horse suddenly appeared alongside. He drew a knife and slashed through the reins, cutting the sunken animal free with the other one continuing to struggle.

The roaring had now reached a terrifying pitch and Cassandra looked over Tray's shoulders to see a wall of water some ten feet high rushing toward them with frightening speed. Before she could think of any action to take, Tray was at her side, his horse swimming with great difficulty. He threw a hand toward her and shouted.

"Gimme your hand, quick, and get on my horse!"

Cassandra clutched Rose in one arm and took hold of Tray's strong grip. She was literally yanked out of the ambulance and found herself behind Tray, astride his horse, water swirling around them in a terrifying maelstrom. But little Rose was not with them—the baby had slipped from Cassandra's arm and tumbled back into the ambulance, screaming in terror.

Eben Carruthers dropped the reins of the remaining mule and grabbed Rose. He thrust the baby into Cassandra's arms and Tray rode them up onto the river bank. Cassandra looked back to see the horrifying tonnage of water crashing down upon the wagon, tearing it apart and spinning the wreckage down river.

"Eben!" she screamed. "No, no!"

Cassandra hugged Rose in one arm with the other around Tray's waist to keep from falling off his horse. She leaned her face against his back and sobbed in despair.

Tray wiped the river water from his eyes. "We'll try to find him tomorrow," he said. "His body might be caught on some bushes growin' along the banks."

Chapter Twenty-Four

Although everyone arrived safely on the western bank of the Pecos, they had little time to make camp; the northern storm began sweeping down on them in heavy sheets of rain. Jagged lightning streaks carried thunder so violent that the ground shook beneath the Manning's ambulance where Cassandra and Rose had taken shelter, cowering in fear.

The rain soon dwindled but lightning continued to slash the dark curtain of night with knives of fire. Lieutenant William Burger, making his rounds of the camp, eventually stopped at the Manning ambulance. He sat on his horse, thoroughly drenched.

"Everybody all right in there?" he called.

Cassandra peered out. "Soaked to the skin, Lieutenant, but we're fine. How is it with the others?"

"Thunder stampeded the cattle and some horses, but they've got them rounded up, now."

Cassandra gasped to see a strange, blue glow of electricity dancing along the lieutenant's hat brim and even around the ears of his horse. Then strands of hair on the back of her neck rose as a bolt of lightning struck only a few yards away. The intense molten light, accompanied by a deafening crash of thunder, threw her back into the ambulance. Anne, blanching with fear, clutched the screaming little Rose to her breast.

"Stay inside!" Burger ordered. "Looks like that hit our

horses—I'd better check!" He turned his horse and disappeared into the wild, black night.

Three soldiers had gathered at a spot where the horses were tethered and Lieutenant Burger saw Colonel Manning hurrying over to the group, pulling a coat over his shoulders. Traylor Doolan was close behind.

"Is anyone hurt?" Burger asked and dismounted.

"I don't know," Manning said. "Let's have a look!"

One of the horses had been killed, its legs still twitching, while not far away lay the contorted body of one of the white soldiers.

"My God!" Manning exclaimed. "It got one of our men, too!"

"Stretch 'im out, quick," Tray said, "and soak 'im with water. Sometimes that'll bring a man to if he's been struck by lightnin'!"

Someone brought a pail of water and poured it over the soldier's body, but unfortunately too late—within minutes, the white flesh had turned the poor man into a blackened corpse. Others arriving at the scene thought a Negro soldier had been killed.

Tom Manning shook his head with a grim expression. "Let's get him into the ground as soon as possible," he decided. "If the rest of our group sees this, it'll be bad for morale!"

Morning finally arrived, bringing an incredible beauty; distant hills took on shades of pink with the sun already turning the ominous purple-red sky into pale blue. No one could have dreamed that the previous night had been ravaged by such violence.

Cassandra, still desolate from losing her good friend Eben Carruthers, gave Rose her milk breakfast and put the baby into the cradle. She turned to see Traylor Doolan ride up on

Pardo. He looked as if nothing had happened.

She said wearily, "I don't suppose there'll be a good cup of hot coffee anywhere in camp this morning—all our matches are still soggy from that downpour."

"No problem," he replied and got down from his horse.

Cassandra watched with curiosity as he gathered up a few twigs that had dried out from the storm. After placing them on the ground in a little pile, he took a bullet from his belt and put it between his teeth, pulling it apart to spill the powder into one hand.

"Now, you got a small rag?"

Cassandra offered him a piece of cloth from the ambulance.

He moistened a corner of the material in his mouth and rolled it in the powder until the cloth was well covered. He then removed one of his spurs and struck it against the wagon wheel, letting the sparks ignite the powder-soaked cloth. It burst into a small flame.

Cassandra beamed with delight. "Why, it's like magic!"

"Now, we can start that pile of sticks to burnin'!"

They worked together at getting a fire going, both on their knees, blowing gently into the tiny flames. As their shoulders touched, Cassandra felt a tingle of warm intimacy.

"Guess I'll be riding with Anne Manning the rest of the way," she said. "At least poor Eben Carruthers won't be driving any more mules."

"I forgot to mention," Tray told her solemnly, "they found his body this mornin' down river 'bout a mile."

Cassandra's heart ached and she remembered her black friend's kind face as he offered his canteen during that scorching day on the prairie.

"When will you bury him? I want to be there."

"They're diggin' the grave up on that hill, now." Tray

145

waved his arm. "He'll be put in the ground right after breakfast."

Cassandra could hardly touch her plate of bacon and beans, the hurt of Eben's loss still lingering. She left Rose in Anne's care, took her Bible in hand and trudged up the hill to where Eben's cloth-wrapped body lay beside an open grave. Traylor Doolan, Lieutenant Colonel Thomas Manning and four Buffalo Soldiers stood at hand.

Two of Eben's comrades gently placed him in the ground and two others began shoveling earth into the grave. Cassandra opened her Bible and started to read:

"Blessed are the poor in spirit: for theirs is the kingdom of heaven.

"Blessed are they that mourn: for they shall be comforted.

"Blessed are the meek: for they shall inherit the earth.

"Blessed are they which do hunger and thirst after righteousness: for they shall be filled.

"Blessed are the merciful: for they shall obtain mercy . . ."

Then she closed the Bible, looked down at the nearly-filled grave and delivered the last line as a tender farewell:

" . . . and blessed is the pure of heart: for Eben Carruthers shall see God."

Chapter Twenty-Five

After a hearty breakfast, everyone began securing equipment before moving on and Cassandra noticed Traylor Doolan tightening a cinch on the Pueblo saddle that fit his lithe body so well. She walked over to him and the horse raised its head with a soft neigh.

Tray gave its neck a calming pat. "Hey, there, Pardo, stop that nickerin'. This here's a nice lady!"

"I hope I didn't scare him," Cassandra said.

"Oh, he's just not used to women. Hardly ever sees any."

The horse stood quietly, giving Cassandra a cautious look with its large brown eyes.

"He's a beautiful animal," she said. "Why do you call him 'Pardo'?"

"Means 'dull brown' in Spanish. Gimme your hand and I'll show you how to make a real friend of ol' Pardo."

He took Cassandra's hand and put it behind one of the horse's ears.

Cassandra started to pull back. "You sure he won't bite?"

Tray laughed. "No—just rub 'im here, right behind the ear. He likes that."

He kept his hand lightly on hers as Cassandra rubbed gently and the horse batted its eyes.

"Why, Pardo, you do like it, don't you!" she said.

Tray dropped his hand and stood back. After a moment she took her hand away and the horse nuzzled her shoulder.

Tray's eyes twinkled. "Y'see, Mrs. Shaw? Now, you've made a friend for life!"

She put her hand back and softly rubbed Pardo's ear again. "We've all become such a family on this trip, Mr. Doolan, I wish you'd call me Cass instead of Mrs. Shaw."

"I'll make a deal. I never felt easy bein' called Mister. I'll call you Cass if you'll call me Tray."

She held out her other hand. "I'd say that's a fair deal, Tray."

He held her hand for a tender shake, then began checking the stirrups while she continued rubbing Pardo's ear.

"Tray," she ventured, "things have been happening so fast, I realize I haven't thanked you for saving my life yesterday . . . and my baby's."

"Oh, I just happened to be there. It was ol' Eben who saved your baby."

She smiled at his unassuming reply and realized that after all this time, she knew very little about Traylor Doolan. She gave Pardo a loving pat on the nose and watched Tray working.

"You know this land pretty well," she continued. "I suppose you've been scouting for a long time."

"Reckon I've spent most of my life on the plains."

"Where's your family?"

"Don't have none. Right after I was born I was taken in by a Tonkawa Indian couple who raised me."

"Then you never knew your parents?"

"Nope."

"Were you able to have any schooling?"

"Only a little from the Tonkawas. Most of 'em are pretty good at learnin' to read and write English. It was the

Tonkawas taught me how to scout."

Their bodies were very close and he turned with a soft gaze, the devilish blue eyes drawing her like a magnet.

She replied in almost a whisper. "From what Colonel Manning says, they did a fine job."

"Well, the Tonks are good scouts," he said modestly.

Cassandra returned to the ambulance, pleased to see that Anne Manning had just put little Rose into a bed of blankets. The child was already sound asleep.

"My, you have the best baby in the world," Anne said. "Why Rose is just no trouble at all. If Tom and I could have children, I'd want a little girl just like her!"

"Well, she takes after her father more than me," Cassandra laughed. "Ian always had an easygoing temperament." Then she grew serious. "I was just talking with Traylor Doolan and learned a sad thing. He lost his mother after he was born and never knew his father. A Tonkawa Indian family raised him. But then I guess you knew all that, since he's such a good friend."

"Tray's a wonderful boy," Anne replied warmly. "Always been like a member of the family to Tom and me." She sighed with pity. "Yes, I suppose Traylor Doolan did have a rather strange childhood. He doesn't really look half-breed at all, does he?"

Cassandra caught her breath. "Half-breed?"

"Yes, he's part Comanche. He didn't tell you that?"

"No . . . it wasn't mentioned."

"Well, I'm not surprised. He's always been kind of resentful about that part of his life. You see, before Tray was born, a band of Comanches raided the Doolan's farm up on the Brazos. They killed poor old Tom Doolan and one of them raped his wife Elizabeth—Tray was the result. You just know he gets those beautiful blue eyes from his mother!"

149

Chapter Twenty-Six

Cassandra climbed into the ambulance beside Rose while Anne Manning settled into a rocking chair, which Tom had tied down for her in the back. The Buffalo Soldier shook the reins and started the mules on their journey while Cassandra sat looking at the passing scene with clouded eyes.

Her growing attraction for Traylor Doolan had been kindled from the moment she fell into those haunting sapphire eyes back at Fort Concho; and after the lifesaving feat yesterday, the infatuation was even stronger.

But now, a cruel knife had been wedged between this feeling and the fact that he was part Indian—a culture that had tragically cut open her heart and filled it with hate. She slumped against the wagon's canvas siding and stared blankly ahead, filled with strange, confused emotions.

Grass appeared more plentiful as they moved up into New Mexico, west of the Pecos River. The refreshing expanse of green came as a welcome relief to the endless dry plains they had left behind.

The party soon arrived at Eddy, a thriving little town of wide streets, many buildings and inevitable saloons. On the outskirts a group of tents squatted like mushrooms—settlers on their way to stake claims in the untamed country north and west.

"Seven Rivers is only about twelve miles north,"

Colonel Tom Manning advised the group. "Since we still have a good day's traveling time, we'll move on and camp there for the night."

Although tired from the arduous journey, Cassandra was glad to endure a few more miles to reach her destination.

The western mountains had begun turning purple under a late afternoon sun as they arrived at Seven Rivers and prepared to make camp at the edge of town.

Cassandra started putting up her tent like dear Eben had done and got onto her knees, spreading out the canvas. She turned to see that Traylor Doolan had walked up and was looking down at her.

"I'd be glad to do that for you," he offered.

She gave him only a glance. "Thanks, Tray. I can't ever do it as well as Eben."

She stood up and watched as he took the hammer.

"I reckon this'll be your last night with us," he said, pounding a stake into the ground.

"I suppose so."

While he worked, her brain still swirled in confusion and she remained silent. It wasn't polite, but she didn't know what to say. Maybe her coldness gave her away. He probably realized that Anne Manning had told her that he had two colors of blood running in his veins. After all, he and the Mannings were close friends and Tray knew how the dear lady loved to talk.

With the tent finally in order she said, "I'm going into town tomorrow morning to find out where my uncle lives."

Tray gave her a serious look. "You ought'n go into a strange town by yourself. I'd be happy to go with you, if you'd like."

"But you can't do that. Colonel Manning will be leaving first thing in the morning."

"Not so. They're spendin' the day here to get supplies and water. They'll be leavin' day after tomorrow."

She had to admit that Tray was right; Seven Rivers was probably full of saloons and rough characters and she hardly knew where to begin with the search for Uncle Emil.

"Well, if you have the time," she said, "I'd be much obliged if you want to help me find my uncle."

Early the next morning, Cassandra's heart ached once more; it was time to say goodbye to the friends who had become like a family. She went to Lieutenant William Burger first.

"It's been a pleasure knowing you," she told the young man. "I'm sorry I won't be at Fort Concho for the wedding—I know Amanda's proud to be your wife."

He took her hand and gave it a little kiss. "The pleasure is all mine, Mrs. Shaw. I'm sure I'm not the only one who's benefited from your wise guidance."

She smiled with embarrassment. "It's not wisdom, Lieutenant. I just look at things from all sides and come to the most practical decision."

"Please send me a letter when you get settled. We Germans have to stick together, you know!"

"And I want to hear about all those beautiful children you'll be raising!"

Now, seeing Anne Manning for the last time, Cassandra couldn't find the words. Instead, the two women hugged each other while tears made their faces shine.

"Oh, Cassandra," Anne finally said, dabbing a handkerchief to her smooth cheek, "I just know we'll never see each other again!"

"Now, you mustn't think of it that way! We'll have to write to each other often . . . we can still be together in spirit."

Cassandra wished she and Rose could go on with the

152

wagon train, but plans had been made and a new life awaited them at Seven Rivers, New Mexico.

She put the few belongings into a wagon and took baby Rose in her arms. Then Traylor Doolan drove them into Seven Rivers, followed by the supply wagon along with Lieutenant Colonel Manning and some Buffalo Soldiers.

Their first stop was the rustic trading post where the supplies would be obtained. Two white-bearded old men leaned back in rickety chairs on the uneven wooden porch, sending an occasional stream of tobacco juice to the yellow-stained steps below. Tray and Cassandra waited for an interval between spits and went quickly inside.

Cassandra's nose came alive at the assortment of musty odors; as her eyes adjusted to the darkness, she saw why.

Barrels of flour, sugar, nuts, kerosene, coffee and whiskey fought for space on the wooden floor covered with dirty sawdust. Weak sunlight from a small dusty window revealed cluttered shelves jammed with bolts of material, kitchen ware, bottles of medicine and various boxes containing hidden surprises.

"Howdy!" a man's voice came from the cavern-like room.

Tray and Cassandra squinted to see the owner, clad in dirty overalls and scuffed boots. He leaned against a wooden counter that had been nicked and scraped by a myriad of goods shoved across its beleaguered surface.

They walked over to the tall, scruffy old geezer who had a broom straw stuck in his mouth.

"Mornin'," Tray said. "We're lookin' for a man named Emil Vosburg. Do you know 'im?"

"Why sure," the man said. "Ever'body 'round here knows ol' Emil Vosburg. Has a little place down near the river. Comes into town to sell me his apples now and then."

"I'm his niece," Cassandra advised. "Can you tell me how I can find his farm?"

"Sure can. It's over on Rocky Arroyo. Just go south outta town 'bout a mile and turn east at the first trail. His is the second house. Built too close to that gully, if you don't mind my sayin'."

"Much obliged," Tray said.

He and Cassandra went back outside and Tray advised Tom Manning that he would join them later. He helped Cassandra back into the wagon and they trotted south, then turned east and soon came to the second farm.

It sat close to a deep gully with a small creek running along the bottom on its way to the Pecos. The only structures were a little sod house and a small barn with a corral holding a milk cow. Two patches of farm land stretched behind. Not far away, a man walked behind a tired-looking mule, plowing neat furrows in the fertile ground.

"Reckon that's your uncle," Tray said.

Cassandra's heart twinged. "He's going to be so surprised . . . I hope he'll accept me!"

They got out of the wagon and Cassandra adjusted Rose onto her shoulder as they walked to a low fence surrounding the plowed area.

The man spotted them and drew the mule to a halt, then came over to the fence. He removed a large-brimmed straw hat, exposing a smooth bald head that glistened in the sun. Not much of his face was visible, for a large, fluffy white beard covered most of it; ebony eyes twinkled out of the whiteness like chunks of coal thrown into snow.

Cassandra could see her dear father's resemblance in the eyes, even though her uncle must now be in his seventies. His thin body, clad in faded blue trousers and shirt, had a slight stoop—from days of hard work building up the farm, she assumed.

"Goot mornin'," the man said with a German accent.

"You Emil Vosburg?" Traylor asked.

"You are correct, vot can I do for you?"

"My name's Traylor Doolan. I brought somebody to see you."

"Uncle Emil," Cassandra said hesitantly, "I'm Cassandra Vosburg . . . your niece from San Antonio?"

Emil Vosburg stared in astonishment, then exploded. "*Mein Gott in himmel*, this I don't belief!" Stepping over the fence, he swooped his niece into a welcome hug.

Little Rose awoke and Cassandra was pleased to see the loving expression on her uncle's face as he lifted the gurgling baby into the air.

"Vy, der little one has Ludvig's smile, for sure!" the kindly man said. "Now, come, come, let us get inside avay from this sun and haf a cool drink of vater. I must hear all about der family!" He turned to the mule waiting with its head down. "You vait here, Ilse! Get some rest—I be back later!"

Uncle Emil carried Rose in his arms while Tray and Cassandra followed him to the modest little two-room home. After Cassandra expressed her hope that Uncle Emil would let her and Rose live with him, he was delighted with the prospect.

"But I varn you, child," Emil said, "this little house, it has not much room for der three of us."

"Oh, Uncle Emil, it's lovely! I can sleep here in the kitchen area with Rose. We won't take up much room, honestly!"

"No, no, Cass, you two are der royalty. You vill sleep in there vere there's a bed. I curl up here by der fireplace in a buffalo skin, be real cozy."

"Well, just for that, I'll cook you some good German meals. I'll bet it's been a while since you've had any *hackbraten!*"

"*Der hackbraten!*" Uncle Emil cried in delight. "All these years I nefer haf it!"

"When my sister Terressa taught me to make it, she said it was your favorite." Cassandra added cunningly, "and afterwards, a little *bienenstich* for dessert?" Her forehead wrinkled. "That is, if I can find almonds in Seven Rivers."

The happy man clutched his fluffy cheeks in ecstasy. "For *der bienenstich* I vill *steal* you almonds! My little *Liebchen,* you haf surely been sent from heafen!"

Tray walked to the door. "Well, now that I know you're staying, Cass, I'll get your things out of the wagon."

He went outside and came back with the few boxes of Cassandra's belongings, then shook Uncle Emil's hand.

"I'll leave Cassandra and Rose in your good care, Mr. Vosburg. Pleased to have met you." He turned to Cassandra. "Tom's waitin'. I better go."

Cassandra watched, astonished, as Tray walked outside where the horse and wagon stood in the warming sun. She left her uncle playing with Rose and quickly followed.

"Wait, Tray," she called, "you can't leave just like that!"

He turned with a faint smile. "I know you and Rose'll be happy here. Your uncle's a nice man."

A pang struck Cassandra's heart. Everyone she knew—all her friends from Fort Concho—were rapidly dropping away, and now, Traylor Doolan, who had stirred a new emotion within her. She felt as if stranded, alone in a strange new world.

"Tray, I want you to know how much I appreciate all you've done for me, and I want to apologize if I've seemed a little distant since we left Pope's Crossing." She looked at the ground, afraid to be pinned by his riveting blue eyes.

He took her by the shoulders and his voice was low.

"You don't have to say it, I understand. I'm half Comanche and it was Comanches that killed your husband."

She finally looked up. "Maybe in time, my feelings will change."

She longed for him to pull her to his chest, squeezing the bias out of her heart, his lips tasting the desire swimming there.

Instead, he gave her a light kiss on the forehead. "By then, who knows where we'll be?"

He released her and jumped into the wagon.

Cassandra watched Traylor Doolan moving away on the dirt road, his virile young body straight in the wagon seat, jiggling the reins.

Her eyes filled with tears and she wanted to tear the prejudice out of her heart, but knew she was the unwilling victim of its gnawing torture.

"Yes," she sobbed to herself, "where will we be?"

PART THREE

- 1880 -

Chapter Twenty-Seven

Cassandra laughed at herself. She had worked so hard to get away from the convent's daily chores back in San Antonio, and here she was, doing virtually the same thing—a cow to milk, crops to take care of and a house to be cleaned. But she was content.

It made her even happier to know that Uncle Emil enjoyed her savory meals and accepted her daughter like one of his own. Little Rose would be five next December, but old enough, now, to ride in front of Uncle Emil on his beloved mule Ilse when they all went to work in the fields.

As they sat in front of the comforting fireplace one evening, Cassandra worked on her mending and Rose snuggled in Uncle Emil's lap.

"Do you see how she viggles her nose?" Uncle Emil said with amusement. He held a tantalizing cookie out of the child's reach. "Venever she gets upset, she just looks at you and viggles that little nose—like a bunny rabbit." He gave her the cookie. "That's vot you are, *Liebchen*, my little Bunny!"

Cassandra looked up with a smile. "If you start calling her 'Bunny,' I hope she won't forget her real name is Rose!"

"Enuff play for now, Bunny," he said and put Rose gently down onto the floor, then rubbed an aching leg. "I be taking another load uff apples to town tomorrow morning, if I can get this leg to moofing!"

Cassandra dropped the sewing onto her lap and graced

him with loving concern. "Uncle Emil, you've been working too hard. Why don't you let me go. I'm caught up on all my chores and you can rest for a change."

"That is kind of you, Cass. But be careful of that man who runs the store—he can drife a hard bargain!"

Early the next morning Cassandra helped her uncle fill the wagon, then she drove it into town.

After trading the apples for supplies and the wagon had been loaded with bags of flour, sugar and coffee, she climbed in, urging the horse forward. Suddenly a roar of gunfire blasted the quiet morning. She froze in terror on the wagon seat, as six trail-hardened cowboys, whooping and shooting their pistols in the air, thundered past on their horses, headed for the nearest saloon.

Cassandra's startled horse reared with a whinny and took off in panic down the street. She pulled frantically on the reins but was unable to restrain the frightened animal as the little wagon careened through town in a cloud of dust.

A man jumped into the street ahead and waved his arms. The horse came to a halt and snorted in confusion as the man grabbed the harness, holding the animal until it calmed down. He patted the horse's nose and talked soothingly until it stood still, panting in the dirt-filled air. The man then walked around to Cassandra.

"You all right, Miss?"

Cassandra breathed with relief and flapped dust from her dress. "Yes, thanks. I do believe you saved me from going miles out of the way—I really wanted to go south!"

"Those cowboys just got into town. After months on the trail, they have to let off steam." He removed his hat. "My name's Fergis Gant. I took over a farm last month, not too far from yours."

Cassandra look puzzled. "Then you must know my name, Cassandra Shaw. I live there with my Uncle."

"Yes, I've seen you and your uncle ride past my place on the way to town."

Fergis Gant was a man in his forties, she guessed, and from his neat clothes she could tell he was a person of some pride. He hadn't come into town wearing dirty overalls like the other farmers.

She felt it rude to leave right after he'd come to her rescue. "Do you have a family there on the farm?"

"Wife died three years ago. Just me and my two boys, now, ten and twelve." He glanced at the horse. "If you're on your way home, why don't you let me ride along. Your horse is still a might skitterish."

"Why, that would be very kind of you."

Fergis Gant walked back to his horse and climbed into the saddle, then rode alongside Cassandra's wagon until they had gone out of town, turned east and stopped at the Gant farm.

"Think you'd have time to meet my two boys?" Fergis asked.

"Why, yes, I can spare a few minutes."

He helped Cassandra down from the wagon and they walked up a gravel path to his large sod home.

Fergis called toward the back yard, "Zack, Jonah! You two come here, now. We got company!"

The two boys came scurrying around the side of the house and slid to a halt like soldiers at attention in their dirty work pants and calico shirts.

"Cassandra Shaw, this here is Zack, he's twelve," Fergis said, laying a hand on the taller boy's silky-blond hair, "and this is Jonah, he's ten."

Cassandra smiled at the two handsome boys. "I live just

down the road. Your father will have to bring you for a visit and meet Uncle Emil and my daughter Rose."

"Yes, ma'am," they answered in unison.

"You two got that hay pitched yet?" Fergis asked his sons.

"We're workin' on it," Zack said.

"'Bout finished," Jonah added. Then he asked with hesitance, "Did you bring us anythin' from town, Pa?"

Fergis took a small paper bag from his coat and held it up. "When you finish with that hay, come inside and find out!"

The boys started to run back to their work.

"Wait a minute!" Fergis shouted.

They stopped, turning to him.

"What do you say to our visitor when you leave?"

Zack gulped in embarrassment. "Please t've met you, Ma'am. If you'll excuse us, we gotta git back to work, now."

Cassandra laughed. "That's all right, you go ahead. We'll continue our visit another time." She turned to Fergis. "I'd better go, now. Uncle Emil will be pacing the floor wondering what's happened to me!"

Fergis escorted her back to the wagon. "Your husband's dead, I take it?"

"Yes, killed by Indians five years ago this March."

"I admire a woman like you, comin' out here, just you and a little baby, to make a go of it." He helped Cassandra into the wagon and she took the reins.

"Well, I'm lucky to have Uncle Emil, otherwise I don't know what I'd do." She flicked the reins and the horse started forward. "You and the boys come by this Sunday and I'll fix you a good dinner!"

"That'd make 'em real happy," he shouted as she drove away, "I sure ain't much of a cook!"

Fergis and his two young boys appeared at Uncle Emil's farm on the following Sunday and Cassandra prepared a delicious meal. Zack and Jonah played tag with Rose in the grass by the house and Fergis had a long conversation with Cassandra and Uncle Emil.

"Me and my wife came out from Missouri nearly twelve years ago," Fergis told them. "Zack was just a baby. We finally settled south of here, near Eddy. That's where Jonah was born." A tiny sadness filled his eyes. "Guess we never should've had the second child—my wife's health started fadin' right away. It wasn't long before I came in from the fields one day and found her at final rest. Eddy was getting too overrun with newcomers, so we came up here to Seven Rivers. Took over that farm I got, now."

As Cassandra listened, she began to realize that this raw land, so far from the comforts of civilization, was no place for a single woman with a child to raise. Even though she felt safe, living with dear Uncle Emil on a substantial little farm, a threatening dark cloud still seemed to hover beyond the horizon.

Chapter Twenty-Eight

Fergis Gant appeared more frequently, helping Uncle Emil dig up rocks in the pasture or to give Cassandra a little gift of candied fruit picked up at the trading post. She enjoyed Fergis' company and tried to keep it on a platonic level, but it was obvious he felt differently about their relationship.

"That man has the sweet eye for you, Cass," Uncle Emil said one day as he bounced little Rose on his knee.

Cassandra tried to hide her embarrassment. "Now, don't start imagining things. We're just good friends."

"I hope you're right," he said. "I vouldn't vant to see you get married and take avay my little Bunny!"

Word of an impending dance at the trading post in town sent a flurry of excitement through the community and Fergis Gant asked Cassandra to go with him. She hesitated at leaving Uncle Emil and Rose alone, but her uncle squashed the notion.

"No need to vorry," he told her. "While you're gone, I can read a story to Bunny by the fire. We be real cozy!"

Cassandra put on her best dress and Fergis, in a rarely seen coat and string tie, picked her up in his buggy. They drove to town with eager expectation.

Ranchers and farmers from miles around brought their wives and children for the night's revelry, unleashing the tensions of a year's hard work. With lively music from fiddle and accordion everyone danced on the dirt floor, which had been packed down hard and smooth with hot shovels. Spiked punch was available for those who imbibed.

Tired and content, Cassandra and Fergis rode home later with the moon guiding their way like a big creamy honeydew melon floating in the sky. It seemed a perfect night for two lovers alone on a dirt road.

"You realize, Cass," Fergis said as if thinking out loud, "we've known each other for some time, now."

Cassandra knew what he was leading up to and stopped him. "Oh, Fergis, I know what you're going to say next and I don't want to hurt you, so please don't say it."

"But, Cass," he pleaded, "I love you, and the boys love you, too. They need a mother, and I want you for a wife, not just a friend!"

"It wouldn't be right, Fergis. For one thing, there's Uncle Emil. And another thing, I can't forget the pain I went through losing my husband . . . I don't want to go through that again, if anything should happen to you."

He searched in vain for a rebuttal. "All right, I'll let it drop for now. But I warn you, Cassandra Shaw, I can be a stubborn man!"

They had passed his own place and Fergis pulled the wagon to a stop in front of Uncle Emil's house. Rose came running out to meet them.

"Rose," Cassandra chided, "it's late—you should be in bed!"

"Mama, Unca Emil's sick!" the little girl wailed. "Come make him better!"

Without waiting for Fergis' usual helping hand, Cassandra clambered out of the wagon and ran with Rose into the house. Fergis quickly tethered the horse and followed.

Uncle Emil lay on the floor with one hand clutched to his chest, the dwindling fire casting a strange orange glow over

167

his big white beard.

Cassandra knelt down beside him. "Uncle Emil, what is it?"

His eyes opened a slit. "Not to vorry, Cass," he whispered. "I haf just the bad pain here."

Fergis helped Cassandra move her uncle into the room where she slept and they lowered him down onto the bed.

"That heart of yours ain't as young as it used t'be," Fergis told the stricken man. "Now, you take it easy for a spell. And don't worry 'bout anything—I'll help Cass do the chores 'round here for a while, till you get better."

Cassandra slept fitfully that night. Every few minutes she awoke to look in on her uncle and thankfully saw that he was resting well. When she lay down again, a new worry crept into her troubled mind: Uncle Emil was succumbing to old age and she wondered what would happen to her if he were suddenly taken away.

Chapter Twenty-Nine

Zack and Jonah worked their father's property while Fergis spent a great deal of time helping Cassandra maintain the farm as Uncle Emil remained bedridden. On a blustery afternoon in autumn they labored together in the field, stooping to collect yellow-red apples that had fallen onto the crunchy, dry leaves below.

"Cass," Fergis remarked, "this just don't make no sense, me workin' one farm, then comin' over here and workin' another. If we were married, your uncle could sell this place and move in with us. We'd have just one farm to keep goin'."

Cassandra stood up, rubbing her aching back, and he walked over to massage her shoulders. She tried to evade his suggestion.

"I'm much obliged for you coming over here all the time and helping out," she said, almost purring under his loving touch, "but I wish you wouldn't . . . I owe you for so much."

"You don't owe me nothin'. I do it 'cause I love you."

"That's just it, Fergis. My feelings aren't as strong as yours. I just don't want to go into a marriage one-sided like that."

"But you could get to love me, I'd see to that!"

She recalled almost the same words she had spoken to Ian when they sat together in the little buggy back in San Antonio. And look how that turned out—she had grown to love him and it ended in tragedy.

"Well, just give me a little more time to think about it."
She sighed wearily. "Right now, we'd best get these apples in
before it gets dark."

Cassandra lay awake that night trying to sort out her
life. Fergis was right. It was foolish trying to run the farm by
herself. A woman needed a man in this hard country and she
had seen loveless marriages at Seven Rivers for that very
reason. Then, Rose was going to be five years old in
December and the child needed a father.

The solution still had not come in the first hours of
morning when Cassandra finally drifted into blissful sleep.

Chapter Thirty

As Seven Rivers grew, so did the violence. Cassandra cringed with each weekly saloon killing, not to mention the drunken cowboys continually shooting up the streets. Also, the vicious feuding between two factions at Lincoln, over a hundred miles to the northwest, had now reached as far as Seven Rivers. A young man involved, named Billy Bonney, was said to have already killed several men before he had even reached the age of twenty.

With all these troubles swirling in Cassandra's head, she took two pails one morning to fetch her water supply. Uncle Emil had situated his small farm between two arroyos; one was a dry bed but the larger one, Rocky Arroyo, always had a steadily running stream that provided good water.

The bright sunshine and singing of birds soon chased away Cassandra's cares. To her delight, she saw that the creek had risen so close to the bank she had no trouble retrieving water. On her return to the farmhouse Fergis rode up in his wagon.

"Fergis," she called, "the arroyo's so high today, I didn't even have to climb down the bank to get my water!"

His face was strangely ominous as he got out of the wagon.

"Cass, there's been stormin' up in the mountains, west. That's why the creek's up. I've just been over to the other arroyo and it ain't dry no more—in fact, it's a river, now. I've heard tell those mountain rains can run down here to the Pecos like a herd of stampedin' cattle and wipe out the whole area!"

Her face clouded with worry. "You think that might happen now?"

"Best not take a chance, since your uncle's house is too close to Rocky Arroyo. I think you two oughta gather up your things and stay at my place till the creeks go down. The boys are loadin' a wagon with our stuff, just in case we might have to make a run for it."

"But your place isn't much farther away from the gullies than Uncle Emil's."

"Even so, it's on higher ground. Now, I don't wanna be firm with you, Cass, but I'm askin' you to do as I say . . . it's for your own safety!"

Cassandra wondered how there could be a flood on such a beautiful sunny day—but then she thought of Rose. If anything happened to her little girl, Cassandra would never forgive herself.

Fergis helped her pack the most important belongings into his wagon and the smaller one Cassandra owned. Then they tied the milk cow behind one of the wagons.

After they helped Uncle Emil into the wagon, the frail man hesitated. "What about Ilse?" he asked with concern.

"Your mule would just drag us down," Fergis told him.

Uncle Emil gave a look of pained shock. "We can't leave Ilse here to die!"

Fergis heaved an agitated sigh. "Look, Uncle Emil, that old mule's so broken down, it really don't matter—besides, we got no time to fool with her!"

Uncle Emil uttered a German word of protest and climbed down from the wagon. "Then you two go ahead. I follow you on Ilse!"

Cassandra took her uncle's arm. "Uncle Emil, please

don't! The water's coming too fast . . . you might not have time!"

He pushed her arm away. "Ilse nefer let me down and I nefer let her down!"

It was useless to argue and Cassandra stood, paralyzed with uncertainty.

Fergis shook his head and forced Cassandra into her wagon. "We'll just have to let him do it his way, Cass. Come on, now, we gotta hurry!"

As they drove the two wagons to Fergis' place, Cassandra glanced over her shoulder but couldn't see her uncle. He was obviously in the barn getting his beloved mule ready to leave.

Cassandra and Fergis arrived at the house to find Zack and Jonah ready with a wagon full of household goods.

At that moment a distant roar caught their ears and Fergis looked back at the once-dry arroyo about a mile away. Unbelievably, water was rushing down its small throughway and spilling up onto both sides of the ground.

Another sound made them both turn to where Rocky Arroyo should have been—in its place, a sea of water grew like a monster, spreading quickly across the land. The roar became deafening as a tremendous wall of water hurtled down both arroyos, carrying uprooted tree trunks, weeds and broken remains of houses in a crashing fury.

Cassandra gasped in terror and clutched Rose to her breast as the dark muddy water and debris turned into a furious giant, rushing toward them. She saw in the distance that her little sod house was engulfed, the mad swirling water dissolving it like a piece of chocolate on a hot griddle.

"Uncle Emil!" she screamed in horror and put hands to her face. There was no chance that he had escaped.

Fergis yelled at his boys, "Zack, you and Jonah take off

up the road—we gotta get outta here fast!"

The water had now reached their wagon wheels as they pushed toward the dirt road leading to town. Cassandra looked back as they raced onward; behind them churned a huge dark-brown sea of turbulence, swallowing everything in its path. Her house had vanished and the apple trees, now washed away, joined other flotsam on its mad rush to the Pecos. Fergis' comfortable home, even on a rise, had been surrounded, his fields destroyed.

They finally reached higher ground where it was safe to stop the wagons. Feeling helpless, they sat and watched the terrible havoc run its course.

The awful noise at last faded to an eerie silence. Only the ugly sucking of water could be heard, finding its way into burrows and small hollows of land. The water finally subsided from Fergis' home to reveal one wall, standing on the hill like a ravaged skeleton.

"Oh, Fergis," Cassandra said, choking on a sob, "do you think we'll find Uncle Emil?"

He gritted his teeth. "Don't see how. Him and that mule of his prob'ly been washed all the way down to Eddy by now!"

Cassandra slumped in the wagon seat. "There's nothing left. What are we going to do?"

Fergis sighed with determination. "Maybe we can find a place in town to stay for the night. We'll just have to take it from there."

They reached town to find everyone talking about the tragic event. The trading post owner would have offered them room at his home, however a preacher and his wife, on their way through the area, were staying with them. The best he could do was to let them have two tents to sleep in, next to the store.

Fergis' mind spun with plans while he and his two sons worked at staking the tents.

Cassandra sat watching, her insides feeling as washed out as the arroyos. Not only her dear Uncle Emil, but everything she had planned and worked for had been torn away. She took a deep breath to force back the tears.

After the second tent had been raised, Fergis dropped a hammer and walked over to Cassandra. A hardness glinted in his eyes.

"If you'll still consider my offer of marriage, I got a plan worked out," he said.

She looked up feebly. "What kind of plan, Fergis?"

"We gotta settle down again somewhere, but you've been complainin' about all the shootin' and violence here in Seven Rivers and you hate to see Rose grow up here. Now, you know I don't have anything to offer you, 'cept my love. What would you say to us gettin' married and goin' up to the Peñasco River area t'make a homestead?"

"The Peñasco?"

"Yes. I hear there's good grass and plenty of water. That's what I'm plannin' to do, whether you marry me or not. 'Course, I'd dang sure rather you came along, too. Now, what do you say?"

She felt speechless. All this in one mouthful took some time to consider. Although Indians were still roaming the plains, she didn't feel safe at Seven Rivers, with all the killing and bullets flying. They would be alone up at Peñasco, easy prey for the redskins. But she would rather take chances against an occasional Indian than place her life in jeopardy at Seven Rivers every time she went into town. And then there was her child to consider; everything she did from now on must be for little Rose's sake. Her throat tightened and the tears finally began to roll.

"I've lost everything," she sobbed. "My child and I don't have any place to go. All right, Fergis. But I want it understood, right here and now, that I am not taking advantage of you. I don't love you like you love me, but I'll stand on my integrity and make you the best wife I possibly can!"

He took her in his arms and she felt like a little lost sheep, crying on his shoulder.

The following day Fergis and Cassandra dressed in their Sunday best and were married by the visiting preacher at the trading post.

That night Cassandra sat in Fergis' tent, holding the Bible on her knees. She adjusted the kerosene lamp in order to see the pages, then with moist eyes, dipped a pen into ink. With great care she wrote:

November 9, 1880: Uncle Emil died in flood at Seven Rivers, New Mexico.

She wiped away a tear and added:

November 10, 1880: Cassandra Vosburg Shaw married Fergis Gant at Seven Rivers, New Mexico.

She blew softly on the page to be sure the ink was dry, and prayed once again that the right path was being taken. But then, she asked herself, what other way was there to go?

Chapter Thirty-One

Cassandra and Fergis replaced their losses by buying some farm equipment and four pigs, together with an old horse and saddle for each of his two sons.

They loaded the equipment and supplies into Fergis' wagon while Cassandra drove hers, crammed with their belongings. Zack and Jonah, excited at having their own horses, rode them with pride as they herded the pigs, along with the cow that had been saved.

The Peñasco River ran cheerfully only ten miles to the north, so they reached it by late afternoon, then turned west to follow the plentiful stream until Fergis found a spot he deemed suitable for their new home.

"My, this is beautiful country!" Cassandra said, gazing at the gentle rolling hills spread before them like a soft blanket of green. She felt a spark of hope as the sun eased itself to rest, painting the few wispy clouds with brilliant colors.

"You don't think this is too close to the river, do you, Fergis?" she asked with concern. "I don't want us to get washed away by another flood!"

"We'll be a lot farther away and on real high ground, here." He shaded his eyes for a good survey of the land. "Look at all that grama grass! This'll be a good place for grazin' when we get started with the cattle." He turned to her with a big smile. "Now, just where would you like your new home to sit, little lady?"

Cassandra had already envisioned a nice big house looking north toward the river. She took a stick and scratched an outline in the earth to show how she thought her home should be laid out. "A sitting room here," she pointed the stick, "and we ought to have three bedrooms . . . here . . . and here . . . "

Fergis laughed at her grandiose plan. "Why, you're wantin' us to build you a palace! That'll take some time. Let's just start out with a plain, two-room sod house. We can add on later."

Settlers customarily built their houses facing north. To make certain his would sit that way, Fergis waited until night and the stars began their faint twinkling. He tied a rope to a stake and drove it at a point where they wanted one corner of the house to be. Then he very carefully lined the rope up with the polestar and staked down the other end of the rope.

"That's true north and south for one side of our house," he told Cassandra.

Fergis and the boys took turns standing guard during the night and Cassandra, eager to begin life in their new home, felt secure in her little tent, nestled with Rose under a warm blanket.

The following morning Cassandra poked her head out of the tent to see Fergis busy tying knots in a long rope.

"What are you doing?" she asked.

"Gotta be sure the corners of our house are perfectly square," he said and continued with his measuring and tying.

When all the corners had been marked as square, Zack and Jonah used a turning plow to cut loose the sod of thick grass nearby. With a spade, Fergis cut big slabs, about two by three feet, and hauled them in a wagon to their house site.

Meanwhile, Cassandra busied herself down at the river, mixing large amounts of thick mud, which she carried back to them in pails. Timbers had been set upright to outline the walls and Fergis broke the sod into uniform bricks, laying them in between the upright poles and sealing them with the mud. The work became slow and tedious, but by sundown they had the shell of a house with two windows and a door.

The next day they found enough rocks from the river bank to build a fireplace at one end of the house.

"There aren't any more rocks," Cassandra said with concern. "How are we going to build a chimney?"

Fergis gave her a wink. "Don't you worry 'bout that. We'll make it outta mud!"

Cassandra's eyes widened in astonishment. "Mud?! But Fergis, it'll never hold up!"

With skepticism, Cassandra watched as Fergis and the boys constructed a chimney of sod bricks and split sticks, thickly plastered with mud.

"Just give it a few days," Fergis told her. "With all your cooking, it'll bake hard as iron!"

Ridge poles were set up inside the house and rafters installed, then beams placed for a roof. Over this came small tree branches, a covering of tar paper from the Seven Rivers' trading post and a topping of sod, laid grass-side down. They finished the roof with a coating of ashes and muddy clay, which would also be used to plaster the inside walls.

Cassandra built a roaring fire in the fireplace to heat the shovels for tamping down the dirt floor, which she had sprinkled with water. The result was a hard, shiny surface, almost as good as the pecan flooring Cassandra remembered at Fort Concho.

"Well, at least this floor won't squeak!" she had to admit.

In just a few days, they had a comfortable two-room house and a corral for the cattle.

Next came the farm, and Zack helped Fergis with the plowing while Jonah trailed behind, planting apples in one plot and corn in another.

On Thanksgiving Day, Fergis and the boys came in tired and hungry. Cassandra felt helpless, being able to fix only a simple meal with the remainder of bacon that had been saved in brine, with cornbread and canned peaches. She slumped in a chair as they began to eat.

"Don't you worry none," Fergis said, noticing the despair in her face. "This time next year, we'll have several pigs and maybe a steer or two. Before you know it, there'll even be a few apples!"

December arrived with its cold winds and Cassandra took Zack down to the cottonwood grove near the river where they selected a small, young tree. Zack cut it down and they hauled the tree back to the house where he nailed it to a wooden stand.

"What're we gonna put on the tree?" Jonah wondered.

"You boys'll have to learn to use your imaginations," Cassandra told them. "For one thing, I've been saving empty tin cans. You take my heavy scissors and cut out long strips, then just curl them around a stick. Take them off and you'll have the shiniest decorations a body could hope for!"

Next came strings of buttons and cut-up labels from the existing cans of beans and fruit. So they would know the contents of the cans without labels, Jonah used his knife to scratch a "B" on cans holding beans and a "P" on those with peaches.

For their Christmas dinner, Cassandra made a peach cobbler and baked a ham roast from one of the pigs Fergis had slaughtered. Berries and watercress growing along the creek's edge added to the holiday cheer, along with the fact that little

Rose celebrated her fifth birthday.

As Cassandra and Fergis cuddled in their bed that night, she felt warmly content. Rose lay asleep in a small cot beside them, and Cassandra knew she had made the right decision. Fergis was a devoted husband and her fondness for him had indeed grown each day. With the farm shaping well, they were a family now. Best of all, little Rose had a father.

PART FOUR

- 1881 -

Chapter Thirty-Two

By February the weather had turned warm enough for Fergis to ride into Lincoln and apply for homesteading. He felt reluctant, leaving Cassandra with just Zack and Jonah for protection, but there was no alternative.

"You stay in the house, now, and don't let the boys get too far away," he told Cassandra. "Zack knows how to use the shotgun." He kissed her lovingly, then rode northward to Lincoln.

Things went along with quiet routine for almost a week. Zack and Jonah worked in the fields, but stayed nearby, and Cassandra busied herself with the few odd chores that kept her close to the house.

One morning, Cassandra called to them. "I can't fix your dinner till the water tub is filled. You boys think you can fetch me some?"

Glad for a respite from their chores, Zack and Jonah raced each other to the house and grabbed two wooden pails, then ran down through the cottonwoods to the river.

"Wish we could go skinny-dippin' while we're down here," Jonah said as he dipped a bucket into the cold water.

Zack frowned at his younger brother. "Ain't no time to play. We gotta take some water back to Cassandra so's she can fix us dinner!"

"Why do we have to call her 'Cassandra,' Zack? If she's married to Pa, don't that make her our Ma?"

"She ain't our Ma. Our real Ma's dead. Cassandra is just Pa's wife."

"But she's like a Ma to me . . . I don't remember my real one!"

Zack set down the pail of water. It was time he had to explain the ways of life to his little brother. "It's just a matter of bein' respectful to your elders," he said. "Cassandra knows we ain't her real boys and she prob'ly don't want to be called 'Ma,' anyway. If she ever does, she'll let us know."

Jonah heaved up his full bucket. "Well, she's still like a Ma to me . . . I don't care what you say!"

"She is to me, too, an' I'm glad she married Pa. But we still gotta show our respect and call her 'Cassandra!'" He picked up the pail of water. "Now come on, Cassandra's prob'ly thinkin' we *did* go skinny-dippin'!"

They had to take the sloshing buckets with both hands, lugging them back up the river bank. As they emerged from the trees, Zack stopped in surprise.

"Look, Jonah, there's some horses tied up at the house!"

Jonah followed his gaze and saw four Indian ponies tethered by the front door. A group of red men, wearing dirty pants and shirts, had just dismounted. One had a cloth tied around the top of his head and was making hand signs to Cassandra who stood in the doorway.

"We'd better git up there quick!" Jonah said. "If anything happens to Cassandra 'cause we were at the river, Pa'll take a switch to us fer sure!"

The two boys left their pails sitting in the grass and scurried to the house. They stopped a respectful distance from the door as Cassandra tried to make conversation with the men.

Zack thought of the shotgun inside, leaning against a corner of the bedroom. "Everything all right, Cassandra?"

She gave the boys a strained smile of assurance. "It's

all right, Zack. I believe they just want something to eat." She made a sign for the Indians to enter.

Zack and Jonah watched from the doorway as Cassandra set plates of food on the table. Her uninvited guests did not sit down but took the cornbread and beans in their fingers and stuffed their mouths full.

Finished, the dirty old man with the filthy cloth on his head grunted approval, then they went outside, mounted their horses and galloped away. Cassandra leaned against the doorway in relief.

"I could've shot 'em if I'd had Pa's gun!" Zack said.

"No, that would be the wrong thing to do," Cassandra told him, "unless, of course, they tried to harm us."

Jonah kept his eyes on the retreating Indians. "I wonder if that old man's a chief?"

"I bet he's Geronimo!" Zack exclaimed. "They said back in Seven Rivers, he's still runnin' around these parts."

Cassandra sighed. "Well, whoever he was, let's get back to our chores. If all the Indians are like that, your Pa won't have to worry about leaving us here by ourselves."

Chapter Thirty-Three

After the impromptu visit by the Indians, the bias in Cassandra's heart eased a little; maybe the ones who had killed Ian back at Fort Concho were just a small band of bloodthirsty Indians, while all the others were harmless. The group that stopped at the house certainly wasn't hostile, only hungry.

Fergis at last returned, all smiles, with Cassandra and the boys grabbing him in welcome hugs.

"I got good news!" he proclaimed. "One hundred and sixty acres of land is all ours—that is, after five years of provin' it up!"

"Oh, that's wonderful!" Cassandra said.

Zack cut in with excitement, "Pa, you should've seen the Indians that came right into the house!"

Fergis' smile changed to alarm. "You had Indians here?!"

"Oh, it was nothing," Cassandra said. "There was no danger, they just wanted something to eat."

"Just the same, those devils will cut off your ears before you can turn around!"

"Well, you're here, now," Cassandra soothed him, "and with Zack and Jonah—and your gun—I don't think I'll have to worry."

Fergis took Zack with him the next day to stake out their precious acres of land and was surprised to see nearly eight hundred head of cattle approaching from the south.

Cowboys, with goading shouts, rode herd as the animals reached Fergis' pasture land and began grazing.

"That's one of John Chisum's danged herds," Fergis said.

"How do you know, Pa?" Zack asked.

"See that brand on their sides?"

Zack squinted to see the brand U—— burned into the skin.

"Also, they're Jinglebobs," Fergis added. "Look at the ears. They're split so the outside flaps down and the other half sticks up."

"Why're they called Jinglebobs?"

"When those cattle were first seen 'round here, somebody said their ears almost jingled when they walked."

Fergis' anger rose as he watched the cattle grazing on his land. "Old John's got probably a hundred thousand head movin' in herds up and down the Pecos Valley, but I don't want 'em eatin' *my* grass!"

He waved his hat urgently at one of the cowboys riding by and the man wheeled his horse to a halt.

"I'd be much obliged," Fergis shouted to the horseman, "if you'd keep your cattle from eatin' up my grass. I got my own stock to feed."

"Sorry, Mister," the man yelled back. "Didn't know we was cuttin' 'cross your pasture. Y'oughta think 'bout puttin' up a fence."

The cowboy turned and shouted at one of the other men to turn the herd and Fergis watched with relief as the huge mass of cattle moved slowly to the north.

Chapter Thirty-Four

Cassandra had just dropped three shirts into the big pot of boiling water beside the house when a gale-like March wind began howling across the prairie toward the Peñasco. She wiped dripping hands on her skirt and went quickly to take washing off the line. The gale tore her bobbed hair loose and it swirled wildly as she called to Jonah, chopping wood by the corral.

"Jonah, help me quick, before our clothes end up in the Pecos River!"

He rushed to the clothesline and they began putting the still-damp shirts, pants and socks into baskets. An ominous darkness spread quickly overhead and Cassandra looked up with a shiver. The sun had begun to fade, engulfed by a soaring wall of black dust rolling toward them from the west.

Fergis and Zack, having seen the frightening pall creeping over the land, brought in the livestock, crowding them together in the shed.

They all ran into the house, where Rose sat playing on the dirt floor. Fergis slammed the door closed and secured the window shutters just as the monstrous dust cloud struck the little sod house like a hungry monster, turning day into night. Flying sand invaded the room, piercing their squinted eyes while the fragile home shuddered against the thundering wind.

Although the water tub had a cover, silt quickly formed on the bottom. That evening they were forced to hold a blanket over their heads while eating out of cans of beans; even so, each bite was full of grit.

They went to bed clutching a handkerchief over their noses and mouths, but the moaning wind became a dirge, making it almost impossible to sleep.

Cassandra lay fretfully on the bed while the overpowering smell of dust dredged up unpleasant memories. During the long night she saw herself as a child again back at the convent, cleaning the small attic above Mother Sabrina's office where they planned to store old record books. The broom she had used stirred up clouds of fine, age-old dirt, mingled with the odor of bat guano, and she thought she would smother.

Cassandra awoke gasping for breath, only to find the smell of dust still there. She heard Rose's crying dry cough and went to console the child.

"It won't be much longer, Honey," she said through the handkerchief. "Just think how much fun you're going to have playing in the sun again!"

Fergis wrapped a bandanna around his head and made periodic trips to the corral, struggling against the heavy winds, to be sure their animals were enduring the terrible storm.

On the third morning Cassandra awoke to find the handkerchief dropped from her face and she was breathing clean air once again. The monotonous droning wind had given up its fight, leaving a blessed silence.

Fergis and the boys had already gone outside seeing to the livestock and Cassandra rose from the dirt-covered bed. She took Rose by the hand, the two making their way through a thick layer of sand to the doorway. Rose ran with delight into the bright outdoors and Cassandra looked up at the clear blue sky, a sight never more appreciated. With a grateful heart, she rushed to join Rose and the two of them rolled with laughter in the soft grass.

"Fergis," she finally called, "we've got to get this house liveable again! You and the boys help me take everything out and I'll give it a thorough cleaning."

Cassandra had to sweep all the walls, windows and the hard dirt floor, then wipe everything down with wet rags before bringing the furniture back inside.

Instead of heating up the big black kettle, Cassandra decided to take all the clothes down to the river and just rinse out the dust and sand. Zack and Jonah went with her, carrying two large baskets filled with dirty clothes, leaving Fergis to mend the corral while little Rose played with her rag doll in the dirt by the front door.

With the terrible dust storm only a memory and the clear day delightfully warm, Cassandra had a cheerful outlook for the days ahead. She and the boys made their way happily across the wide expanse of grama grass, then down through the large grove of cottonwoods to the river bank.

The Peñasco splashed gleefully on its way to the Pecos, as if sharing Cassandra's joy of the fresh new day. Zack helped her wash out the clothing while Jonah folded the washing in the baskets to take back for drying. It took some time to finish the chore before they began their walk back through the purple shade of cottonwoods.

Emerging from the dense trees, Cassandra stopped with a gasp; in the distance, black smoke poured from the house windows and doorway. She and the boys stood in disbelief as they saw a group of Indians rush out of the house and jump onto ponies tethered at the corral. One of the red men picked up little Rose who dangled, whimpering, from his arm as he got onto a horse.

"Rose!" Cassandra screamed and ran toward the house.

Zack and Jonah dropped their baskets of clothing and followed.

The Indians began riding off, except the one holding Rose. He sat astride his horse, struggling to place the child in front of him.

As Cassandra ran up to them the little girl saw her mother and began to cry, "Mama . . . Mama!"

Cassandra grabbed the Indian's ankle. "Give me my baby!" she shouted, but the hostile gave her a push with his foot, sending her sprawling to the ground. She sat up while the Indian galloped off to join his fellow braves, little Rose's cries fading in the dry air.

"My baby!" Cassandra screamed, "Bring back my baby!" She sat in the dirt with anguished tears turning dust to mud on her cheeks. Then she heard Zack cry out.

"Pa! My God, Pa . . . no, no!"

She turned to see the two boys vomiting on the ground. Before them, to her horror, Fergis' naked body hung tied to the corral gate. Almost unrecognizable, he had been scalped and mutilated—like a butchered steer with its stomach slashed open and the entrails spilling out onto the dirt.

Chapter Thirty-Five

Anne Manning had looked forward to a pleasant new Army post and was not disappointed with Fort Union in northern New Mexico Territory. Although sitting at the fork of the Santa Fe Trail on a flat lifeless plain, it seemed huge compared with Fort Concho.

As a supply depot for most of the southwestern forts, ample quarters built of adobe served all personnel, including the laundresses. Comfortable homes for the officers stood along flagstone walks, neat as a line of soldiers, and separated from company quarters by a large parade ground. Across a wide breezeway spread another area with quartermaster facilities, storehouses and corrals.

But civilization was not too far away; the bustling railroad town of Las Vegas lay a few miles to the south and quaint Santa Fe was just over the beautiful Sangre de Cristo Mountains.

While Tom grappled with his new duties as post commander, Anne fell into the position of entertaining various officers of the fort and supervising its social affairs. Even though she was given the extravagance of a Mexican housekeeper and cook, she still had never been so busy in her life, and never so happy.

Traylor Doolan felt tied to the fort, with scouting jobs becoming less in demand. The best time of the day came when he shared the evening meal with Tom and Anne Manning.

"The only thing that keeps me at this danged fort is your cooking," he said to Anne.

She gave him a teasing look. "That's just an excuse. I know you're itching to get away from this military life. And it's not really my cooking, I only supervise."

After they were seated at the table and Tom poured their wine, Anne, as was her custom, began to rehash the day's events.

"Some interesting mail came in today. That young Lieutenant Burger and his wife Amanda are expecting a little one this December! They're still at Fort Concho." She sipped the wine as the housekeeper served their meal. "I also received a letter from Cassandra Shaw, and guess what—she's no longer Mrs. Shaw, but Mrs. Fergis Gant!"

Tray looked up in surprise. "She still livin' at Seven Rivers?"

"No. She married a nice man with two young boys and they're building a farm on the Peñasco."

"Well, I hope Fergis Gant is a good man," Tom said. "Cass deserves the best!"

"How I wish she would have come with us," Anne worried. "I hate to think of her living in that wild country. They say Chief Victorio has escaped from the reservation and is doing terrible things down that way!"

"Well, you really can't blame the old chief for raisin' Cain," Tray said. "The government promised to let his people stay in their homeland at Ojo Caliente, with all the mountains and forests. Turned out to be a lie and they got penned up at that desert reservation in Arizona instead."

Tom Manning refilled their wine glasses. "You needn't worry, Anne. Colonel Grierson's got Victorio on the run. Last I heard, Grierson had the old chief holed up near the Mexican border."

Tray perked with interest. "I'd sure like to go down there and give the colonel a hand . . . think you could arrange it, Tom?"

Anne gave him a frown. "Oh, please don't think of getting mixed up in all that shooting, Tray!"

"Beats putterin' around here!"

"I think it can be done, Tray," Tom said, "but it may take a while. You know how slow the government moves."

Anne sighed in resignation. "It's obvious I don't stand a chance, with you two in cahoots. I couldn't hold you down, anyway, Traylor Doolan!"

After the housekeeper had cleaned away the table, Anne put a shawl around her shoulders. "Captain Petersen's wife Mary isn't feeling well, and I promised I'd look in on her. You two go ahead with your Army talk while I run over there before it gets too dark."

Tom gave her a troubled look. "Anne, I don't think that's wise. I've heard reports of smallpox in Santa Fe and Mary Petersen likes to shop there. She could very well have picked it up."

"Oh, she's probably just come down with a cold from this night air. Besides, I'll only stay a minute."

A pall of anxiety swept over Fort Union the following day—the post surgeon diagnosed Mary Petersen's illness as smallpox and placed a quarantine order on the Captain's residence.

"I want everything that Anne touches to be boiled immediately!" Tom told their housekeeper. "We're not taking any chances."

However, Anne's strength began to ebb and her skin eventually broke out in the dreaded splotches. She took to her sick bed while the cook and housekeeper fled in panic.

"You're gonna need some help," Traylor Doolan said to Tom Manning. "Would you like me to move in for a while?"

Tom looked helpless. "That's mighty generous of you, Tray. I'm so concerned, I hardly know what I'm doing any more!" He looked around the small room. "But we don't have another bed."

"Heck fire, Tom, I've slept on the hard desert most of my life. A blanket here by the fireplace will beat that any day!"

Together, the men continued to sterilize Anne's bedding and eating utensils with boiling water while the post surgeon administered the only medicines available.

Anne Manning's low resistance proved unable to cope with the dreaded thing that had invaded her frail body. In not long she withered to almost a skeleton, hardly resembling the kind and gentle woman Tray once knew.

On the seventh day a cold, December wind moaned through Fort Union like a foraging coyote. Tom Manning sat before the fireplace with head in hands.

"I thought I'd prepared myself for a time such as this," he said wearily. "Now, I don't know what to do!"

Traylor Doolan looked down at his friend, a man who'd treated him with kindness and respect he'd never known from anyone else.

"It's just somethin' we all gotta face, Tom. Anne knows this, and you've gotta be as brave as she is."

Tom raised his stricken face. "She *is* a brave little lady, and she always loved people." A tiny smile trembled at the corner of his mouth. "I used to tell her she talked too much. But you know, she never said anything that would hurt anybody."

Tray felt helpless to say any more and went to the bedroom where he sat at Anne Manning's bedside. He took a damp towel and placed its coolness on her forehead.

Anne looked up with eyes like two red stones sinking in a darkened pool, her voice barely audible when she spoke.

"I want you to know the happiness you've brought me, Tray. I was never able to give Tom a son, but God was kind enough to let you come along instead."

Tray fought to keep his eyes dry. "My life wouldn't have been the same without you, and I thank you for that. But don't talk, now . . . you've gotta rest."

"No," she protested. "There's no time and I have only a few words left. Never think you're less than you are, Tray. There's not a better man alive, what with that unselfish heart of yours." She took a small breath and closed her eyes. "Now, would you ask Tom to come in . . . please?"

Tray patted her hand and went to the sitting room. "She wants t'see you, Tom," he said with a tightened throat.

Manning raised his tired face and saw that no other words were necessary. He went with resignation to his wife's bedside.

Chapter Thirty-Six

Christmas came to Fort Union, but instead of an aura of good cheer, it brought a vacant sadness. Anne Manning lay at rest in the post cemetery and all the happy activities she had planned were forgotten.

Tom Manning threw himself into work, trying to minimize his grief. Before he realized it, the eastern Turkey Mountains were turning green again under a gentle spring sun as if to ease his pain.

Good news arrived for Traylor Doolan and Tom delivered it with mixed emotions.

"The assignment came through for you to join Colonel Benjamin Grierson," Tom said, "but I hate to see you go."

Tray was both relieved and sad. "I don't like the idea of us partin', but you know me and my itchin' feet! Is Grierson still on the heels of that old Indian?"

"Yes. You're to help him on a sortie against Chief Victorio near the Mexican border. The colonel wants you to report at Fort Davis by the end of the month."

Tray began immediately to prepare for departure, putting his few belongings into the saddlebags.

"What's your hurry?" Manning asked jokingly. "Shouldn't take more than twelve days to get down there. And you don't even have an extra pair of clean clothes. Anne would never let you get away like that!"

"Thought I'd stop at Peñasco on the way an' say hello

to Cassandra. Maybe I can get her to wash out somethin' for me."

"Well, you go ahead, and please give Cass my regards. I'll keep an ear to the telegraph to see how you're doing with Colonel Grierson."

They went outside and Tray threw his saddlebags over Pardo's back.

"You know, I never really thanked you for all your help while Anne was ill," Tom said.

Tray jumped into his Pueblo saddle. "I'm the one oughta be sayin' thanks. You and Anne are what's made my life worthwhile!" He reached down and grabbed Tom's hand with a firm shake. "But you ain't seen the last of me! Our trails'll be crossin' again one of these days."

Stifling a pang of remorse, he tipped a goodbye finger to his hat and trotted Pardo south toward the Peñasco.

Chapter Thirty-Seven

One chore followed another for Cassandra, but she had little time to reflect on her accomplishments. Heavy work kept the horror of the Indian raid from her mind and things were shaping well. She thanked God for Zack and Jonah; they were doing the work of men twice their size. Even with all the activities to see to, Zack had been able to fix up the chairs and table that were partially burned by the Indians and Cassandra felt safe, now, with the boys at her side.

On this particular Monday morning she stirred some lye soap into the large, black iron pot of simmering water, then added the clothes, swishing them around with a heavy wooden stick.

As she stood up, stretching her aching back, Jonah came running in from the fields, pressing one hand on the other, which was dripping blood.

"Jonah, what happened?" Cassandra asked. "You're bleeding!"

"Cut it on the scythe. Zack said I oughta get back to the house and you could wrap it up for me!"

Cassandra knelt down to examine the wound, relieved to see it wasn't a major cut. But it did need a bandage. "Come inside and I'll take care of it."

They went into the house and Cassandra took out a strip of clean cotton cloth she always kept for such emergencies, then dipped up a bowl of water and put it onto the table.

"Sit down, now," she told him, "and let me clean that blood away."

Jonah sat in a chair and held out his injured hand. His dark blue eyes softened as he watched her work.

"Zack says just 'cause you married Pa, that don't make you our Ma," he said quietly.

"Zack's right, in a way. I'm what they call your stepmother."

"Zack says it ain't respectful to call you 'Ma.' But since my real Ma died when I was a baby, you're the only Ma I ever had."

"Well, even though you and Zack aren't my real children, I think of you two as my own boys." She tightened the cloth strip around his hand.

"Then it's all right if me and Zack call you 'Ma' instead of 'Cassandra?'"

She looked at him with a warm smile. "I'd be mighty proud if you would!" She tied the bandage. "Now you'd better get back and help Zack, but be careful with that hand!"

Jonah got out of the chair and wrapped his arms around her for a big hug. "I'll watch out . . . and thanks for fixin' my hand, Ma!"

Cassandra's loving eyes followed him as he ran out of the house and back to the field.

After cleaning up the table, she returned to the simmering kettle outside and saw a man on horseback approaching the house. Unable to distinguish his face Cassandra started to go inside for the shotgun, an instinct acquired after that terrible day last March. She stopped when the man called her name.

"Howdy, Cass! Don't you remember an old friend?"

"Traylor Doolan!" she breathed as he rode up to her. "I can't believe it . . . it's been so long!

"But you're still pretty as ever!" He had to swallow the lie, saddened to note the hard lines around her eyes.

"Well, get down from there and come inside. I'll fix you something to eat." She walked up to the horse and rubbed behind its ear. "Hello, Pardo, how've you been?" Pardo gave her a friendly nuzzle.

Tray jumped down. "Ain't hungry, but I'll take a drink of water if you don't mind."

They went inside and he sat at the table while she poured him a cup of water, then settled into a chair opposite. "What on earth brings you to this neck of the country?" she asked.

"On my way to Fort Davis. Gonna help Colonel Grierson run down Chief Victorio. Anne Manning told me you got married and started a homestead. Thought I'd stop by an' pay my respects." Then he added somberly, "Don't know if you heard about Anne . . . she died of smallpox last December."

"Yes, I got a Christmas greeting from Tom. I must have moped around for a week after I read it!"

Zack and Jonah, having seen Tray's arrival, ran in from the field and stuck their heads through the door.

"You all right, Ma?" Zack asked.

His words gave Cassandra a warm feeling; Jonah must have done some talking, for it was the first time he'd called her that.

"Come in, you two," she said, "and meet an old friend of mine."

The two boys entered shyly and Cass introduced them. "Traylor Doolan, these are my husband's boys, Zack, the bigger one, and Jonah."

The brothers said their hellos and dipped themselves a drink. "You stayin' a while, Mr. Doolan?" Jonah asked.

"Just passin' through," Tray replied. "Wanted to say hello to your Ma."

"Now you two finish your drink," Cassandra told them, "and get back to your chores. Mr. Doolan and I want to chat a spell."

Zack and Jonah nodded their heads politely and left.

"I'd like to meet that husband of yours," Tray said: "Where you keepin' him?"

Cassandra leaned back in the chair, looking very tired. "On a little hill down by the river. Buried him last March."

Tray's blue eyes softened. "Sorry to hear that. What happened, a sickness of some kind?"

"Indians killed him . . . cut him to pieces. Took my little girl Rose, too." She turned to gaze through the window at Zack and Jonah working in the field. "I can still hear my baby crying, 'Mama, Mama!' when they carried her off." Then she looked at Tray. "They made a mess of the house. Burned the furniture, cut open our mattresses and the sacks of flour and sugar. Even took my books . . . my Bible! Why do you suppose they'd want those? They can't read!"

Tray set down his cup. "They use the paper to stuff in their shields. It's lightweight and with the hard buffalo-hide cover, the shield's almost bulletproof." He tried to change the subject. "Cass, why don't you go back to Seven Rivers, or even up north? It ain't right for just you and those two boys livin' out here on the plains by yourselves. The Indian wars may be comin' to an end, but there's still some of 'em runnin' around."

She gave him a determined look. "Papa told me I had his stubbornness in my blood. This is my registered homestead and I refuse to be run off. I've got Fergis' gun and Zack has taught me how to shoot. If any Indian comes around here again, it'll be his last stopping place!"

Tray grinned. "I hope that don't include me."

Cassandra looked startled; she had forgotten his heritage. "Of course not, you're my friend. After all, you saved my life and I owe you that. But I'm still going to stay here and build this place into a ranch, Indians or no Indians!"

Tray shrugged in defeat. "Well, if you need any help gettin' the place in shape, reckon I could spend a day or two here."

Cassandra glanced through the window again at Zack and Jonah working with the plow and horse. "There's a lot to be done and it's hard on the boys. You know you're welcome to stay as long as you want, and we could use another strong back." Then she studied him ruefully. "Besides, it looks like those clothes of yours could stand a good washing."

He looked sheepish. "Guess it's been a spell since they've seen water, but I only got one other change of clothes, and they're grimy, too."

"Well, you came at a good time, I've got the pot boiling. The boys'll show you down to the river and you can give yourselves a bath while I wash all your clothes. In this sun they'll be dry by the time you're finished."

Zack and Jonah returned from their chores and showed Tray down to the river. In a few minutes, Jonah brought Tray's clothes back to Cassandra.

"Now, you get back down there and wash, too," she told the boy. "When these clothes are dry, I'll bring them down to you."

Cassandra later hung out the freshly washed clothes, which dried quickly in the glaring sun, then she gathered them up and made her way to the river.

The boys were still frolicking in the cold running water. Tray had just emerged from the stream, and stood naked on the bank, watching them with amusement.

His back was to her when Cassandra approached and she smiled at the sight of his bronzed body. The strong shoulders and muscles glistened in the sun while sparkling droplets of water coursed over the firm roundness of his buttocks. She had to admit that the Indian half of him gave his skin a pleasing masculine color. She laid the neatly folded clothes on a large rock and silently returned to the house.

Chapter Thirty-Eight

Zack and Jonah took an immediate liking to Traylor Doolan. When they were not sharing chores in the field, he taught the youngsters some of his scouting lore, and at night held their rapt attention with stories of his exciting adventures.

Meanwhile, Cassandra sat by the fireplace, working with needle and thread on an extra shirt for Tray. The warm, family atmosphere began to ease the ache in her heart over Rose's absence.

After the boys had gone to sleep in their beds on the other side of the room, where Tray also slept, he joined Cassandra at the fireside. They spoke in low voices.

"Tray, you don't know what a boost you've been to my spirit," she murmured, and rethreaded the needle.

"I 'spect it does get lonesome out here, just the three of you."

"It wouldn't have been so bad if I still had little Rose here with me." She concentrated on the sewing and continued. "I wish you could have seen her with Uncle Emil . . . that man loved her like his own daughter. He always called her 'Bunny,' because Rose had a habit of wrinkling her little nose whenever she was provoked. It got to the point where even I was calling her 'Bunny' once in a while." She looked up with a dark face. "I wake up at nights, now, wondering if my little girl is dead or alive . . . and if she is still alive, what she must be going through!"

207

"Best you don't think about it," Tray consoled her. "One of the good things 'bout Indians is that they love children and treat the captured ones like their own."

On the third day of Tray's visit, Zack and Jonah had gone to the river for water and Cassandra popped an apple pie into the wood stove. Through the window, she saw Tray out by the corral throwing the Pueblo saddle over Pardo's back. With concern she wiped her hands on an apron and rushed quickly to the corral.

"Tray, what are you doing?"

"Well, seems to me things are pretty much in control 'round here, now," he said, cinching the straps. "Reckon I'd better git myself down to Fort Davis. Colonel Grierson's waitin' for me."

Cassandra sighed in resignation. She had told herself it wouldn't last and now the time had come. She put a hand on his arm. "Couldn't you stay on, Tray . . . please?"

"Ain't a place on earth where I wouldn't get itchin' feet after a few days. You'd just end up seein' me and Pardo ridin' off some mornin'."

"But we all love you and you're just like a father to the boys!" His penetrating eyes made her blush at what she had implied.

Without a word, he took her shoulders and lowered his head so that their lips met. She put her arms around him and they held each other tightly.

With his growing strength pressing against her, she recalled the sight of his bronze naked body sparkling in the sun. Now, she wanted him more than anything in the world. But then the realization pierced her heart—she was embracing an Indian!

He sensed the feeling and released her. "It's still there,

ain't it?"

She looked down, ashamed. "When we first came to the Peñasco, some friendly Indians stopped for food and I thought maybe I was wrong to hate them." She raised her face to him. "But then I saw what the others did to Fergis . . . the same thing they did to Ian!"

His hands tightened on her shoulders. "The Indians were here long before the white man, free to roam the plains, hunt their buffalo and live as they pleased. Now, they're bein' lied to, starved and forced to live in a world they don't understand. Can you blame 'em for fightin' back?"

"But why do they have to do such monstrous things?!"

"Not all of 'em do it. Even ol' Geronimo won't take a scalp. Some of 'em think by cuttin' up their captives, the enemy goes to the Big Sky like that—in disgrace."

She could only look at him through tear-filled eyes, her heart torn by a mixture of love and resentment.

He gritted his teeth. "I'm sorry if I got you upset, I shouldn't have kissed you." He put his foot into the stirrup and threw himself up onto Pardo. "You're a fine stubborn woman, Cass, but you've got a lotta learnin' to do. We're all just plain human beings. It don't matter what color we are!" He tipped his hat. "Please tell Zack and Jonah goodbye for me." He turned his horse and trotted away.

Cassandra doubled her fists in self hatred, wanting to beat out the prejudice that still lurked inside. Frustrated tears spilled down her cheeks as she watched Traylor Doolan once more fading out of her life.

Chapter Thirty-Nine

"We've chased Victorio all over southern New Mexico," Colonel Benjamin Grierson said after Traylor Doolan had arrived at Fort Davis. "Now, he's hiding out across the border again, in Mexico."

"Don't reckon he'll be any happier there," Tray replied. "From what I hear, Mexico's after his hide, too!"

"He'll have to come back up into Texas for water—and I plan to block every water hole he makes a try for. My guess is he'll go for Eagle Springs. I already have some men stationed there and tomorrow morning we'll take the nine men who came with me from Fort Concho to join those at Eagle Springs."

The headquarters door opened and a young boy of seventeen stuck his head in. Excitement shone in the dark-brown eyes. "I've got my gun cleaned and my pack all ready, Father. When do you think we'll leave?"

"Early in the morning," Ben Grierson said. "Come in, Robert, I want you to meet Traylor Doolan—he'll be one of the scouts." He turned to Tray. "This is my son, Robert. He just graduated from high school back east and wanted to come out west looking for adventure."

Tray and young Robert Grierson shook hands.

"Pleased to meet you, Mr. Doolan," the boy said.

"Likewise." Tray looked at the gun in Robert's hand. "You plannin' on helpin' your father catch old Chief Victorio?"

Ben chuckled. "Alice was against it, but Robert insisted. I'll keep an eye on him, though."

Robert gave his father a look, as if being treated like a child. "You and mother needn't worry. I've been practicing with my rifle and I'm a pretty good shot!"

"I know you are, Son, but I'm hoping there'll be little or no gunfire."

The small group left early in the morning, traveling southeast. All rode horseback, except a disappointed Robert Grierson who expected to have his own horse. Instead, he had to find space in the supply ambulance.

Near sundown they made camp at a water hole called Tinaja de las Palmas and started a campfire for the night. After their evening meal, the men sat around the fire, talking in low voices while Robert cleaned his rifle one more time. His father and Traylor Doolan squatted next to each other, finishing their Arbuckles coffee.

Ben Grierson asked casually, "Whatever happened to that delightful Cassandra Shaw? The last I saw of her, you were all on your way to New Mexico."

That eventful trip brought a fond memory to Tray. "Oh, she remarried, but her husband was killed by Victorio's men up on the Peñasco."

Ben scowled. "I'm sorry to hear that. Too bad we couldn't have caught that Indian while we were up there. Is Cassandra all right?"

"I saw her on my way down here. She and her two stepsons have a nice ranch coming along real good, now."

"And her baby girl . . . she must be five or six years old, now."

"Indians carried her little girl away after they killed her husband."

Grierson was stunned, recalling the beautiful baby he had seen in Cassandra's arms back at Fort Concho. Before he could reply, a courier rode into camp.

The rider, Lieutenant Henry Flipper, the first black man to graduate from West Point, fighting prejudice and degradation all the way, dismounted and reported to Colonel Grierson.

"I just rode in from Fort Quitman, sir," Flipper said. "Captain Nolan says to tell you that Chief Victorio has crossed the Rio Grande just below the fort. He's not going to Eagle Springs like we all thought!"

Ben gave a sardonic smile. "Of course! That smart Indian knew we'd expect him to hit one of the prominent water holes—he's going for a smaller one instead!"

Tray grinned. "And we're probably sittin' right in his path!"

"You're right, Tray. This Tinaja water hole depends on rainfall and is usually low or dried up. No troops would likely wait for Victorio here. We'll just stay put till that old devil comes looking for water and then grab him!"

Tray raised an eyebrow. "But there's only ten of us."

"It'll take Victorio a while to get here." Ben looked up at Flipper. "Lieutenant, I want you to ride back to Fort Quitman as fast as you can and tell Captain Nolan to send all the men he can to help us out!"

Henry Flipper had just covered ninety-eight miles in twenty-two hours and was exhausted. He took a deep breath of cold night air. "Yes, sir, but could I have a fresh horse?"

Grierson looked chagrined. "I'm sorry, Lieutenant, I wasn't thinking—you've had a hard ride. Please help yourself to some food and hot coffee while we have another horse saddled."

Thirty minutes later, Lieutenant Henry Flipper took off again and Traylor Doolan rode Pardo out into the night, looking for any signs of the approaching Indians.

At four o'clock in the morning Grierson was surprised to see a small group of soldiers ride into camp—Lieutenant Finley and ten of his troopers from Eagle Springs.

"Knowing you had a small party, we came to escort you to the springs," Finley said.

"That was thoughtful of you," Ben told him. "We can use all the help we can get! We're almost certain Victorio is on his way here. I'm having my men lie in wait for him."

Tray returned to camp as the hills changed to pink under a rising sun. "There's an Indian camp about ten miles to the south," he told Grierson. "They oughta be here by late mornin'—and it looks like a big party!"

As soon as his small group of men finished breakfast, Grierson had them climb up into the surrounding rocky ridges and wait with their guns ready.

"Robert, you stay here in camp with Lieutenant Finley and his men where it's safe," Ben told his son.

Robert frowned in protest. "But, father, I want to go, too!"

Grierson shook his head. "No use arguing. Your mother would boil me in oil if I let you go up there!"

Robert stayed reluctantly in camp while Tray and Colonel Grierson crouched with the others behind rocky fortifications and watched the pass below.

Finally, at nine o'clock, the first group of Indians appeared, riding slowly and covering the area with their sharp eyes. The sun must have glinted off a soldier's rifle, for the Indians suddenly stopped and turned their horses around.

Ben Grierson was determined not to let them get away. "Finley!" he called down to the lieutenant waiting at the camp. "Take your men after them. Hold them up till Nolan's

213

reinforcements arrive—they should be here any time, now!"

Lieutenant Finley and his men leaped onto their horses and took off after the Indians. Gunfire broke out and two Indians fell, but then Finley was surprised by another group of the enemy rising up from the crags behind him.

"We're almost surrounded!" Finely shouted to his men. "Get back to the rocks and they'll follow!"

The lieutenant and his troopers began racing back toward the rocky ridge where Grierson waited.

While the Indians gave chase, howling like wild coyotes, Finley and his men lured them into range and Grierson's men opened fire. The startled Indians turned in panic and retreated to hide in the nearby ravines.

Chief Victorio had now seen the extent of his enemy and decided they could not deter him and his warriors from reaching the water hole. The Indians regrouped and surged forward in a huge mass of screaming red bodies and galloping horses.

"My God!" Colonel Grierson sputtered. "We don't have a chance!" But his spirits rose when companies of soldiers from Fort Quitman appeared, riding into the foray with blazing guns.

The startled Victorio and his braves whirled their horses, racing back across the plains.

"I'll follow 'em and see which way they're goin'," Tray said to Grierson.

Tray gave Victorio a head start and then rode after them, careful to remain unseen. After making sure of the direction they were taking, he returned to camp.

"They're headed toward Rattlesnake Springs," he said.

"Then we've got to move fast and get to Rattlesnake Canyon before they do," the colonel replied.

Tray looked around at the dead bodies. "They'll be

slowed down a little to take care of their wounded. And with seven of his braves killed, he'll have a few less to fight, anyway."

The men quickly broke camp, then left for Rattlesnake Canyon. They rode all day without a stop. When darkness arrived, Grierson kept pushing them.

"We can eat hardtack while we ride," he told the group. "We've got to get there before Victorio does!"

Robert sat in the jostling ambulance, chewing on a tasteless biscuit and swigging from his canteen. The desert turned into mysterious shapes under a clouded moon and his scalp crawled.—in the passing shadows, fan-like tops of giant yuccas looked just like Indians in headdress. He put a hand on his rifle, but soon monotony brought relaxation and he leaned back to grab a few minutes of sleep.

The boy awoke at daybreak to find they were still traveling. His body ached from the long ride, so he climbed out of the ambulance to walk alongside, stretching his cramped legs while chewing on a breakfast of more hardtack.

By late afternoon the group arrived at Rattlesnake Canyon after twenty-one hours of hard riding, pleased to see they had reached the springs ahead of Victorio.

The men took the saddles off their beleaguered horses and everyone settled down for a welcomed rest around the campfire.

"After I feed and water Pardo," Tray told Grierson, "I'd better ride out and watch for those Indians."

"Good idea," the colonel replied. "I wish I could get by with as little sleep as you do!"

After Tray left, Colonel Grierson looked down at his son who had stretched his tired body out on a blanket.

"You see, Robert," Ben chuckled, "adventure isn't as glamorous as you thought it would be!"

Robert grinned back at his father. "I'll make up for it when we fight the Indians again!"

One of the men walked over with a bottle of whiskey. "Colonel, would it be proper for us to have a sip after that hard ride?" He offered the bottle to Grierson.

Ben smiled and took the bottle. "I think it would be in order—but only a sip." He tilted the bottle for a gulp and then handed it to Robert. "Looks like you could do with a little, Son."

Robert took the bottle and swallowed some whiskey like a man. With a grimace he gave back the container and wiped his mouth. "Why do they call this place Rattlesnake Springs?"

The soldier laughed. "That's why we'd rather drink whiskey. The water here would sooner kill a rattlesnake if he drank it! It don't hurt the Indians, though. They'll drink anything."

Guards took turns during the night and early next morning Grierson positioned Companies C and G under Captain Viele among the crags of Rattlesnake Canyon. The remaining companies were held in reserve.

A few hours later, Traylor Doolan returned from his scouting. "They're on their way," he told the colonel. "We oughta be seein' 'em by midafternoon."

Grierson had orders relayed through the men to hold their fire until the Indians were in easy range.

At two o'clock the first vanguard of Victorio's braves appeared on the horizon, approaching cautiously. The soldiers, hiding among the crags, tensed and positioned their rifles while the reserve troopers remained hidden below.

Robert had been ordered to stay with the reserves and keep out of the gunfire, but he lay behind some rocks with his rifle gripped in readiness; he was not about to pass up this opportunity to shoot an Indian.

His father stood some distance away, watching anxiously with Captain Viele and Traylor Doolan.

Tray glanced at the eager Robert holding the gun and walked over to the boy.

"You ain't really plannin' t'use that thing, are you?" Tray asked.

"I can't go back east and say I didn't get myself an Indian!" Robert said. He noticed Tray's gun still in its holster on his hip. "Aren't you going to fight them?"

"Ain't my job. I don't fight 'em, I just find 'em."

"Haven't you ever killed an Indian?"

"Only when I had to."

Grierson broke the conversation. "Tray, they've stopped. You think they've seen us?"

Tray looked ahead at the line of Indians on their ponies; they were shading their eyes and scanning the area. "They're just bein' cautious. But they can smell us if they get close enough!"

The Indians started forward once again, headed toward the spring, and when they were in range, the men on the ridge opened fire. Some of the Indians fell from their horses while the others wheeled around and galloped off with yelps of surprise.

The firing ceased and Grierson fidgeted with his revolver. "That was only part of his men. You think Victorio will get away, now, Tray?"

"He probably thinks those soldiers on the ridge are all we have with us. But he's mighty thirsty. I'll wager he'll fight his way to the spring, just wait and you'll see!"

As Tray predicted, the entire party of Indians soon rose from the horizon, Victorio in the lead, all racing with war hoops toward the spring.

"Now's the time!" Ben said to Lieutenant Viele. "Let's

217

take your men against them—I think we've got him!"

Grierson joined Viele and his troopers as they mounted quickly and galloped forward with guns blazing.

Victorio and his braves, astonished at the appearance of more soldiers, reined to a halt, their horses rearing with snorts and whinnies.

Tray and young Robert watched. However, the boy had waited long enough; he jumped up and ran out with his rifle firing.

His father shouted with alarm, "Robert, get yourself back to camp!"

Tray drew his revolver and raced after the boy just as an Indian turned on his pony and took aim at Robert. Tray hoped he was close enough and fired; the Indian dropped from the horse.

"Come on, now," Tray yelled and started to grab Robert's arm.

But Robert lifted his rifle and let go a blast. Tray turned to see that the Indian he'd shot from the horse had raised on an elbow to shoot, but Robert's bullet stopped him and the Indian now lay dead.

By the time Tray and Robert got back to the camp, Victorio and his warriors had fled in panic, leaving at least thirty Indians killed or wounded.

The soldiers returned and Ben Grierson faced his son with a mixture of rage and relief. "I ought to skin you alive for running out there like that!"

Tray put a hand on Robert's shoulder. "Now, don't be too hard on him, Colonel. After all, he saved me from gettin' shot!"

"And I got my Indian!" Robert added with pride.

Ben had to smile. "Even so, when we get back to Fort Concho, I'm going to ship you back east immediately!"

Outnumbered and in danger of being cornered, Victorio went back across the border again into Mexico. Many of his warriors were wounded and most of the stock broken down.

American troops were not allowed to pursue Indians across the border, so Grierson posted his men along the Rio Grande while Victorio hid out in Tres Castillos Mountains.

"I wonder how long we'll have to wait," Ben said. He was as restless as the others.

Traylor squinted his blue eyes at the rugged terrain across the river. "The Mexicans just might take 'im off our hands. They want 'im as bad as we do!"

True enough, a courier arrived two days later with the news. Mexican troops had found the wily Indian. After a furious battle, Victorio and sixty of his warriors were killed with sixty-eight women and children taken as captives.

At their camp on the Rio Grande, Ben Grierson slumped down on a large flat rock and heaved a deep sigh, but Traylor Doolan knew it wasn't because of weariness; Colonel Benjamin Grierson had lost the satisfaction of winning a brave fight.

"I suppose now, Mexico will claim a great victory," Ben muttered.

"Everybody'll find out later," Tray consoled him. "It was you that gave 'em that victory!"

True, the real victors were Lieutenant Colonel Benjamin Grierson and his 10th Buffalo Soldiers. They had frustrated the great Indian chief at every turn, drained him of resources and driven him, sorely crippled, into Mexico where he was an easy target for the Mexican soldiers.

Grierson called his men together and said, "I guess that does it. It's all over. But I want to thank every one of you for helping me so tirelessly. No matter how one looks at it, we've all accomplished a great task!"

The large group broke up, with parting words of camaraderie, and started back to their respective locations.

Ben looked forward to returning to Fort Concho and seeing his wife Alice again, but before parting company, he shook Traylor Doolan's hand. "What about you, Tray? What are your plans, now?"

Clay shrugged. "Well, first, I'll have to go back to Fort Davis and get my pay for this job."

"And then?"

"Danged if I know. All the forts are closin' down, and there's hardly any more Indians to chase."

"Why don't you stay on at Fort Davis? They're still gathering up some Apaches. Maybe they could use someone with your rare talents."

"Thanks, Colonel. I got nothin' to lose."

They said their farewell and Tray climbed into the Pueblo saddle. He rubbed Pardo behind the ear and breathed a heavy sigh, for he was tired and the future looked blank. "Well, Old Fella, if you can keep goin', reckon I can, too."

He gently nudged the faithful horse and they headed northwest.

PART FIVE

- 1884 -

Chapter Forty

Traylor Doolan relaxed in the Pueblo saddle while Pardo carried him in a steady gait over the lower Llano Estacado. The horse's rhythmic clip-clopping eased Tray's mind into thoughts of the past like an eagle skimming over the plains searching for prey.

The Victorio campaign had ended successfully three years earlier, but Tray had some regret for having been a part of Chief Victorio's defeat; another great warrior had vanished from the West's troubled plains.

With the Indian wars diminishing, the Army forts began closing down, one by one. Scouting jobs tapered off and Tray had stayed at Fort Davis, helping the few Army units round up any remaining hostiles. While there, a welcome message came in over the telegraph. It was from Tom Manning:

> *Fort Union deactivated and am now at Fort Concho.*
> *Need you here soon as possible to help catch our old*
> *friend Gray Panther. Signed, Colonel Thomas*
> *Manning.*

Tray had to smile, realizing Tom was now a full colonel. Then he thought about the message. It was hard to believe that any Indians were still surviving on the empty plains with almost no buffalo left to sustain them. However, if Gray Panther was still on the prowl, he'd probably be down to just a few warriors and squaws. With his elimination, and the last of the Apaches subdued in New Mexico and Arizona, the west would truly be wide open for all the land-hungry settlers waiting to rush in.

Tray felt a wave of nostalgia as he rode into Fort Concho on a late afternoon. Although Colonel Benjamin Grierson had left the place two years earlier, the neatness and order he had begun were still evident. But nobody could erase the curse of bleakness that still permeated the garrison.

Tray went directly to the new headquarters building that Grierson had constructed in 1877, after finally scrounging money from the tight-fisted government.

Inside, he found Colonel Thomas Manning and an Infantry captain studying a large map tacked to the wall.

Tray gave a small laugh as he entered. "Don't tell me you need a map, Tom. You oughta know this country like the back of your hand!"

Manning turned at the sound of his friend's voice. "Traylor Doolan!" He grabbed Tray's hand. "Colonel Grierson said you might still be at Fort Davis—I see you got my wire."

"That's right. And congratulations, by the way, on makin' it to full colonel."

"A few years too late, I'd say!" Manning turned to the captain. "Tray, I'd like you to meet Captain Nicholas Tyson. He'll be one of my commanders on this campaign."

Captain Tyson, a good-looking young man with a shock of sandy hair, took Tray's hand with a smile.

"It's a great pleasure to meet you, Mr. Doolan. The colonel here's told me a lot about you. From what he says, you're the best scout they've got in these parts!"

Tray uttered another laugh. "Tom talks too much."

"Well, I'm certainly glad to see you, Tray," Manning said, "although this may well be our last scouting party together. It's old Gray Panther, still raising hell down here.

He's the last of his kind and with him out of the way, I imagine we'll all be out of jobs."

"We're both gettin' kind of long in the tooth for this kind of thing, anyhow. Time for us to retire, don't you think?"

"I'm only forty-nine and you're, what—fifteen years younger? There's a lot of fight left in both of us. But just what'll you do, Tray, when there aren't any more Indians to run down?"

"Thought maybe goin' out to California. Heard you can pick up gold right off the streets!"

Manning's smile faded. "Funny you should say that. Anne and I had planned to settle down somewhere in California after I retired from this confounded Army."

Tray kindly changed the subject. "Now, tell me, what're your plans for chasin' down Gray Panther?"

Manning turned back to the map. "I was just showing Captain Tyson. Gray Panther's down here in our area attacking wagon trains moving toward the Pecos. His party consists of only about twenty or more warriors, but he's a vicious scoundrel—killed at least fifteen white men and women just last year."

Tray glanced at the map. "This is mostly flat country, shouldn't be too hard to track 'em down. If you don't mind a suggestion, my guess is he'd show up at Monument Spring more'n anyplace else."

"I was thinking of just that premise. The Infantry's Sixteenth Regiment's stationed at Fort Concho, now. Captain Tyson can take one company on a southern route and you and I can take another one, swinging around up north, then we'll all meet at Monument Spring. If Gray Panther isn't found on either route, we'll just wait for him there."

Preparations were made and they started out in the early

morning, going their separate ways, Captain Tyson with fifty men of Company A, and Manning's party with forty-five men from Company C.

While the Manning group traveled north to Five Wells, they took their time, hoping to discover any small sign of Indian activity. But the arid land seemed to be bare with no trace of animal life in the last several days. Tray kept his keen eyes to the ground, watching for tracks.

"What do you think Gray Panther and his people are doing to survive?" Tom Manning asked as they rode slowly over the wide dry plains. "I've seen no evidence of buffalo."

Tray assumed with regret that the white man must have succeeded in driving the magnificent animal to extinction. "They'd have to be saving on their tepees and clothes since buffalo hides ain't available anymore." He shook his head. "I'd bet a dollar to a horned toad they're havin' a rough time!"

"And what do you suppose they're eating?"

"Well, they don't prefer rabbits. Even if they could catch a prairie dog, it ain't very tasty. There's the mesquite bean they grind up to make bread, and berries on bushes that grow sometimes on the Brazos or Pecos. I reckon they're mainly livin' off the cattle they stole durin' raids on white settlers."

Manning and his group finally reached Five Wells and found the area dry as the dust blowing over the cracked lake bed.

"Well, it's no big disappointment," Tom Manning said. "We've been skimping on our water, although it'd be nice to fill the water barrels."

"That'll make the pack mules happy," Tray added. "We oughta have just enough water to get us to Monument Spring."

"Then we'll make camp here and go west before sunrise."

Tray was the first one up next morning and rode Pardo out in the dim light, searching for Indian signs. He discovered hoof prints in the cool sand a mile from camp and rode back in time for breakfast.

"Looks like they found us before we found them," he told Manning while they ate. "I'd say their scouts have gone back to report us bein' here."

Manning stroked his short beard, which the years had turned a silvery white. "The thought just struck me . . . do you think Gray Panther knows I'm the one who's on his tail?"

Tray grinned. "If the scouts got a good look at you, then Gray Panther knows. Your face is stamped in his memory."

"And I'll never forget *his* face!" Manning recalled the last encounter with the old chief at Fresh Fork. "As I remember, you said he swore to get even with me!"

During the next three days Tray followed the pony tracks heading toward Monument Spring and knew his hunch was correct.

In not long Colonel Shafter's white stone monument appeared on the horizon, sparkling in the bright sun. Manning drew his company to a halt so that Tray could ride unseen for a closer reconnaissance.

"Who knows what you're going to find down there?" Manning said. "I expected Tyson and his company to arrive before we did. If they found Indians, there should've been a conflict."

"We'll see." Tray rode off for a look.

The mesquite soon became thick enough to offer a good cover and Tray dismounted, dropping Pardo's reins; the faithful horse would wait for him. Tray eased himself through the brush until he had a view of the spring some distance away. He saw only two lodges, with faint smoke coming from their conical openings. Tray realized that with a party of twenty or more, they must be down to their last bits of buffalo hide to have just two tepees. Several horses and two head of cattle stood tethered nearby. Tray crawled back to his horse and returned to Manning and the soldiers.

"Their camp is down there, all right," Tray said, "but I couldn't tell if all the Indians were there. There's a lot of horses, but they could be stolen ones. Old Gray Panther and his boys just might be roamin' the area lookin' for us!"

"Well, I'd like to get this thing cleaned up," Manning said with determination. "Let's rush down there and take the camp—we should have them outnumbered if they show up!"

The company split in half, using the tactic of attacking from two sides, and loped down to the Indian encampment.

They entered at full speed, shouting and shooting into the lodges, with only a few squaws stumbling out in terror, two fatally hit by the flying bullets. The soldiers leaped from their horses and began ransacking the two tepees, but no warrior was present.

Suddenly Tom Manning realized he had been outwitted, for the twenty warriors had waited until the white men were off their horses and distracted. Although twice outnumbered, the Indians now advanced into the camp screaming and releasing a volley of arrows and gunfire.

Manning saw the dreaded Gray Panther in the lead; his ugly face with its crooked nose twisted in a mask of intense hatred.

The soldiers began firing back, dropping at least four Indians, however two soldiers were struck down by arrows in the chest. It looked like a fight to the death for each and every man, both red and white.

However, the odds changed quickly as Captain Tyson and his fifty men appeared from out of nowhere. They galloped into the melee, shooting and clubbing Indians off their horses. The hostiles were now clearly overwhelmed and one of them began riding off to the west.

Manning saw that it was Gray Panther. The colonel was not about to let the old chief get away and he leaped onto his horse, striking out after the Indian who headed up the rise toward Shafter's stone monument. Tray wheeled his horse around and galloped in pursuit.

As Gray Panther approached the rise, Manning fired; but the chief had raised his shield and the bullet glanced off, leaving a shredded path on the buffalo hide. While Manning began to reload, Gray Panther reined to a halt and fitted an arrow into his bow. With a scowl of vengeance, he coolly aimed at the colonel.

At that moment Traylor Doolan rode up with his gun drawn. Just as the arrow was unleashed, he blasted Gray Panther off his horse with a fatal bullet in the chest.

Captain Tyson had arrived on the plateau directly behind Tray. The two quickly dismounted and rushed to catch Tom Manning as he slid from the saddle, Gray Panther's arrow protruding from the colonel's neck. Tray and the captain helped Manning over to the monument, easing him down to lean against the pile of white rocks.

"How bad is it, Tray?" the colonel gasped with pain.

Tray shook his head as he studied the ugly arrow lodged in Manning's neck. "If you'd been hit straight on, we could push it through, but it's pointed up toward your brain pan."

"Then see if you can pull it out."

"If it's barbed, we can't."

"Try it and see."

"It'll hurt like hell!"

"Go ahead, Tray. Get this damned thing out of me!"

Captain Tyson held Manning's head and jaw while Tray

took hold of the arrow shaft and gently tugged. Manning gritted his teeth to fight the unbearable pain until he finally had to cry out. Tray stopped.

"Go ahead," Manning panted, "just let me holler!"

Tray pulled again, harder, but the arrow was obviously barbed and would not be extracted. Manning's face turned white with agony and he slumped forward.

Tray put an ear to the colonel's chest and listened for a moment, then looked up at Tyson.

"He's okay, just passed out. Get a wagon up here fast! We've gotta get 'im back to Concho soon as possible."

"Right on!" the captain replied. He jumped onto his horse and galloped it down to the spring.

Tray broke off the arrow shaft, leaving about four inches protruding from Manning's neck. Then he sat down and leaned against the monument, cradling the colonel's head.

Minutes later Tyson returned with a wagon and driver. Tray and the captain carefully placed Manning into the wagon, then watched it trundle back down the rise.

Captain Tyson walked over to Gray Panther's body and picked up the dead Indian's shield. He ran a thumb over the torn spot created by Tom Manning's bullet.

"Think I'll take the old boy's shield, as a reminder. This was my first Indian fight, y'know."

"Might as well," Tray replied. "He won't be needin' it any longer."

Captain Tyson took the shield and rode his horse down to the spring.

Tray threw himself into the Pueblo saddle, but before leaving he turned to gaze at Gray Panther, sprawled in death. Tray's blue eyes glinted in the sun; he had satisfied a vengeance, carried all his life without realizing it.

His eyes moved for a last look at Colonel Shafter's stone

edifice. It was meant as a beacon to all those yearning for a new life, but Tray noted with sadness that one side of the proud, white monument now carried the red stain of blood.

Chapter Forty-One

Captain Tyson now took command of both companies and supervised the burial of two unfortunate soldiers while Tray sat in the wagon, watching over Tom Manning.

Tom finally regained consciousness and feebly raised a hand to his neck to see if the arrow was still there. He felt the broken-off shaft and asked in a husky voice, "What's happening?"

"We're takin' you back to Fort Concho as fast as we can," Tray replied.

"That'll take days. If the arrowhead's hoop-iron, I could be dead by then."

"It was the last arrow Gray Panther had in his quiver, so we don't know if he was usin' hoop-iron or not. But, it *is* barbed and we can't pull it out. If we push it through, it'll hit your brain and you'll be dead for sure. We'll just have to pray it ain't hoop-iron and take a chance."

Five Indian warriors, two squaws and a little girl had been taken prisoners and put on horseback, then the group started back to Fort Concho.

Tray rode alongside the wagon carrying the colonel and kept an eye on his friend, stopping now and then to give him a sip of water. Tray's heart felt like a piece of lead for he knew the chances of Tom cheating death were not good.

In the late afternoon of the third day Manning went into delirium and fever. Tray asked that the party halt for the day.

While the men went about their chores, he sat in the wagon with a blanket on his lap to rest Manning's head and patted the colonel's face with a damp kerchief.

As evening grew dark, the soldiers squatted around their campfires, talking in low voices, but Tray remained in the wagon. Tom Manning's fever had not gone down and Tray ached with helpless pity. He closed his eyes with fatigue and drifted into half sleep.

Near midnight Tray awoke to the sound of a gurgling cough and looked down.

Manning took Tray's hand in a weak grip and looked up through glazed eyes. "I want you to know," he managed to say, "you've been like one of my own all these years . . . they've been good ones."

Tray swallowed the knot in his throat. "And you've been the father I should've had." He knew he'd spoken for the last time to his beloved friend.

Tray spent the rest of the night digging a grave. In the dull light of morning, thunder growled from a desert storm on the horizon with charcoal clouds smudging downward in long, slanting streaks of gray, carrying moisture to a thirsty land.

The cool air held a clean smell of fresh rain as four soldiers lowered Colonel Thomas Manning into the ground. Tray stood to one side watching, hat in hand. His face glistened from rain drops lightly spotting his cheeks and unashamed tears spilling out of his eyes.

Chapter Forty-Two

The short morning rainfall spread a grateful coolness over the military unit edging in a long line across the damp plains.

Traylor Doolan and Captain Tyson, leading the group, rode in silence. Tray didn't feel like talking and the captain knew Tray's heart still ached with the loss of his good friend. Hoping to free Tray's mind of the tragedy, Tyson finally spoke.

"That little girl they took with the squaws—one of the men said she looked like a white girl."

Tray's glum expression didn't change and he remained silent.

"Said she's got red hair and green eyes. I've never seen an Indian like that, have you, Tray?"

Tray finally stirred in his saddle. "Indians are always takin' children captive."

"Must be hard on their folks. Wonder if that little girl remembers her ma and pa?"

The image of Cassandra flashed through Tray's mind, telling him how it almost killed her, seeing little Rose taken away. He wondered what Rose's age would be today.

"How old you reckon that girl is?" he seemed to think aloud.

"Looks eight or nine to me."

Tray's thoughts began to roll. It couldn't be what he was thinking; Rose was captured by Apaches over in New

Mexico and this was Texas Comanche territory.

"That shield you took from old Gray Panther," he said, "let me have another look at it."

The shield dangled on the far side of Tyson's saddle horn and he moved it around so Tray could see it.

Tray studied the symbols painted on the tough buffalo hide. "That don't look Comanche to me. I'd say it's Apache." He turned his eyes forward again. "When we make camp, I wanna talk to that girl."

After the evening meal, Captain Tyson brought the captive girl to Tray's campfire.

"I think I ought to stay here with her," Tyson said.

"Fine with me."

Tray looked at the child. She wore a filthy, one-piece buffalo skin dress that drooped from her shoulders to just above the soft moccasins on her feet. Her face and hair were so dirty it was difficult to see that she was not true Indian. If given a good scrubbing, Tray thought, the child might have pretty red hair and a decent white complexion.

Tray asked her in Comanche to sit, and she lowered herself to the ground with legs crossed, eyes glinting like emeralds in the firelight.

"My name is Traylor Doolan," he continued in the Indian tongue. "I want to be your friend. Will you tell me your name?"

A moment of silence passed before she answered, also in Comanche. "I have many names. I am now called Snow Cloud, for that was the way of the sky when I was found by my new family."

"Your other family, where are they?"

"They are a different people . . . Apaches who live across the big river."

"Do you remember another family? A white family?"

235

The girl's eyes drooped and she made a small frown. "I do not remember."

"Please try to remember where you were before you lived with the Apaches," Tray urged softly.

The girl raised her eyes but did not answer. She stared at him without emotion.

"Do you remember your mother?" Tray persisted. "A white mother who called you Rose?"

She repeated, "I do not remember."

Tray sighed futilely and motioned to Captain Tyson. "You might as well take her back to the others."

"Did you find out about her folks?" Tyson asked.

"No, I didn't get anywhere."

"But what did she tell you?"

"She was taken by the Apaches on the other side of the river, to begin with. The Apaches and Comanches hate each other—their territories are divided by the Pecos River. Two years ago there was a battle between the two of 'em on the northern Pecos in New Mexico. That's probably where she was taken prisoner again, this time by Gray Panther." Tray shrugged in defeat. "Her first capture must have been at such an early age, she can't remember her real family."

After Captain Tyson had taken the girl away, Tray sat staring into the campfire. He still wasn't convinced; if only there was some way to find out who she really was.

The unit arrived at Fort Concho days later and the Indian prisoners were sequestered to await transportation to the Fort Sill reservation in Oklahoma.

Tray and Captain Tyson made out a full report on the tragic expedition, with a final summation that the Staked Plains were now clear of any hostile Indians. For Tray, the price paid had been dear.

236

The post commander, Colonel Matthew Blunt of the 16th U. S. Infantry, a firm but kindhearted man in his early fifties, wore his hair long with a heavy beard almost completely white. He had known Thomas Manning and received news of the colonel's death with resigned sadness.

"Tom Manning was a good man and a dedicated soldier," Colonel Blunt said. "Many brave men have given their lives during these years of conflict . . . I hope this is the end of it."

Captain Nicholas Tyson and Traylor Doolan took rooms above the hospital and that afternoon the captain tapped on Tray's door. When Tray opened it, Tyson held up a bottle.

"Look what I found at the sutler's," the captain said with pride. "The last bottle of good Irish whiskey at Fort Concho till the next shipment comes in! Thought you'd like to share the first drink with me."

"I ain't really a drinkin' man, but if you say it's that good, I'll have a sip or two."

"Good! Grab your water glass and come to my room."

Tray took his glass and followed Tyson next door. The captain poured whiskey into both glasses and they sipped from them with grimaces of pleasure.

Tyson picked up Gray Panther's shield that was leaning against his bed. "You said this is Apache, yet a Comanche chief was carrying it." He studied the shield. "If this thing could talk, I bet it'd have quite a story to tell!"

"Maybe it *can* talk," Tray said.

"What do you mean?"

"Indians pack their shields with pages of books they steal from the white man. That there shield just might tell you where it came from."

Tyson ran his finger over the ripped area made by Manning's bullet. "Looks like there really is some paper inside this thing. I hate to tear up a souvenir, but now you've got me curious—I'm gonna see what I've got here."

He took out his knife and made a careful slit around one edge of the shield, revealing several compressed sheets of paper. He removed a handful and read them.

"Well, I'll be damned! Looks like they took some poor soul's Bible." He handed the pages over to Tray and then took out some more paper.

Tray leafed through the pages and saw one with handwriting on it. His heart quickened as he read the words:

March 20, 1875: Cassandra Vosburg and Ian Shaw married, San Antonio, Texas.

December 25, 1875: Rose Terressa Shaw born, Fort Concho, Texas.

March 10, 1876: Ian Shaw killed by Indians.

Buried at Fort Concho, Texas.

November 9, 1880: Uncle Emil Vosburg died in flood at Seven Rivers, New Mexico.

November 10, 1880: Cassandra Vosburg Shaw married Fergis Gant at Seven Rivers, New Mexico.

Tray could remember Rose as a baby, smiling at him with her auburn hair and olive green eyes. *Just like Ian's,* Cassandra had told him. Tray looked at the dates on the page once more; Rose would now be about the same age as the captive white girl.

The next morning Tray took the Bible pages to Colonel Blunt's office and asked, "Have those captives been sent to Fort Sill yet?"

"Why, no," Colonel Blunt replied. "They'll be leaving in another two days."

Tray showed him the pages. "I think this might help us find out who that little white girl is that we took prisoner. With your permission, I'd like to talk to her."

The colonel scanned the pages. "Of course. We should do everything we can to return that poor child to her real mother and father!"

An Infantry sergeant brought the captive girl to Fort Concho's new headquarters building and into the stark room used for court-martial proceedings.

Photographs of U. S. President Chester A. Arthur and General William T. Sherman, Commanding General of the United States Army, looked down from one wall while across the way hung a portrait of General C. C. Augur, Commander of the Department of Texas. A United States flag was tacked to a third wall and before it sat a long, rustic wooden table with three chairs. It was deemed that too many people would scare the child, so only Traylor Doolan and Colonel Blunt sat at the table.

After the sergeant had escorted the girl into the room, Tray asked her in Comanche to take the wooden chair facing him and the colonel.

"You may leave us alone, now," Colonel Blunt told the sergeant, "but please stand guard outside."

The little girl, now clad in a fresh buckskin dress and with the grime washed from her face and hair, sat stiffly, hands in lap. She stared with solemn green eyes at the two men as Tray began the interrogation in Comanche tongue.

"Snow Cloud, your real mother and father were white and your father was killed by Indians when you were a baby. Later, your mother married another white man named Fergis Gant. He had two sons, named Zack and Jonah, and you lived with them . . . do you remember any of this?"

She simply stared with no response.

"Try to think back," Tray urged. "Before the Comanches called you 'Snow Cloud,' what was your other

239

name?"

"Across the big river, my other family called me 'Red Deer.'"

"But that was your Apache family. Before that, when you lived with your white mother, what did she call you . . . do you remember her calling you 'Rose?'"

The girl shook her head irritably. "I have told you before, I do not remember."

Tray saw her nose twitch—much like a rabbit's. He felt a surge of hope and continued quietly.

"Do you remember your Uncle Emil? You lived with your mother in Uncle Emil's house at one time."

A strange glimmer entered her green eyes and he kept pushing.

"Your Uncle Emil loved you. He called you 'Bunny.' Do you remember, Bunny?"

Her lips parted into a faint smile and the eyes widened. "Unca Emil," she said slowly, and then pressed a hand to her breast. "Bun-nee . . . Bun-nee!"

Chapter Forty-Three

After little Rose Shaw had been taken away, Tray explained to Colonel Blunt.

"An Indian brave's shield is his sacred possession. The only way you can get it away from him is to kill him. Durin' the Pecos River battle in northern New Mexico, Gray Panther obviously killed the Apache who'd captured the girl. He took the shield, not only for a prize, but to disgrace the dead owner's spirit."

"Amazing!" the colonel said. "But, now, we've got to find that poor girl's mother."

"No problem. I know who she is—and where I can find her!"

Rose, reluctant to leave the old Comanche woman who had taken the girl as her own, pleaded to remain with her people and go with them to the Oklahoma reservation.

"We can't let you do that," Tray told her as gently as he could. "Your real mother has been crying for you all these years. Let me take you to her. You'll see it's the best way."

The Indians knew they had to do what the white men said. Before the captives were taken off to the reservation, Rose hugged the old Comanche squaw for the last time and the two said goodbye with tears staining their cheeks.

To ease the shock of confrontation, Tray sent a letter to Cassandra, saying that he would be bringing her daughter back. He also told of Thomas Manning's death.

"Before I take the girl to her real mother," Tray said to Colonel Blunt, "I think it'd be a good idea if she could stay here at the fort a week or two. Maybe take in some of the classes at your school here."

The colonel pulled at his beard in thought. "You mean ease her back into the white man's society? That's very good."

Against her will, Rose Shaw reentered the white man's world with controlled defiance. Short memory flashes occurred from time to time, but they only added to the frustration of her confused new life. The English language did not prove too difficult. What she had learned prior to being captured seemed to come back and she picked up the words quickly.

"I think we're ready to go," Tray at last reported to the post commander. "Rose is pretty good, now, with the white man's talk. I'd like to get started for New Mexico tomorrow morning, early."

Rose had become a seasoned rider during her Indian years and was given a pony to ride along with Tray. She had no trouble keeping up with his fast pace and they covered a good distance the first day, stopping for camp by late afternoon.

The cobalt sky took on pastel brush strokes of red and orange at sundown while Tray gathered up some dried mesquite for a fire. Rose sat cross-legged, her back resting against a saddle. She watched Tray as he worked at the fire.

"Soon's I get this goin' we'll have somethin' to eat," he said. "'Course, it ain't raw deer meat like you're used to but it'll keep you goin'."

The twigs soon turned a hot glow and Tray filled a small pot with water from his canteen, tossing in a handful of ground Arbuckles. While the crude coffee pot heated on the fire, he unwrapped a roll of salt pork and cut off two slabs, then opened a can of beans, putting the contents onto a tin skillet next to the coffee.

Rose had not spoken during the entire day and mutely studied Tray as he leaned back on his saddle, waiting for the food to warm. At last, she broke her silence.

"You have the skin and hair of the red man, yet you have the eyes and ways of the white man."

Tray smiled. "That's 'cause my mama was white and my daddy was Comanche."

"You lived with the Comanche?"

"No. With a Tonkawa family . . . till I grew up."

She frowned. "The Tonkawas are cowardly. They bend to the will of the white man. You did not wish to live as a Comanche?"

"The Tonks are peaceable. They want the white man and Indians to be one people. That's why the Comanches hate 'em. I figured maybe workin' with the white man's Army, I might get the Comanches to think the same way."

"But this land belongs to the red men, not the white men."

He gave her a long, wise look.

"You're just a little girl, now. And, bein' raised by the Indians, I don't blame you for feelin' the way you do. But when you get older, I think you'll understand the only way for us all to get along is for the Indians and white men to work together."

While they ate their simple meal, the sky became a huge mural of spotty magenta clouds against an ocean of dark turquoise; an ivory fingernail-clipping of a moon seemed pasted in the middle. Finally, Tray rubbed their empty tin plates in the sand to clean them and Rose spoke again.

"What is my real mother like?"

With a smile, Tray fetched their two blankets.

"Cassandra? Well, did you ever see an Indian brave cut a limb off the bois d'arc tree to use as a bow? It's a mighty pretty-lookin' tree, but the limb just won't bend the way he wants it to. That's your ma, beautiful and stubborn. But her heart's full of love and I know she's just pawin' the ground to see you!"

In the glow of the dying fire, a look of dread marred Rose's young face.

Tray tossed her a blanket. "Now, let's get ourselves some shut eye." He brought out a short length of rope and said, "Give me your foot."

She looked up in surprise. "What are you going to do?"

He put the rope around her right ankle, then his left one, and made a tight knot. "Just in case you plan to get on your horse durin' the night and go find your people."

As the evening chill crept in, Tray and Rose nestled in their blankets, listening to the warble-like call of a burrowing owl that had taken an abandoned prairie dog hole for its home. After a few minutes Rose spoke in a low voice.

"Traylor Doolan, are you asleep?"

He shifted irritably. "No. You need to do somethin'?"

"No, it isn't that. I am curious. Part of you is that of the red man . . . have you ever taken a squaw for a wife?"

"You sure ask grown-up questions for a little girl just goin' on nine."

"Have you?"

"That's personal and I don't talk 'bout personal things."

"I have seen you at moments when I think your heart is heavy. Sometimes it calms one's heart to talk about it."

There was a long silence and finally Tray responded. "Maybe I'll tell you about it sometime. Right now, you go to sleep. We've got lots of ridin' t'do tomorrow."

Chapter Forty-Four

Traylor Doolan and Rose Shaw traveled through Pope's Crossing, north along the Pecos River, up through Eddy, then Seven Rivers and northwest, finally to Cassandra's homestead on the Peñasco.

Tray marveled as the ranch came into view. Fields stood rich with fruit trees, corn and alfalfa. He saw in the distance two whitewashed wooden buildings. A long house with a breezeway separating its two sections stood next to a good-sized barn with a corral containing horses, pigs and chickens.

In one field, two young men worked at filling a wagon with bright red apples. They paused as Tray and Rose ambled up on their horses. The older one's face broke into a wide smile and Tray recognized him as Zack.

"Traylor Doolan!" Zack exclaimed. "Ma said you'd be showin' up pretty soon!" He ran up to Tray, grabbing his hand.

The younger one, Jonah, ran over with a grin and also took Tray's hand. "Sure good to see you again, Mister Doolan!"

Tray smiled down at them. "Now why did you two have to grow up like this! Kinda makes me feel like an old man! How old are y'all, anyway?"

"I'm nineteen," Zack said proudly, "and Jonah's seventeen."

Tray looked around at the land. "Looks like you've

been a might busy since I was here last! You got quite a spread!" He turned to Rose who had been sitting quietly on her horse behind him. "Zack and Jonah, I brought your stepsister Rose back with me. 'Course, she probably don't remember you. She was just a tad when the Indians took her away. Rose'll be livin' with you, now."

The brothers said their "how do's" but Rose only nodded without comment.

"Now, we better find Rose's mother," Tray said. "Reckon she's up at the house?"

"Yes, sir," Zack replied. "Just follow the road up that-a-way. Goes right to the house."

Tray put a finger to his hat brim in thanks. "See you later." He spurred his horse forward and Rose followed without a word.

Cassandra spooned dumpling batter on top of a stewing hen and glanced through the kitchen window at the two riding up. Her heart leaped—little Rose had come home! She quickly replaced the pot lid, wiped her hands on an apron and ran out to meet them.

"Tray!" she exclaimed as he dismounted. "I've been on pins and needles! I got your letter two weeks ago."

Tray wrapped her in a hug, then held her at arms length, pleased to see that the harsh facial lines had smoothed out into a contented look.

"Thought I oughta prepare you. Didn't wanna just come bustin' in." He went to Rose's horse where the girl sat staring at Cassandra with curiosity. Tray held the animal's reins while she climbed down. "Well, Cass," he said, "this here's your daughter Rose."

Cassandra rushed over, taking the girl in her arms. "Welcome home, Rose!" she cried with moist eyes.

But it was like embracing a limp rag doll. After a

moment Cassandra released her to stand back in confused disappointment.

"You'll have to be patient," Tray said. "She learned a lot of English at the fort, but it's still kinda rusty." Then he addressed Rose. "I think you know how to say hello to your mother, Rose."

The girl stared blankly at Cassandra and said, "Hello . . . Mother."

Cassandra wiped her eyes with the apron and forced a bright smile. "Well, you've grown up some, after all these years. Reckon we've got a lot of catching up to do. I guess you two must be mighty hungry after such a long ride. It's almost dinner time, anyhow, and the boys'll be coming in from the fields. Let's all go inside."

Zack and Jonah soon arrived and washed up from the pump by the house; they came in and sat at the table with Tray and Rose.

While putting on the plates and silverware, Cassandra found it hard to keep loving eyes off her daughter.

"I Hope you and Rose like chicken and dumplings," Cass said to Tray. "It's Zack and Jonah's favorite." She removed the chicken from the stove and placed it on the table, then sat down and smiled at Rose. "I don't know if you're in the habit of saying Grace, but that's what we do here."

They bowed their heads—all but Rose, who sat watching while Cassandra started with the Grace.

Tray glanced at Rose out of the corner of his eye and saw the girl's nose give a little twitch. Maybe it was wrong bringing her here; she no doubt would have been happier to remain with the Indians. He realized a difficult time lay ahead for both Cassandra and her daughter and he wondered if it would actually work out.

They all ate hungrily, except Rose who took the food

gingerly with her fingers, ignoring the alien fork and spoon.

"There's a lot you're gonna have to teach Rose," Tray said. "It'll be kinda hard at first since she don't know much English but she understands more'n she can speak. If you have any problems, just use sign language."

Cassandra felt her disappointment growing; it was not the joyful homecoming she had hoped for. Rose was like a complete stranger in the house—like an Indian! Maybe after a good bath, her stringy hair braided and the crude animal skin replaced with the little girl's dress Cassandra had sent off for, Rose would look like the white girl she really was—and accept Cassandra as her mother.

"Maybe I oughta stay on for a few days," Tray said to Cassandra after dinner. "Until you and Rose understand each other better."

Cassandra took his arm. "Oh, Tray, would you?! You can sleep in the shed next to the barn. It's small but you'll have room." She shook her head in confusion. "I think I'm going to need all the help I can get!"

Jonah gave his room to Rose and bunked with Zack, but Rose ignored the bed, choosing to sleep on the floor, wrapped in a buffalo skin. Tray talked to the girl in Comanche only when necessary, hoping that the English language would quickly be absorbed from Cassandra and the boys.

"Zack and Jonah," he suggested, "maybe you two can help by showing Rose around the ranch . . . how you take care of the livestock and harvest apples."

The little girl's dress arrived and Rose put on the hateful clothing only because her mother insisted. Tray looked at the girl with doubtful eyes; she seemed miserable and completely out of place in the foreign clothing.

But Cassandra appraised her daughter with a satisfied

smile and later said to Tray, "I'm so pleased. My daughter looks like the white child she really is! The thing we have to overcome, now, is getting her to use a bed."

Tray could smell trouble in the air. "Cass, slow down a little. Rose is goin' through a big change in her life. These things are gonna take her a while to get used to!"

"But she *is* learning fast," Cass told him with pride. "She helps me in the kitchen, she uses a knife, fork and spoon during meals, and her English has improved remarkably!"

After the evening meal, while Zack and Jonah explained to Rose the wondrous things pictured in the mail order catalog, Tray and Cassandra stepped out onto the porch. She leaned against the railing and a warm breeze gently lifted her honey-colored hair as they gazed at a lavish sunset spreading before them.

"I think I oughta take my leave tomorrow mornin'," Tray said.

She turned with desperation. "Oh, Tray, I wish you wouldn't! How am I going to cope with Rose without you?"

"You'll get along. You can understand each other, now, and she's learnin' real good." He frowned slightly. "Just don't push her."

Cassandra's face clouded. "I thought everything was going all right, but it's like there's a barrier between us. I want her to love me but she keeps fighting me. Oh, I don't mean literally, but I see it every time I look at her. There's a resentment . . . like she'd give anything to be someplace else besides here!"

"You sure there ain't resentment on your part, too?"

She looked surprised. "What do you mean?"

He didn't answer but only looked at her with those incredible, all-knowing blue eyes.

She put hands to her face. "I hate it when you put me

on the spot like this, Tray! You're always so right! Yes, I do resent the fact that my daughter is an Indian girl, not the white girl that I gave birth to!"

He took her by the shoulders. "You think she doesn't know that? It shows in your face every time you look at her, everything you do. That dress you put her in, and her braided hair. Why don't you just let her be herself? Would it hurt to let her run around in a buckskin dress? Even go barefoot if she wants to? Yes, and even say she's Indian and proud of it. Ask her about the ways of the Indian. If you try to understand how she feels, you'll get her confidence."

Cassandra's eyes filled with tears and she put her face on his chest.

"You had me thinkin' for a while maybe you'd changed," he said, "but that old Indian hate is still in your eyes, Cass. I'm just hopin' that after you get to know Rose, you'll lose all that bitterness." He kissed her lightly on the forehead. "Right now, I think we better get back inside before they start wonderin' 'bout us."

At the crack of dawn, Zack and Jonah went out to milk the cow and check the livestock, waking Tray in his little shed by the barn.

After visiting the outhouse and washing up, Tray made his way to the house, wondering if any coffee was waiting, but found the kitchen empty. Undaunted, he prepared a coffee pot and put it on the stove.

In not long, Cassandra appeared, wrapped in a robe and looking as though she had worked the fields all night.

"Sorry if I woke you," Tray said. "I wanted to leave before anybody got up. I hate sayin' goodbyes."

She gave a tired sigh. "That's all you and I ever do. Let me fix you some coffee."

"Already got it brewin'. Should be done 'bout now. Care to join me?"

"Yes, thanks, I will."

She brought down two cups from the cupboard and he filled them, returning the coffeepot to the big black stove. They settled into chairs opposite each other at the table.

"Tray," she began and looked into her coffee cup, avoiding his overpowering eyes. "What you said last night . . . I thought about it all night long. Hardly slept a wink." She looked up with tired determination. "I want you to know that I'm going to try . . . I really will!"

He sipped his coffee, searching for an answer, but was spared the trouble—Zack came bursting in through the kitchen door, his eyes full of excitement.

"Ma, Rose's horse is gone! You think the Indians stole it?"

Cassandra set her cup down in surprise. It was not likely Indians since almost all of them were now on reservations. There could be only one other possibility.

She got up from the table and went quickly to the bedroom where Rose slept. The room was empty and she looked into the closet; it held only the two dresses and shoes that Rose had been forced to wear.

Tray had walked in behind Cassandra and she turned to him. "Rose is gone," she said limply. "I've lost my little girl again."

"She couldn't have gotten far," he replied, "even if she left during the night. I'll saddle Pardo and track her down."

Cassandra put a hand on his arm. "No, don't. She's gone back to her people where she really belongs. It would only be cruel to make her stay here." Her eyes became watery. "Rose never truly thought of me as her mother. It's my fault . . . I didn't know how to make her love me!"

251

Tray felt helpless and said, "The Indians know how to warp the minds of white children when they capture 'em. It just takes a little time to turn 'em back."

"I can't help resenting them for doing this to me!" She raised her teary face. "Can't you see, Tray? They've taught my child to hate me!"

He took a deep breath, feeling tired and defeated, for there was nothing more he could do. "Cass, I'm sorry . . . I'm just sorry!"

He walked out of the house and to the corral where he threw his saddle over Pardo and cinched it up, then got his saddlebags from the little shed. With a firm jaw, he leaped into the saddle and rode quickly down the dirt road, away from the ranch.

Cassandra stood in the bedroom, listening to the fading hoof beats, then collapsed onto the bed. She broke into heavy sobs, wondering why God was punishing her like this. Everything she ever loved was always being cruelly taken away.

PART SIX

- 1892 -

Chapter Forty-Five

Apache Chief Geronimo, old and tired of fighting, finally made peace with the white man, striking a final blow to the Indian wars. As a crowning tribute by his oppressors, Geronimo and his people were herded onto trains and shipped to a reservation in Florida; a far cry from the beloved plains they had roamed since childhood.

Almost all of the Army's forts now sat empty. Even dear old Fort Concho, deactivated in 1889, found its buildings converted to civilian housing and commercial business.

Traylor Doolan, in his forty-second year, could still smell out a water hole, or Indian for that matter, twenty miles away; but it would be the last time he'd do so when the Army asked him to help round up the final group of Apaches in New Mexico.

Tray and the Cavalry unit found only ten Indian lodges nestled among the piney hills of Capitan Mountains. The weary Indians offered no resistance, although their tired eyes failed to hide a deeply embedded hatred and their children cried from hunger.

The soldiers and their commander waited on horseback as Tray dismounted to greet the wrinkled Apache chief in his own language.

"We have come to help your people," Tray said to the haggard-looking old man and looked around at the shabby living quarters. Skinny children stared with large ebony-eyed curiosity. "Can you not see that if you hold out another week—even another day—your children will die of hunger and your people freeze to death? We offer you food and a warm place to sleep."

The proud red-skinned man remained silent, as if weighing the honesty of the words.

Tray saw the need for more urging. "You are wise and have been your people's leader for many seasons. My heart tells me you will see it is the right thing to do . . . to save your people from more suffering."

The old chief studied Tray's face for a moment before speaking. "You have the eyes of the white man, but I feel you also carry our blood and would not tell us lies. I am tired of running. My people are tired. I will tell them to trust you so we may finally lie down in peace."

He turned and gave orders to some of his braves who, in turn, circulated the decision to others. Soon the motley group began rounding up their scant animal skins and meager belongings, then dismantled the lodges; the soldiers got off their horses to help load equipment onto Indian ponies.

One determined young brave, seeing a last chance for freedom, dug a heel into the flank of his horse and took off into the nearby trees. An enlisted man saw him and gave chase.

Tray stiffened; he'd seen too often the havoc wreaked by a young trigger-happy soldier. He jumped onto Pardo and rode after them, hoping to avoid bloodshed.

The Indian had not been able to go far, zig-zagging through a stand of dense pines. The soldier brought his horse to a halt and took aim with a rifle. Tray spurred Pardo forward into a fast gallop, forcing his horse to collide with the other, just as the rifle cracked. Both men were thrown to the ground.

The bullet ricocheted off a tree near the Indian brave

who stopped in his tracks, fearing another shot.

"What the hell'd you do that for?!" the soldier bellowed at Tray and staggered to his feet.

The company commanding officer, having seen the chase, arrived in time to witness the incident. He reined his horse to a halt.

"We're here to take them back, not kill them!" he shouted at the enlisted man. "Now you get back to camp and wait for me—we're going to have a little chat!"

Tray still lay on the ground. A searing pain raced up his leg and he was unable to get to his feet, he turned to the Indian, addressing the brave in Apache. "It was a mistake. It's all right. Come back in peace, we will not harm you!"

The young warrior saw the futility of escape and rode back to the camp while the officer helped Tray up and into the saddle.

They returned to the village where an Army medic eased Tray down from his horse and set him on the ground. The medic removed Tray's boot, examing the foot.

"Looks t'me like you've got a broken bone in that foot, Mister Doolan," the man advised. "Reckon you'll be out of commission a spell. Better keep the boot off while we take you back to the hospital at Fort Stanton. That ankle's gonna swell, for sure!"

A young Indian girl had been watching and timidly walked over to them. "Mister Doolan?" she asked. "Traylor Doolan?"

Tray looked up and saw that she had long auburn hair and her green eyes shimmered in the sunlight flickering through the trees.

"Yes," he responded. "Do I know you?"

She flashed a tiny smile. "You may remember me as 'Snow Cloud' . . . or perhaps 'Rose Shaw.'"

257

"Rose, of course! But you've grown a mite since the last time I saw you."

She laughed. "We all change with time. I am of seventeen years, now." Then she saw the pain in his face. "But your foot, it needs medicine. I can help if you wish."

"I'd be obliged if you could stop the damned lightnin' from runnin' up my leg!"

She took the rolled blanket from his saddle cantle and put it behind him. "Lean back, now. I will return with something to soften the pain."

While the Cavalrymen grouped everyone for the short ride to Fort Stanton's Indian reservation, Rose Shaw applied a poultice of mud and sliced prickly pear to Tray's ankle.

"You speak good English, now," Tray said while she worked.

"After you last saw me, I found a tribe that took me in. Years later we were captured by the white men and taken to a reservation in the north where I learned more of the white man's tongue. But they gave us little to eat and many of our people died of the white man's sickness."

"Well, I'm glad to see you were spared," he said.

"Some of us escaped, and we lived on the plains and in the mountains, but there was little food and we were always being hunted. Now, as our chief says, we are tired of running. Our only hope is that the next reservation will be good to us."

She took the kerchief from Tray's neck and wrapped it around his ankle. He winced as she tied a knot.

"Rose, you'll never be happy on a reservation. Why don't you let me take you back to your mother. You'd have a good life there."

She looked up, a vacant sadness in her misty green eyes. "My mother does not like me because I am Indian."

"But you're a white girl, only raised by the Indians."

"I am very much like you. We are both part Indian. Tell me . . . how do you live among the white men when you still have the red man's blood in you?"

"There's only one way. Each of us has to accept the other one as just a person, not red or white. Some find it hard to do this. Your mother's one of those, but it was because the Indians had done her great harm and no one can blame her. If I take you back now, I know she'd meet you half way if you'd do the same . . . won't you give it another try?"

Rose made a last tie in the dressing. "I would like to, but there would always be resentment in my mother's eyes. No, the only thing for me to do is go to the reservation."

Chapter Forty-Six

Fort Stanton, about seventy miles west of Roswell, nestled in a picturesque valley against the 12,000-foot Sierra Blanca peak, the serenity belying its turbulent involvement in the Lincoln County war. Attractive, white buildings stood around the fort's parade ground with corrals and stables to the rear. A few scraggly pecan and elm trees did their best to offer a bit of shade.

The company medic helped Traylor Doolan into the sparkling clean hospital, situated at one end of the establishment.

"You'll have to remain in bed for at least a month," the post surgeon said to Tray after wrapping a tight bandage around the foot.

"A month?!" Tray exploded. "I never laid on my back more'n one night at a time!"

"That bone has to set. If you don't want to have a limp the rest of your life, you'll do as I suggest!"

For two weeks, Tray felt like a caged rabbit. The hospital walls closed in and the odious smells of medicine threatened to strangle him. He finally demanded the use of crutches and hobbled out onto the covered porch, filling his lungs with the pure clean air a man was meant to breathe.

But the fate of Rose Shaw kept dwelling on his mind. Against the surgeon's wishes, he made his way to the post commander's office.

"You think I could have permission to visit one of those people on the reservation?" he asked.

The commander was curious. "Really? Which one would that be?"

"She's a white girl. Been livin' with the Indians. They call her 'Snow Cloud,' but her real name is Rose Shaw."

"Why, I didn't know we had a white girl on the reservation!"

Tray didn't want to go into details. "Well, I know her mother . . . but it's a long story."

Tray could still ride, but needed the crutch for walking. On arriving at the reservation, he learned that the girl called Snow Cloud and several others had been taken to the sick ward.

Tray hobbled into the building and found a young orderly in dark-blue trousers and soiled, white hospital smock, lounging in a wooden chair, feet propped up on a battered desk.

The boy looked up nonchalantly from a magazine in his hands. "Mornin'. What can I do for you?"

"I'm lookin' for a girl called 'Snow Cloud'," Tray told him. "Is she here?"

"Yeah, she's that pretty one they brought in a few days ago. Why d'you wanna see her?"

The boy was still wet behind the ears, and his attitude quickly irked Tray.

"She's a friend. I'd like to see her, if you don't mind."

The young man's smile was almost a smirk and he didn't bother to get up. "She's in that ward there," he nodded toward a doorway. "Third bed on the right. How come she's a friend of yours?"

"I don't think you'd have time to hear about it!"

Tray walked through the door on his crutch and found

himself in a foul-smelling room with a number of Indians crowded on makeshift beds. Looking around, he made his way to a crude army cot where Rose lay; the sheet was stained with urine and perspiration and there was no pillow for her head. The auburn hair spread in a tangle around her fever-inflamed face.

"Rose," he said quietly, "it's Traylor Doolan."

She opened her eyes with a weak smile. There was an attempt to speak but no words came out. Tray could see that the illness had taken a strong hold on the girl and her throat was obviously swollen with infection. A dirty glass and tin pitcher sat on the small bedside table and he poured some water into the glass, then raised her head for a sip.

"I think I oughta let your mother know you're here," he said. "She'd want to see you."

Rose swallowed with difficulty, closing her eyes against the pain. Finally, a whisper emerged. "No . . . she would not care."

"Well, then, I'll see to it you get better."

He set the glass down and squeezed her hand with affection, then put the crutch under his arm and thumped out of the room, his gut boiling in anger. He found the orderly leaning back in the chair with a cigarette dangling from his lip.

"Mister," Tray said firmly, "that girl in there called Snow Cloud is seriously ill. I want her taken to the post hospital where she can get the right kind of treatment!"

The young man laughed. "What makes her anything special? These are all Indians—none of 'em belong in the post hospital!"

"She's not Indian," Tray answered through clenched teeth, "she's a white girl." He looked back through the doorway at the filthy surroundings with its beds of dying humanity. "And whether these are Indians or not, they deserve to be cared for better than that!"

The young man looked at him in dismay. "Just who the hell are you, anyway?"

Tray dropped his crutch and snatched the cigarette from the man's lips, then took him by the collar, tightening it around his neck.

"The name's Traylor Doolan and I'm givin' you fifteen minutes to get that girl to the post hospital and then get this place straightened up . . . or I'll have the commanding officer of Fort Stanton kick your ass clean to Texas!"

Chapter Forty-Seven

Cassandra pushed open the screen door and threw soapy water from a dishpan onto gravel that bordered the walkway; with luck, the strong lye would kill the invading buffalo grass poking up after last night's rain. Two little boys slopped with glee in a mud puddle under the large elm and she broke into laughter.

"Arlene! Take a look at those kids of yours . . . you're going to have some more clothes to hang out!"

The young girl, pinning clothes on the line, turned with exasperation and blew the dark hair from her plain but lovely face. "Oh, no!" She set down her basket. "Todd and Torrence, y'all were clean right after breakfast, now look at you!" She walked over to the children and took one by the hand, pulling him out of the wonderful slimy mud. "You two just wait'll your daddy comes in for his dinner!"

The little boy stood crying while his brother was also extracted from the pool of dark brown ooze.

Cassandra watched with amusement from the porch steps. "I swear, if you'd tell me which one of them has the dirtiest face, maybe I could tell those twins apart!"

True, the two-year-olds were identical; nearly two feet tall, bright chubby faces with their mother's hazel eyes and their father's platinum-blond hair that would put corn silk to shame.

"I have a good mind to leave 'em like this so Jonah can see what they've been up to when he comes in," Arlene said.

"Then, they'll get it!"

"Now, you know that daddy of theirs wouldn't lay a hand on those boys."

A man on horseback appeared at the far gate, riding toward them.

Cassandra studied his face for only a moment before breaking into happy dismay. "Traylor Doolan!" The dish pan dropped with a clang and she rushed to greet Tray as he reined his horse to a stop. "Tray, get yourself down here so I can give you a big hug!"

"You'll have to give me a minute," he answered. "Ain't as quick as I used to be."

He eased himself down, favoring his left foot and she wrapped her arms around him for a fond embrace, then stood back to look at the slightly raised foot.

"Now, what've you gone and done to yourself?"

"Fell off my horse."

"Fell off your horse?!" She put a hand on Pardo's neck. "Old Pardo probably just got tired of having you on his back all these years and threw you off!"

Tray watched fondly as she gently rubbed the horse behind its ear and the animal gave her a pleased, baleful look.

"He looks tired, Tray. Do horses feel their age like us humans?"

"It's more'n that. I had to run 'im into another horse up at Capitan to save an Indian from gettin' shot . . . 'fraid I got ol' Pardo's leg hurt, along with mine, doin' it."

Another horseman rode up and the tall blond man in his early twenties dismounted. "Well, if it ain't Mister Doolan!" He walked over, grabbing Tray's hand.

"I hope you'll remember Jonah," Cassandra said, "and this is his wife, Arlene. Traylor Doolan, here's, an old friend, Arlene."

265

Arlene still had little Todd by the hand. "Pleased to meet you, Mister Doolan. These two dirty children are our twins, Todd and Torrence . . . this one's Todd. Soon's I get 'em cleaned up, you'll see they're right nice-lookin' boys."

Cassandra took Tray by the arm. "Well, come on, everybody, let's put another plate on the table and we'll have dinner!"

Arlene washed and changed the twins while Cassandra laid out the food. As they ate, Tray asked about Zack.

"Oh, he got married and moved out on us," Cassandra said. "Owns a livery stable over at Miller. He and his wife have a little three-year-old girl, now. With all these young ones running around, it makes me feel like old Mother Hubbard." She laughed. "What *would* you call me, step-grandmother?"

"Your place sure has gotten a lot bigger since I was here last," Tray said. "You must be doin' all right for yourself."

"Well, after they hit pay dirt with that big artesian well at Roswell a couple of years ago, everybody started digging wells with good water. I even got one of my own. Things just kept growing with more people coming in. We sell them meat and produce from the ranch, here."

"You were lucky to have Zack and Jonah help get you started."

"Yes, but when Zack left I had to hire a couple of Mexicans to help out, they live in a little house out back." She gave Jonah a reproachful look. "Now, Jonah's talking about leaving—going in with Zack since he's doing so well. If Jonah leaves, I don't know what I'll do."

"Now, Ma," Jonah said to his stepmother, "I told you I won't go till you find somebody to take over for me."

After dinner, Arlene went to work cleaning up the kitchen and Jonah returned to his chores in the field.

"Why don't I saddle up a horse and show you around the place, Tray?" Cassandra asked. "Not every day I get to brag a little!"

She got a paint horse ready and the two rode out to the fields.

"I bought up a hundred more acres over the last few years," she told him as they ambled along the roads separating various fields of fruit and grain. "The big 'dry up' in eighty-six took most of my cattle, but now I have five hundred head, a slew of pigs and a few milk cows. With so many ranches around, I don't get as much as I used to for the meat. But I do believe I have the best apples and pecans around!"

"I'm proud of you, Cass," Tray said. "Looks like you've done everything you set out to do. Wish my life had turned out as good!"

She studied him with concern. He had put on many hard years and it showed in the tiny lines around his steady blue eyes, but they still held their captivating charm. His lame foot added to the care in her heart. Even his beloved horse Pardo looked like he'd had it, roaming the plains.

"This country's civilized now, what with all the trains running around," Cassandra said as they continued slowly along the dirt path. "I can't see there'd be a need for scouts anymore." Then she asked seriously, "Tray, just what are you planning to do with the rest of your life?"

He shrugged with indecision. "I told Tom Manning before he died that I might go west . . . see what California has t'offer."

"California?! It's time you stopped all that roaming around. You need to settle somewhere, Tray, and be content with what's left of your life. I've been thinking since dinner time . . . with Jonah leaving, you could step in and help me run this ranch. There's everything here you'd want. Even a nice

267

pasture for Pardo to roll in."

He smiled at her kindness. "It's a temptin' offer, but that's like takin' in a stray dogie." Then he pulled his horse to a stop. With puzzlement, she stopped hers alongside.

"Cass, my comin' here wasn't all for just a friendly visit. I wanted to tell you . . . I've seen Rose again."

"Rose?!" Her face lit up for a moment, then turned dark. "Where is she?"

"Up at Fort Stanton, on the reservation with some other . . . " He caught himself. "With some Indians she'd been livin' with."

Cassandra turned to gaze at the neat rows of apple trees and spoke as if thinking out loud.

"I told myself years ago that she was dead . . . that I'd never see her again. It was the only way I could go on living without my little girl." A thought made her smile. "Little girl! Why, she'd be seventeen, now, I reckon . . . how does she look, Tray?"

"She's a beautiful girl. Been on the reservation 'bout three months, now. I was goin' to let you know, but she didn't want me to. She thinks you still don't like her."

Cassandra slumped in her saddle. "There was always that something between us. It shut out the love I had."

"Cass, all the old Indian chiefs are tired of fightin' and have given themselves up. Rose feels that way, too. All she wants is for you both to love each other as mother and daughter. Don't you feel the same way? Ain't you tired of fightin', too?"

Cassandra bowed her head. "Tray, I've known you for a long time. Anybody'd think I'd have the sense to learn something from you after all these years. Your heart may be half white and half Indian, but it's a good heart . . . wiser than mine will ever be." She looked into his gentle eyes. "I'm thirty-four now. Guess I just had to grow up to learn. Yes, I'm tired of fighting."

"Rose has grown up, too, and she has better thinkin', now. Cass, the only reason I came to tell you about Rose is that she's at the Fort Stanton hospital."

"She's ill? What is it?"

"Indians call it the white man's sickness. I was worried about her condition when I saw her last. I think if you'd go see her, it'd help a lot."

Chapter Forty-Eight

Tray's nose wrinkled in a frown as he and Cassandra entered the Fort Stanton hospital. It still reeked with the gagging smell of medicine and he wanted to get out as soon as possible.

"We'd like to see that girl you brought in last week," Tray said to the post surgeon. "The one named Rose Shaw, from the Indian reservation. This here's her mother, Cassandra Gant."

The doctor took Cassandra's hand. "Pleased to meet you, Mrs. Gant. I'm happy to say your daughter is much improved!"

Cassandra relaxed under his compassionate smile. "I'm relieved to hear that, Doctor!"

"She still needs attention, but if you can take her with you, I think we can release your daughter tomorrow."

They were shown into the ward and directly to the bed holding Rose Shaw. Tray was glad to see that her dark-orange hair was clean and the sheet on which she lay was fresh and white. Best of all, her face glowed with the color of health.

"Rose," Tray said, "I've brought someone to see you. It's your mother."

Rose looked up with surprise.

Tray saw anxiety in her eyes and added, "She loves you and wants you to get well real soon."

He helped Rose to a sitting position, moving the pillow

behind her head, while Cassandra sat in a chair next to the bed.

"I'll wait outside so you two can talk," Tray said. He limped quietly out of the room.

Rose glanced down meekly. "I did not wish to cause you trouble."

Cassandra took her hand. "I wanted to come, Rose. It would have been sooner, if I'd known you were here."

"I am your daughter, but I am still Indian."

"Please believe me, Rose, that doesn't matter any more! As Traylor Doolan says, whether we're red, white or black, we're all human beings."

"Traylor Doolan is a wise man. I have learned from the pain he carries in his heart that we must all love each other as one people."

Cassandra looked perplexed. "What pain do you speak of?"

"Even though the Comanches killed his wife and baby son, Traylor Doolan still wants the Indian and white man to live together in peace."

Cassandra gasped. Why hadn't he told her? Tray had borne his suffering with courage all these years while she, with the same kind of loss, had let it eat her heart away. She swallowed her astonishment and said, "Rose, I love you very much. The doctor says you can be released tomorrow. I'll come back for you, then . . . if you'll come home with me."

"Home?"

"I have a nice large place, now," Cassandra said, "where you can ride horses and run around just as you like." She added with a rueful smile, "You won't even have to put on an ugly dress!"

Rose stared without expression and Cassandra tensed —maybe she'd failed again. "You *do* want to come home with me, don't you Rose?"

Cassandra held her breath and then, for the first time, she saw a loving expression on her daughter's face.

"Yes, Mother," Rose said. "I want to go home!"

Chapter Forty-Nine

Tray didn't understand. Cassandra should have been thrilled that tomorrow she and Rose would be together again. Instead, Cassandra remained strangely quiet.

"It may be a short ride back to the ranch," he said, "but I ain't gonna let you go by yourself."

She put a grateful hand on his arm. "There's really no need for you to come with me, Tray, but I'd like that."

They rode in silence all the way. Finally, after they'd put their horses in the stable at the Peñasco ranch, she spoke again.

"It looks like we're going to have another beautiful sunset. Let's go up the hill and enjoy it, Tray."

They walked through the fields of waving grain to the summit of a small rise and stood close to each other.

The lowering sun hid behind a bank of heavy gray clouds while lightning streaked through their darkness like fiery cracks in a mirror. Soft thunder rolled and a giant fan of gold spread over the remaining patch of blue sky. To frame the remarkable scene, a crisp-clear rainbow of blue, green, orange and red appeared in a completely unbroken arch, from one end of the earth to the other.

Cassandra gazed at the plains stretching endlessly west of the ranch.

"Tray," she said in a soft voice, "Rose told me you had lost a wife and son at the hands of the Comanches . . . I wish you'd have said something about it."

He followed her eyes to the fading horizon. "Didn't see it'd make any difference."

She turned. "But it would. I'm sure I would've taken a different outlook on things." Her heart melted with tenderness. "Did you ever see your real father?"

He kept looking into the distance. "A few times. His name was Gray Panther, a mean no-good Kwahadi Comanche who'd raped my white mother to show his hate for the white men . . . and I turned out to be his son! I was told later that my mother's husband, Tom Doolan, had kicked Gray Panther in the face at the time. Tom Doolan got burned alive for defendin' his wife, but old Gray Panther carried that broken nose all his life!"

Cassandra, stunned by the revelation, thought she knew the rest of the story. "I know that a Tonkawa Indian couple took you in when you were born . . . but what about your mother?"

"The Tonkawas were Quiet Bear and Blue Dove. They found my mother where Gray Panther left her to die and took her to live with them till I was born. But my mother didn't want me 'cause I was half Indian. She ran west with a wagon train . . . left me with Quiet Bear and Blue Dove. They raised me and loved me like I was their own."

"I learned most of that from Anne Manning," Cassandra said.

"Did she tell you about my wife?"

"No. I knew nothing about that part of your life."

"She was a Tonkawa girl, real pretty and lovin'. I can't tell you how happy I was when she gave me a son! We all lived on Quiet Bear's little farm. One day I went down to the Brazos, huntin' deer to get a skin for my baby. When I came back I found 'em all killed, except for Quiet Bear—but he was almost gone. Before he died he told me it was Gray Panther who'd done it. He'd taken my little son by the heels and bashed his head against a rock." Tray gave a derisive laugh. "He didn't even know he was killin' his own grandson, but it wouldn't have mattered to 'im, anyhow."

Cassandra wiped a tear from her eyes; she knew too well the pain of recalling tragic memories.

Tray took a deep breath and finished the story. "Tom Manning and I fought Gray Panther a couple of times. The last time was down at Monument Spring, where I shot 'im dead."

"So you ended up killing your own father?"

"Had to. He was gonna kill Tom. But it wasn't like killin' my father. I was just gettin' even for him bringin' me into a world where most people won't accept me . . . even my own mother hated me. And then him killin' everything I loved." He finally turned his eyes back to her. "All this time I've been preachin' to you about 'resentment.' I'm not any different from you, Cass. I was carryin' resentment all my life and didn't know it."

"Tell me, truthfully," she asked, "if you didn't *have* to kill Gray Panther to save Tom Manning, would you have killed your father, anyway . . . out of revenge?"

He thought for a moment. "No, I don't believe I could've done that. It just turned out that way."

"So you see, Traylor Doolan, the only difference between you and me is that your heart's bigger than mine."

He looked up at the sky, embarrassed for spilling his guts. "Looks like that storm's decided to come this way. I don't like the idea of ridin' back in the rain. You mind if I stay over and go with you in the mornin' to pick up Rose?"

She followed his eyes to the rolling black clouds and put an arm around his waist. "Of course not. But if we're in for a storm, I hate to think of you sleeping in that barn shed!"

275

Chapter Fifty

They got back to the house just as heavy raindrops began pelting dust off the porch steps. Cassandra was pleased to see that Arlene had supper about ready.

"We'll have another mouth to feed," Cassandra told her. "Traylor Doolan has to stay till the rain lets up."

The young girl turned with a smile. "I was wonderin' if you'd be comin' back, Mr. Doolan. We always fix enough, so it's no problem!"

Jonah walked into the kitchen, their tow-headed twins hugging his legs with loving squeals.

"Good to see you again, Mr. Doolan! Hope you and Cass found Rose all right."

"She's fine," Cassandra told him. "In fact, Tray and I are going to Fort Stanton tomorrow morning and bring her back home."

Arlene put a hand to her forehead. "My goodness, that girl's gonna need a place to sleep! Maybe Todd and Torrence can bunch up with us and Rose can use their room."

Cassandra shook her head with a laugh. "No such thing. Rose and I can share my bedroom till Jonah takes that job with Zack at Miller and you all have to move out."

Arlene put another plate on the table and moved to the stove. "Well come on, everybody, let's sit!" She glanced at Tray. "Hope you don't mind eatin' early, Mr. Doolan. We like to go to bed right after supper so we can get to our chores before the sun comes up!"

The storm reached its height while they ate, rain beating against the house and lightning flashing through the windows. Afterwards, Cassandra and Arlene cleaned up the kitchen, then Jonah and his wife were ready to retire.

"Mr. Doolan," Jonah said, "with this storm ragin', you ain't plannin' on sleepin' in that barn shed again, are you? Why don't you use Todd and Torrence's room? They can sleep on the floor with us."

Tray laughed. "Thanks, but I've slept through worse than this—and on the open prairie without a tent!"

Jonah and his family said their goodnights and disappeared to the bedrooms.

Cassandra went to the doorway. She opened it a crack to peer out and said, "Tray, you'll be soaked to the skin just going to the barn!"

He walked up close and looked over her shoulder. "It does look mighty wet out there. You got anything else in mind?"

She turned and their bodies touched. "I . . . I don't know . . . "

He pulled her close and she said no more, for his mouth had found her lips. Her arms went around his neck and she felt a searing flame burst to life, melting away any prejudice that had lingered all these years.

They finally parted for a breath of air and she put a shushing finger to his lips, then led him by the hand to her bedroom.

Quick flashes of lightning shattered the darkness, their bareness gleaming in the split-second brilliance as they quickly undressed.

They lay on the bed and Tray took her in his arms, moving his lips, hungry but gentle, over her breasts. Cassandra ran her hands around his shoulders and down over the firmness she had encountered on his first visit to the ranch. The passionate fire seemed to be exploding in both their souls. As Cassandra reached her moment of ecstasy, she remembered that day, so long ago, when she stood on the vast Staked Plains and had never felt so free in her life. Now, it was the same. Her mind, her entire body, was cleansed. Free. No bias. No hate. Only love.

Chapter Fifty-One

A ray of morning sunlight peeked through the bedroom window, moving slowly across Cassandra's face. She awoke and stretched with a warm glow not felt in years.

Her arm moved to the other side of the bed and found it empty; Tray had already gotten up and dressed, for his clothes were not on the chair. The little clock showed eight o'clock. They were to pick up Rose at the fort hospital and she berated herself for staying in bed so late. She quickly got out of bed, threw on a robe and went to the kitchen.

Tray stood beside the table, pouring himself a cup of coffee.

"Tray, you let me oversleep!"

"We got plenty of time. You want a cup?"

"Yes, please." She took a chair at the table.

"Jonah and Arlene already took the boys with them to the field," he said and filled another cup. He gave it to her and sat across the way. "No need to get the buggy ready. If you got another horse to take along, Rose is a good rider."

She sipped the coffee, knowing this was probably their last bit of intimacy.

"Tray, I wish you'd think about that suggestion I made the other day . . . staying on and helping me turn this ranch into one of those big cities I've always dreamed about."

He toyed with his cup without looking at her. "Cass, I love and respect you more'n anybody I ever knew. But runnin' a ranch just ain't the kind of life for me. If I tried to make a go of it here, I'd only end up hurtin' you!"

Her eyes were pleading. "But you might change your mind. Won't you at least give it a try?"

He shook his head. "Some men can't put down roots anywhere. I guess I'm just one of 'em." His eyes had turned soft blue again. "This place is what you've been wantin' all your life, Cass, and you'll have Rose with you, now. You oughta be content with what you've got. You don't need me."

She breathed a sigh of resignation. "I *do* need you, Tray. But it was foolish of me to even think about it. Anne Manning always said no one could hold you down. Then you're going on to California?"

He shrugged. "And parts in between."

Tray saddled up a pinto, then led it behind on a lead rope as they started their ride to Fort Stanton. Sharp emotions tore at Cassandra's heart along the way. It would be wonderful having her daughter again, but she was also losing Traylor Doolan.

Chapter Fifty-Two

They walked into the Fort Stanton hospital office and Cassandra gasped in surprise. Rose sat waiting in a simple but attractive dress, with a matching ribbon that held back her long auburn hair. A warming smile only added to her beauty.

"Rose, where did you get such a pretty dress?" Cassandra rushed to give her a hug.

"The doctor's wife gave it to me. She wanted me to look nice for my mother."

"You didn't have to dress up for me—I love you, no matter what you wear!"

They all went outside where the horses waited.

"I brought you your own horse to ride back with me," Cassandra said.

Rose beamed in delight. "He's really mine?"

"All yours and anything else you want."

Tray bent down and gave Rose a kiss on the cheek. "You be good to your mother, now."

Rose looked at him with confusion. "You are not coming with us?"

"No, my job's done."

Cassandra offered her hand to Tray in farewell, but he ignored it and took her gently by the shoulders.

"You know I don't like goodbyes," he said and gave her a gentle kiss on the lips. "We've had one helluva life, Cass. I wish it could've been different, somehow."

Her eyes filled with tears. "We lived it the only way we knew how."

He climbed up into the Pueblo saddle and tipped his hat, then Pardo took him slowly out of Fort Stanton.

Rose watched with regret. "Traylor Doolan has been good to me. Will we ever see him again, Mother?"

Cassandra smiled and brushed at a tear. "He'll show up again, he always does. It may be a while, but I know we haven't seen the last of Traylor Doolan!"

Epilogue

Fort Concho, immediately after being deactivated, was taken over by private concerns. Therefore, it stands today in remarkable preservation in the thriving city of San Angelo, once the wicked little town of Saint Angela.

One of the most unrecognized post commanders at Fort Concho was Lieutenant Colonel Benjamin H. Grierson, a devoted military man whose painstaking endeavors were ignored due to his sympathy for the Indians. Fearing that the grave of his beloved little daughter Edith would be destroyed in the area's rapid growth, her coffin was exhumed from the post cemetery and moved to one in San Angelo. After his wife Alice died on August 16, 1888, from malignancy due to a leg injury, Grierson finally received the long-overdue appointment of Brigadier General on his sixty-fourth birthday, July 8, 1890. He remarried seven years later and died on August 31, 1911, at the age of eighty-five.

The hard-driving Lieutenant Colonel William R. Shafter campaigned for many years in the wild southwest and later, in 1897 as brigadier general, he conquered Cuba in the Spanish-American War. With the rank of major general, he retired on July 1, 1901, at the age of 66. His wife Harriet died in 1898 and Shafter passed away on November 12, 1906, at Bakersfield, California.

The proud monument of white stone, which William Shafter and his courageous Buffalo Soldiers built in 1875 to guide settlers west, was dismantled by two grizzled buffalo hunters in 1883; the stones were hauled down to the spring and used to build a one-room house and corral. When newcomers settled in the area, the little rock house was turned into a schoolhouse, then a post office and the community was given the name *Monument*.

The town grew into a major stopping place for travelers, with a large hotel noted for its lavish meals. Today, Monument, New Mexico, is spread out into farms and ranches. Gas wells can be seen pumping on the plateau where Colonel Shafter's "pile of rocks" once stood.

As a fading testimony to the shaping of our southwest, the small rock house and nearby Monument Spring still remain on private property in the community of Monument, New Mexico, six miles southwest of Hobbs.